THE
GOLIATH
RUN

BRAD SMITH

The Goliath Run

Copyright © 2020 Brad Smith

Design by M. C. Joudrey and Matthew Stevens.
Layout by Matthew Stevens and M. C. Joudrey.

Published by At Bay Press May 2020.

At Bay Press acknowledges the generous support of the Manitoba Arts Council.

CONSEIL DES
ARTS DU
MANITOBA
ARTS COUNCIL

Library and Archives Canada cataloguing in publication is available upon request.

ISBN 978-1-988168-21-0

Printed and bound in Canada.

This book is printed on acid free paper that is 100% recycled ancient forest friendly (100% post-consumer recycled).

First Edition

10 9 8 7 6 5 4 3 2 1

atbaypress.com

THE
GOLIATH
RUN

ONE

His name was Arthur Walker Hays. He lived in a trailer on the edge of the town, behind the house where he was born, the house where his mother still lived. He was forty-seven years old and weighed nearly three hundred pounds. He hadn't worked since his mid-twenties, when he'd been a laborer on a paving crew for a few years, until he'd been knocked down by a slow-reversing dump truck, injuring his back. For that he got a pension.

He almost never went into town during daylight hours, choosing to do his shopping, mainly for food, at night when he would walk to the QuikMart two miles away. His mother's sister later told the press that she was quite certain that the two of them hadn't spoken a word for almost ten years, although he would occasionally leave a note for her when he was upset about something, the grass not being cut or his mail not coming through. He became particularly irate when his disability check was late and often accused his mother of stealing it.

He owned a '77 Chevy van, which hadn't turned a wheel since sometime in the nineties. It was parked alongside his trailer and served as a kennel for his two beagles, which he used to run cottontails in the woods to the north of town. He got a litter of pups, sometimes two, from the dogs each year and he sold them along the roadside, sitting there in a lawn chair with a sign and a cardboard box full of whimpering six-week-old pups.

On a Monday night in early October he walked into town to buy groceries and then, uncharacteristically, stopped at a tavern on the way back, a small place called McPhee's Country BBQ, at the intersection of the county road and the town line. He had not, to anybody's knowledge, bathed in years and nobody came near him as he sat alone at the bar. He drank two glasses of beer and when settling up got into an argument with the bartender over the price of the draft. The bartender finally told him that the beer was on the house, as long as he promised never to return. He furthermore suggested that Hays, with the money saved, might invest in a bar of soap. Hays told the man that he would be sorry for that and then told everybody in the place the same thing.

There was no way of knowing if he went to sleep that night although a neighbor from down the road, out walking her dog after midnight, reported hearing a loud discussion from inside his trailer as she passed. That didn't mean he had company. He was often heard arguing with himself, sometimes while walking into town or in the woods with his dogs.

Whether he slept or not, he was up and on the move by nine o'clock. He shot the dogs first, at close range with the shotgun, and then went into the house for the first time in fifteen years and shot his mother with the .45 while she sat in front of the TV, drinking coffee and watching *The Price Is Right*. He left her bleeding out on the recliner and started to walk.

A man on the county road saw him around ten o'clock that morning, at McPhee's Country BBQ, banging on the door, a rucksack over his shoulder. The place didn't open until noon and there was nobody there.

It was just coincidence that he arrived at the school during recess, when all the kids were on the playground outside. He stopped by the edge of the woods and assembled the Bushmaster, slid in a thirty-round clip and walked onto the school property and started shooting. He emptied the clip and then pulled the .45 from his belt and emptied it as well, save one round, which he used on himself.

That slug tore through the skull of Arthur William Hays and

lodged itself in his brain, a brain that no one could or ever would understand. When the police showed up, they found Hays lying on his back on the grass, with the holocaust all around him. By nightfall, everybody in the country, the world even, would know his name - and the name of the quiet little community of Laureltown.

TWO

One week earlier

The birthday party was at two o'clock, an appropriate hour for an eight-year-old, Jo thought. It was a five-hour drive so she left the farm shortly after eight that morning, giving herself a buffer against thruway construction or a flat tire or natural disaster. Henry was killing chickens as she left, standing beneath the awning off the barn, in his shorts and rubber boots and Grateful Dead T-shirt, his gray hair tied back in a ponytail to keep it from falling over his face as he bent to his work. They had an order of two dozen birds for the market in Monticello the following day.

She dropped down to 84 and took it across the state, skirting Scranton before picking up the Pennsylvania Turnpike and taking it all the way west to the Pittsburgh suburb of Laureltown. It was the first she'd driven the Explorer since Stan at Mooretown Tire & Lube had replaced the brakes and she could notice the difference. For eight hundred dollars and change, she should notice something, she thought. Stan fancied himself both a ladies' man and a master mechanic and to hear him tell it, replacing the brakes on a ten-year-old Ford fell just short of fine-tuning an Apollo spacecraft. Whatever his expertise in the field of auto mechanics, his technique as a charmer left a lot to be desired. If he was under the impression that talk of scored rotors and seized calipers was the way to get Jo's blood running, he was seriously mistaken.

It had been six months since Jo had seen Susan and Dave and the birthday girl, Grace, and she felt considerable guilt over the fact. Where did the time go? It was the same old story; they vowed to get together more often and they meant it when they said it but it never happened. Jo, running the farm with Henry, rarely went anywhere socially, especially between the months of April and November. Susan and Dave had their own work, and Grace was involved in too many things for Jo to count—school and soccer and camping and dance and baseball, and undoubtedly a bunch of other activities Jo didn't know about. Jo did speak to Susan on the phone once a month or so, and always talked to Grace at the same time, so she felt close to them, closer than to most people in her life. She had first met Grace a few hours after she came into the world and had been quite in love with the very thought of her ever since. The summer before this one, she had come to stay with Jo at the farm for three days while Susan and Dave had gone to California for one of a work thing of Dave's. Jo and Grace had spent every waking hour together, and the sleeping ones too, as Grace, then just shy of seven, hadn't wanted to sleep alone in the old farmhouse, with the creaks and groans of the building and a grumbling hirsute man down the hallway, even if the hairy grumbler was Jo's grandfather.

She arrived in Laureltown a little past one so she drove directly to the hotel to check in. In the past Susan had always insisted that Jo stay with them, but each year the party grew bigger—Dave's parents drove up from Florida, Susan's sister and family from Boston—to the point that there was no room at the house. For the past couple of years Jo had taken a room at the Radisson on the south edge of town.

In her room she washed her face and changed into a dress. She still had a little time to kill and knowing that there was nothing worse than showing up early for a party when the parents are still hurrying about doing last-minute things, she drove around the town for a quarter hour, past the high school where she and Susan had first met, past the bars downtown where they'd occasionally been served under-age, by the canning factory where she'd worked after her senior year, before heading off to her short-lived academic career at Penn State.

The subdivision was just ten years old but it felt older. The lots were large, a couple of acres on average, and the houses were all of a vintage design—two-story for the most part, with exteriors of brick or fieldstone or stucco. A lot of functional shutters and leaded glass. When Jo got to the house there were eight or nine cars parked in the drive and along the road out front. The place was a saltbox design of red brick, sitting well back from the street. The lawn on either side of the concrete drive was freshly cut and trimmed for the party, and the pleasant smell of the grass clippings hung heavily in the air. The flower beds were full of color, late bloomers like hibiscus and camellias and mums.

Walking up the drive, Jo heard commotion from around back and so she skirted the house to follow the sound. There a dozen or so kids were running around the yard, all holding plastic rings above their heads, the rings producing great soapy bubbles that either floated through the air into the branches of the trees, or were popped by squealing children. Jo spotted Grace in the crowd but Grace, focused on her bubble ring, didn't see her. A number of adults, all holding drinks both alcoholic and not, were standing around watching. Jo knew most of them by sight but couldn't manage any names offhand. She went through the French doors into the house and found Susan in the kitchen, arranging wedges of cantaloupe and watermelon on a platter.

"Shit," Jo said when she saw the food.

Susan looked up. "Nice to see you too."

Jo shook her head. "I mean shit, I put together a hamper for you. Tomatoes and peppers and zucchini, bunch of stuff. It's sitting on my front porch."

Susan gave her a hug. "Guess you're going to have to come back."

Dave had gone into town for pizza so Jo helped with the snacks. The party went on for a couple of hours. There were presents for Grace and then the kids gorged themselves on pizza and what was announced as gluten-free cake. Some of the men were into the beer by then and it looked as if they might hang in a while. Jo waited until the main crowd thinned out before giving Grace her gift. The two of them walked over to the open gazebo perched on a rise in the lawn, next to a row of pine trees that marked the rear property line. They sat and Jo gave the little girl the bag.

"It's a book," Grace said, looking inside. She was still a little wound up from the party. And she had received a lot of presents, a number of them books. Jo watched as Grace gave the cover a quick glance before opening it. The little girl's eyes widened.

"Hey, that's me," she said slowly. She took a moment. "And that's you!" She stared up at Jo. "That's us in this book!"

"That's us."

Grace looked toward the house, where Susan was standing on the patio, talking to her sister. "Mom!"

By the time Susan walked over, the little girl had already flipped through the fifteen pages of the book and started again. "Aunt Jo gave me a book about me and her on her farm. This is so cool. Look, there's Buster! I told you about Buster."

Susan looked at the illustrations a moment before smiling at Jo. "Finally putting that artistic bent to work?"

Jo shrugged. "Slow but sure."

Grace looked up, realizing. "*You* made this book? No way."

"I made that book."

"Like, you did all the pictures and everything?"

"It's the story of your visit to the farm, start to finish." Jo reached over and flipped to a page. "That's when you got your soaker down at the pond."

"My first soaker ever," Grace said. "Look at Buster, Mom. When you have a rooster, you don't need an alarm clock."

Jo smiled. She was quoting Henry.

Grace turned the page. "Here's Aunt Jo and me collecting the eggs. Sometimes you have to clean a little poop off them. But they're fine to eat."

Jo was aware that Susan was looking at her as if she'd just won a

Nobel Prize for something. Grace sighed and closed the book, then held it for a moment in both hands.

"This is the best birthday present anybody ever got," she decided.

By eight o'clock the birthday girl was tired enough that she offered to go to bed without prompting. Jo took her up and tucked her in. Grace had been carrying the book since she received it and had gone through it with everybody there more than once. Jo sensed a saturation level with the uncles and aunts and cousins and grandparents but nobody let on. Now Grace lay the present on the pillow beside her and reached out for a hug, her eyes already closing.

Susan was emptying the dishwasher when Jo went back downstairs. Dave and the others were in the family room, watching football. Both Dave and his father were Gator alumni and would rather—in Susan's words—sever an appendage than miss a game. Jo poured herself a cup of coffee and sat at the island. She would have had more wine but she had to drive to the hotel. Susan, finishing up, sat across from her.

"The best birthday present ever."

"Hyperbole," Jo told her.

"It's not hyperbole if it's true."

Jo nodded. "It might have been better if she hadn't kept mentioning it in front of all the other people who gave her stuff."

"Screw 'em," Susan said. "Not your fault you're original. How'd you go about getting it made anyway?"

"It was amazingly simple. I did the story and the drawings and turned everything over to one of my summer workers, a girl taking art at Columbia. She did it all on her computer and we found a place in town to do the binding."

Dave came up from the family room, looking for another bottle of wine.

"Gators are up by six."

"We don't care," Susan reminded him.

He cut the foil from the wine. "What are you guys talking about?"

"Kids," Jo said. "Your kid."

9

"Look at you," Dave said to her. "I can practically hear your ovaries crying out in the wilderness."

"Nice," Susan said. "Have another beer, hon."

Dave sat down, the corkscrew half in the bottle. "Seriously, Jo. Why don't you just do it? You know you want a kid more than anything."

"You do understand the process, don't you?" Jo asked. "Takes two to tango and all that."

"Get inseminated. It's the twenty-first century, for Chrissakes."

"I raise organic food for a living," Jo said. "Wouldn't it be bad for my business model if I produced a genetically modified human being?"

"Just do it." Dave twisted the corkscrew a couple more turns and pulled it to no avail. Susan took it from him. "It's not genetically modified anyway. It's real sperm. You want some of mine? I'll whip you up a batch right now."

Susan pulled the cork from the bottle and handed it over. "Goodbye."

He was laughing as he left the room.

"Like you needed that image in your head," Susan said when he was gone. "But maybe he has a point. Have you thought about it?"

Jo nodded. "I've considered it. There's something so…antiseptic… about it though. Is that really how I want to make a kid?" She drank some coffee. "I'm pretty sure my car mechanic would take a shot at knocking me up."

Susan's eyebrows lifted. "Oh?"

"But then he might want to hang around afterward."

"Well, there's always a catch."

Jo sighed. "Maybe I'm destined to live vicariously through you guys and Grace. I could never produce a child that beautiful anyway."

"Wait until she becomes a snotty teenager. See what you think then."

"She will never be a snotty teenager," Jo said. "She's perfect."

THREE

Renata sat in the control booth and pinched the bridge of her nose with her thumb and forefinger as he asked the question again. She wondered how many times she'd heard him ask it. Eleven years, roughly two hundred and twenty shows a year. Had he asked it a thousand times of a hundred guests? Twice that? Half that? Renata didn't know and couldn't know. Well, she could know—if she wanted to go back through the archives, show by show, and take a count. Nobody was that much of a masochist. She did know that she'd heard it enough. She also knew that it didn't mean anything, just as surely as the woman sitting across from him at this minute knew that.

"Do you love your country?" he persisted.

"Of course I love my country," the woman, whose name was Natalie Marks, replied. "I didn't come here to discuss my love of country, or yours. I came here—"

"I don't think you do," Sam cut her off. "You don't love your country. If you did, you wouldn't expend so much energy trying to destroy it."

"That's a ridiculous statement."

"Is it?" Sam demanded. "Is it really? From this chair, it's an accurate statement. From this chair, it's right on the money. I've seen people like you in action. You have an insidious agenda, you undermine, you infiltrate, you insinuate. Today you're trying to remove God from our classrooms. Tomorrow you'll go after another of our freedoms. You'll go after our guns, or our right to assemble. That is, if we *let* you. But we're not going to let you do that. You might not have noticed, ensconced in your pie-in-the sky bubble, but there's been a change in this country. We have a President who is on to people like you."

"Could we please get back to the matter at hand?" the woman asked.

Sam slammed his fist on the table. "This *is* the matter at hand! Do you love your country? Do *you* love your country? You do not! Because in order to love your country you are required to also love and support its constitution, the document that guarantees that the Christian religion be studied in our schools."

"The constitution guarantees no such thing."

"Don't you dare presume to educate me on our constitution," Sam warned her. "How many books have you had on *The New York Times* bestseller list? I've been writing about the history of this country for twenty-five years. I know how my country works. And I know that it is not going to lie down while you try to destroy it."

Renata saw the familiar frustration on the woman's face, the realization that she would not be allowed to speak her piece. What did she expect, coming here? For Chrissakes, the show was called *The Right Thing with Sam Jackson*. It wasn't *Meet the Press*.

Still the woman tried. "Our coalition is overwhelmingly Christian. But, whatever our beliefs, we feel that teaching religion in our schools is a waste of taxpayers' dollars, money that could be better spent educating our children. We're falling behind—"

"You're trying to remove God from the conversation and I won't have it," Sam snapped. "We're going to a break."

When they were off, Sam got up and left the studio, as was his custom, not wanting to engage with the person he'd spent the last eight minutes or so eviscerating. He'd pace the hallway, smoking a cigarette while checking his phone.

Renata walked out into the studio, where Natalie Marks sat, fuming. Renata would be fuming too. But then Renata wouldn't have been foolish enough to show up.

"Are you up for another segment?" she asked.

"Is he going to let me speak?"

Renata couldn't answer the question. Not truthfully anyway. "You realize it's all an act. We're in the entertainment business."

"So in real life he's not a bully and he's not an asshole?"

Renata sighed and made a point of looking at her watch. Yet another scene she'd suffered through too many times to count. "If you leave, he might keep talking about this issue anyway. And you won't be here to present your side."

Natalie Marks got to her feet and removed her mike, tossing it onto the table. "What's the difference? I *am* here and I can't defend my side. Goodbye."

When they went back on air, Sam did just what Renata had predicted, rehashing the previous debate before dismissing Natalie Marks as just another agent for the creeping socialism in the country, and one who had run away when confronted about it. Presumably the woman was in a cab by that time and wouldn't have to hear it, although it could also be assumed that her friends and colleagues back home in Iowa were watching and recording it.

The final segment was a feel-good piece about a high school quarterback who'd come back from a car crash to lead his team to a district championship. Sam loved stories like that. He seemed to think that they could happen only in America, that there had never been a Scottish or Turkish kid who had recovered from a broken leg or fractured collarbone. The piece held no interest for Renata, who passed the time texting her daughter, who was traveling in Australia.

When they were clear, Sam came into the control booth, something he almost never did. But it was Monday, and the ratings had been posted. He stood in the middle of the small room, not looking at anybody in particular. Renata's new assistant, Kevin, sidled up to tell him, as he had every night for the two weeks he'd been there, what a fantastic show it had been.

"The constitution doesn't say that," Will offered, after a moment. He was tucked defensively in his corner, the research rathole, as Sam called it.

"Doesn't say what?" Sam asked, not looking over.

"It makes no guarantees regarding religion." Will was typing something into his laptop while he spoke.

"I never said that." Sam pulled at the knot in his tie.

"He never said that," Kevin chimed in.

"Was somebody talking to you?" Will asked.

"I never said that," Sam said again.

"Yeah, you did." Will continued slowly, "And, um, Trump never actually said he would send troops to Guatemala."

"He inferred it," Sam replied, tossing the tie onto the console, where it caught the edge of the chrome and hung there for a moment before sliding to the floor.

"He didn't *say* it. You said that he did."

"You're going to correct me once too fucking often," Sam said, ending the discussion. He looked at Renata and his eyes went to the door to his office. She nodded slightly.

Once inside, he moved to sit in the leather chair behind the desk. Renata remained on her feet and watched as he pulled a bottle from a desk drawer and splashed a couple of ounces of scotch in a glass. When he offered the fifth toward her, she shook her head.

"Well?"

She shrugged. "No change really."

"I want the number."

"One point seven average."

"The week before was one point eight," he said. "So there was a change."

"Slight."

"Slight *downward*," he said. "Downward. I don't have much use for the word. Unless we're talking about my cholesterol."

"We've been over it," Renata said. "Everybody's down. A million stations out there, Sam. How many ways can you cut a pie?"

"My slice of the pie used to be bigger," he replied. "All I've done, I deserve a bigger slice." He gestured toward the door, indicating the empty studio beyond. "Doesn't help I'm interviewing some Bolshevik from Idaho. Who gives a fuck whether some school board in Idaho wants to teach the Bible? As long as they don't teach the Koran, who gives a fuck?"

"Actually, she was from Iowa." She watched his eyes go dark. "And things will improve, with the campaigns heating up. Your numbers have always been great at election time."

Sam sat quietly fuming. In 2016 he had beat the drum on a nightly basis for Trump and as a result had scored his highest ratings in the six years he'd been on the air. Trump's base had made sure of that. Given the controversies that surrounded the administration, the numbers should still be up but they weren't. Sam's audience seemed to be looking elsewhere—presumably to Fox and other rightwing news outlets that seemed to be more vociferous in their defense of the guy in the White House.

"The problem," Renata began, "is that you're competing against your imitators. All these guys acquired their tropes by watching you. And now they're chipping away at your numbers, when they should be sending you thank-you cards every week. I guess it would be flattering—if it wasn't so frustrating."

"You're telling me I don't stand out anymore. Thanks for that."

"If we believe these guys are a bunch of copycats, which I do, then that's true. You're still the alpha male of the pack but you're not unique…because they've made themselves in your image."

Sam took a drink of scotch. "This is a discouraging conversation. But now that you've identified my problem, that I've become common—"

"I did not say that."

He wouldn't be derailed. "Now that I know I am garden variety, then what is your solution? How do I reinvent myself? Maybe I'll move to the left. Bernie Sanders and I can hand the country over to the fucking socialists."

"When pigs fly," she said smiling.

Glancing at his watch, he downed the drink and got to his feet.

"Where you off to?" she asked.

"Meeting Mikey boy."

"You coming by later?"

15

"I don't know," he said after a moment. "I have things to do. You know—like creating a new persona more palatable to the public."

"For Chrissakes, Sam."

He walked to the doorway and stopped. "There's one thing everybody needs to know. I'll decide how this plays out. I will not be pushed. I might jump, but I will not be pushed."

"And you think I don't know that?" Renata asked.

"It's not you I'm talking about."

FOUR

When Jo got home from Laureltown Henry was back from the farmers market in Monticello and was working on the Ford tractor in the machine shed. She changed her clothes and walked down to see if she could help. She found him standing at the rear of the building, staring at the shelves above his head. He wore coveralls and rubber boots and his battered straw cowboy hat.

"What are you looking for?"

Without turning he held up the thing in his hand. "Fuel pump."

"You have a spare?"

"Someplace."

"Imagine my surprise."

Jo went over to look at the same shelves. Henry was seventy-one years old and had never—to Jo's knowledge—thrown away a single thing over the course of those seven decades. That meant that he in all likelihood had a spare fuel pump for a 1952 Ford tractor. It also meant that the fuel pump might be hard to locate, tucked away as it undoubtedly was among the cluttered collection of carburetors, pumps, electric motors, pulleys, belts, chain saws, jacks, vises, hammers, axes and hundreds of other items crammed onto the shelves.

"How was the birthday party?" Henry asked, his eyes fixed narrowly on the shelves. Like Ahab, scanning the horizon for the great whale.

"The party was good."

"She like the book?"

"She loved the book. She said to tell you hello."

Henry nodded, handing Jo the fuel pump he'd been carrying before moving across the floor to a wooden stepladder, which he propped against one of the posts that held the shelving in place. He climbed up and pulled forward a wooden Pepsi crate, had a look inside and put it back. He pulled down another, this one Orange Crush, and did the same. The third time was a charm; the crate he brought down had inside eight or nine fuel pumps of different sizes and designs. Two matched the one Jo was holding.

"How was Monticello?" she asked as he went to work bolting the used pump onto the tractor.

"About four hundred," he said.

"What moved?"

"Tomatoes, potatoes," he said. "Summer squash. Little bit of everything."

He dropped a bolt and it rolled under the tractor. With his creaky knees, he had trouble kneeling down to look for it. The lighting in the shed was as old as Henry and that didn't help. Jo went around to the other side of the tractor and found the bolt where it had lodged in a crack in the concrete floor.

"So what did she say?" he asked.

"Grace?"

"Yeah."

"She showed everybody the book and explained everything in it. Buster and the goats and the chickens. Gathering the eggs. The frogs in the pond. There are a couple dozen people in Pennsylvania who have heard enough about this farm to last them a lifetime."

"She never said nothing about me?"

"You are something else," Jo said. "Yeah, she told them about the old guy with the beard who makes his own wine and beer. She didn't mention you growing ganja back by the bush because she doesn't know you do that."

"I'll show her when she's old enough."

"You will not."

The pump was in place. Henry threaded in the two fuel lines and tightened them with a wrench. "Did you invite them for Thanksgiving?"

"Yeah. They're coming."

The old man wiped his hands with a rag and then reached over and hit the starter button. After half a minute, the tractor coughed and fired. He revved it until it would idle on its own, then shut it down. He looked at Jo.

"I was thinking," he said. "We should head over to the livestock auction in Britnell and buy a pony. We could hitch it to a cart and haul root vegetables from that back field."

Jo nodded. "We've got a tractor to haul root vegetables from that back field. You want to buy a pony for Grace."

"Maybe I do."

"That's a good idea, Henry."

FIVE

Rachel Jackson was sitting outside at Galliano's in the Village, with Lila and Mary Louise. They'd met for lunch at one-thirty and had been sitting there ever since. It was nearly four now. They'd had wine with lunch and then coffee and then, when they decided they had no place they needed to be, more wine.

"Okay, that's the third bottle," Mary Louise said as the waiter refilled their glasses and took the empty away. "I just want to know how much wine it's going to take for Lila to give us the deets on her wild weekend in Maine."

"More than three bottles," Lila said. "You might have to throw in a couple shots of tequila and a Percocet."

"Oh, come on," Mary Louise pleaded.

Rachel sipped the wine and watched the two of them. They had spent the morning tying up loose ends for the upcoming *Fashion for A Cure* auction event at MOMA and they were all a little giddy with accomplishment. That and three bottles of Prosecco.

"Whatever would you like to know?" Lila asked.

"Everything," Mary Louise said. "Tell us about the food, the hotel, the view. While you're at it, you might mention the mystery man you went with. Any little details—height, weight, hair color. The size of his penis."

"The view was spectacular," Lila offered.

"We still talking about his penis?" Mary Louise asked.

"We never were."

Rachel put her glass on the table. Since they had arrived the sun had moved across the sky to hide behind the high-rises to the west and now they were cast in shade. It was a cool day. She wished she'd brought a sweater.

"You could start by telling us the guy's name," she suggested.

"Oh, I don't think so," Lila said.

"Why not?" Mary Louise asked. "Is he a spy?"

"No."

"Then why not?"

Lila took a drink and smiled. "Because you might tell his wife."

Mary Louise looked over at Rachel. "I fucking knew it! Didn't I tell you?"

"You did," Rachel said.

"Okay," Mary Louise said. "Now we're going to have to guess who it is. We know it's somebody we know because you just said that we might tell his wife. We couldn't do that if we didn't know her, right?" She hesitated, thinking. "Okay, this is going to require more wine."

She waved across the courtyard, trying to get the waiter's attention. As he made his way over, Rachel's phone rang. She looked at the display and answered.

"Hi, honey."

"I'm standing outside the school and he's not here."

"Again?" Rachel looked at her watch and glanced at the other two, now flirting with the waiter, who was gay and therefore somewhat immune to their lewd suggestions. "Listen, I'm tied up in a meeting, the charity auction. Give him a few minutes and then call your father. He's finished taping by now."

She heard the little girl sigh. "Okay."

"Love you," Rachel said and hung up.

"Eric suggests we switch to the Australian red," Lila said. "What do you think?"

"He's never failed us yet," Rachel said.

Michael was waiting for Sam in the bar of the Empire Hotel, at a table by the windows. He was sipping red wine, his drink of preference, and reading something on his tablet. He wore a plaid shirt and tan khakis. What a writer looked like these days, Sam thought as he walked across the room. Whatever happened to real writers— the whiskey drinkers, the barroom brawlers, the skirt-chasers? They had vanished, gone with antenna television and the full-sized sedan. If somebody got drunk and took a swing at Michael Ewen, he'd burst into tears and speed-dial his fucking therapist.

Sam sat down and nodded to Walter, standing quietly a few feet away, who nodded back and went to the bar. Walter was the last of his breed, a black man of indeterminate years who knew that his job was to deliver three fingers of single malt scotch, along with a dish of pistachios, and not attempt to strike up a conversation about the Knicks or the Mets or the situation in Afghanistan. He and Sam were not equals, in a way that had nothing to do with race. Neither were they buddies. In paying an exorbitant amount of money for three ounces of liquor, Sam was fundamentally Walter's boss. Walter understood that dynamic, even if his younger co-workers did not.

"How was the show?" Michael asked. He'd turned the tablet off and set it aside.

Sam took a moment before replying. "Forgettable."

"Okay." Michael had a sip of wine and touched his lips with his fingertips after drinking. He was sporting the beginnings of a wispy blonde mustache and a couple drops of wine clung to it. "Did you get the draft?"

Sam's phone rang before he could reply. He pulled it from his pocket, looked at the display. "Hey, Nessa."

"He's not here…again," the little girl on the line said.

Sam looked at his watch. "It's only a few minutes past. Give him another five. Did you call your mother?"

"She told me to call you. She's at a meeting someplace."

"Give him another five and call me back if he doesn't show."

"This sucks."

Sam hung up and looked at Michael. "My daughter's driver. All he has to do is drive her to school in the morning and pick her up in the afternoon, tasks that seem to be beyond his range of capabilities. I hope his resume is up-to-date."

"How old is she now?" Michael asked. "Vanessa, right?"

"She's ten."

"A ten-year-old," Michael said. His son was about to turn five. "What's that like?"

Sam, watching the approaching Walter, shrugged. "Don't ask me. I can't talk to her. What the hell am I going to talk to a ten-year-old about? She talks to her mother, when she's around. She talks to the nanny. Maybe when she's twenty, she and I can have a conversation. What were you saying?"

"The draft."

Sam took a drink of scotch and reached for a handful of nuts before answering. "It's still not where it needs to be in terms of his philosophy."

"You mean his political philosophy?"

"I don't know that we can differentiate between how he felt personally and politically," Sam said. "One leaches into the other. I'll say it again—Jackson was the first president to understand Manifest Destiny. He was the first to know that it required ruthlessness, a take-no-prisoners, fuck-the-consequences attitude. And that's not coming through in my book. All I'm seeing is some backwoods cracker who fought a few Indians and got elected president. This needs to be a political book, how it relates to what's happening today. Do you think that any of these pissants on the left today would do what Andrew Jackson did? Do you see them booting the Cherokees out of the Carolinas? Christ, they'd be down there weaving baskets alongside them."

"Nicole likes this draft," Michael said tentatively.

"Nicole?"

"Your editor," Michael reminded him.

Sam had a drink and set the glass down. "Nicole couldn't edit a fucking grocery list." He opened some pistachios, allowing the hulls to fall on the table. "The books until now have echoed my political viewpoints. The Lincoln book, the Jefferson book, all of them. This one is going to be no different. I wouldn't do this otherwise. I wouldn't put my name on the dust jacket otherwise. You've been with me from the start and you know that."

Michael drank more wine, glancing at the tablet as he did. Sam could see he had an urge to turn it on, to go in to see what he had missed on Twitter or Facebook in the last five minutes. He was like a fucking teenager.

"How do we connect him somehow to Manifest Destiny? The term never existed until after he left office."

"The idea existed!" Sam exploded. "*Because* of Jackson. Why don't you get that? You and that dim-bulb Nicole? When he crushed the Seminoles in Florida, you don't think that was Manifest Destiny? When he wiped out the Creeks? He didn't need the fucking term."

Michael looked around the bar. Several people were watching, drawn by Sam's outburst. They didn't pay a lot of attention, though, or display any alarm; presumably most of them would have recognized him.

"I'll take another pass at it," Michael said.

"Do that."

"Do you want to talk to Nicole about this?"

"Why would I want to talk to Nicole?"

"See if she's on board?"

"Nicole has been acknowledged as editor of my last five books, all of which made it to the bestseller list," Sam said. "Her contributions to those books have been virtually non-existent yet she's received praise for them. Trust me, Nicole's on board. I can call her up and tell her to kiss my ass if that makes you feel better."

"No."

"No what?"

"That would not make me feel better."

Sam's driver dropped him off as the black limo was pulling up to the brownstone. Vanessa got out and started up the walkway.

"Hey kid," Sam said.

"Hey." She kept walking, up the steps and into the house.

Sam slapped the rear fender of the limo as it started to pull away, stopping it. Sam walked around the car as the driver, Sean, powered the window down.

"Late again, are we?" Sam asked.

"The car was in for brakes," Sean said. "I told the guys—hey I need it by three-thirty at the latest. These guys don't listen. What do they care?"

"Brakes. Last time it was tires."

"Gotta keep it up," Sean said. "The agency—they're safety first over there. Good thing for the customer if you ask me."

"I am asking you." Sam knelt down, closer to Sean's level. "Last driver we had wasn't late once in two years. So what's your problem, pal? You a boozer, crackhead, unable to tell time, what is it?"

"No sir," Sean said. "None of those."

"I think I can smell beer on your breath, son," Sam said. "Under the Tic Tacs. Were you wetting your whistle this afternoon?"

"No sir. Like I said, the brakes were getting done. I can give you the number of the garage if you want. Hopefully they'd tell the truth."

"It's Sean, isn't it?"

"Yes, sir."

"You born here?"

"Here?"

"In this country? Were you born here?"

"Yeah, I was born here."

"But your people are Irish," Sam said and he didn't wait for a reply. "So you've got alcoholism in your family. Right?"

"I wouldn't say that. No sir."

Sam straightened. "You've got the simplest job in the world. Just do it."

SIX

Biblical inferences aside, Sunday was not a day of rest, not on a produce farm in the middle of harvest season. The next day was the farmers market in Carsonville, and there were tomatoes and squash and corn to pick for that. There was also cultivating to do, as the recent rain had sprouted weeds, and product pricing and any number of little repair jobs that were part of the bargain when running a farm with aged equipment. Fortunately, working the Sabbath was not an issue, either for the agnostic Jo or for Henry, who worshipped only at the altar of Willie Nelson.

It was late in the afternoon when Karl arrived, driving his huge diesel-powered Dodge pickup, still wearing his suit from church earlier that day. Apparently, he hadn't gone home after the service but he had—by his breath—gone someplace where rye whiskey was being poured.

Henry was changing the oil in the seven-ton GMC they used to transport produce to the various markets in the area, while Jo was loading the back of the truck, using a wheeled dolly to run up the ramp. She had twenty hampers of red russet potatoes ready for sale and had spent the past hour washing them in the large water trough in the shed before transferring them into baskets.

"You ever hear of taking it easy for a day?" Karl asked as he got out of the Dodge. He hadn't noticed Henry beneath the truck.

Jo came down the ramp and passed close enough to smell the booze on him. "I was off just yesterday."

"Off all day and couldn't find time to return my calls?" he asked.

She'd known that was coming when he'd pulled into the driveway. He'd been leaving messages for three weeks now, ever since she had relented and gone to dinner with him on a Saturday night. She'd gone because she'd been bored and had a feeling that she needed to socialize and because he was a good-looking guy, kind of sexy in a lumbering manner, and because she realized it had been a year or more since she'd actually had dinner in a restaurant. However, the meal had been lousy and she'd discovered that she and Karl had philosophical differences significant enough that she couldn't see herself dating him or going to bed with him, even for purely recreational reasons. Unfortunately, he hadn't come to the same conclusion. In fact, he had managed—somewhere between the overcooked chicken and the bland apple cobbler—to develop a crush on her, one that had only grown as Jo had ignored his advances.

"I was out of state," she said now.

"Really? Doing what?" There was a hint of jealousy in his tone.

None of your fucking business, Jo thought. "Birthday party for my goddaughter."

"You could've taken me. I love kids."

Jo had no response for that, so she went into the shed for more potatoes. He followed, as she knew he would while hoping he wouldn't.

"Careful," she said. "You'll get your Sunday suit dirty. Church run a little late this morning, did it?"

"I stopped by Wayne and Shirley's for a bit. I'm not afraid of getting dirty, Jo. I grew up on a farm. How about I help with your loading and then we can go for a bite somewhere?"

"I have too much to do, Karl." She watched the disappointment on his face. "You realize you shouldn't be driving, right?"

"Why the hell not?"

"I'm thinking you and Wayne cracked a seal."

"I can drive," he said. "That what you're worried about?"

"I'm not particularly worried about anything. But how would you get those millions of bushels of soybeans to market if you lost your license?"

"I'd call you," he said smiling. "You can drive a truck."

"Not your truck."

She went past him again, pushing the cart up and into the van.

"Millions of bushels," he said then, catching on finally. "Is that why you don't return my calls—because you don't like how I farm?"

Jo was of a mind to tell him the truth, thinking it would be the fastest way to get rid of him. But she wasn't interested in hurting him. He was just a big clumsy doofus who happened to farm a couple thousand acres he'd been handed by his father. He was using modern methods and making a lot of money in the process. Jo was of the opinion that his way was the wrong way but she wouldn't try to convince him of it. He wouldn't listen if she did.

"When I say I'm busy, I mean it," she said instead. "You know it's just Henry and me here."

Karl, touchy under the booze and the rejection, was growing irritable. "Where is the old pothead anyway, if you guys are so busy?"

"Under the truck, you fucking Kraut," Henry barked.

Jo tried not to laugh. At that point, Karl decided to depart the field. As he was driving away, Henry slid out from beneath the engine, a dripping oil filter in his hand. He watched the diesel pickup disappearing down the county road.

"You shouldn't encourage him."

"For Chrissakes," Jo said and went back to work.

SEVEN

Sam had a drink as he considered what he'd just heard. They were sitting at a corner table in the clubhouse, having just come in off the course. It was late afternoon and the PGA stop was on the big screen against the far wall.

"And who told you this?"

"Ann McCoy," Burt replied. He was looking at the menu.

"She told you he was supporting Welles?"

"According to her, he's introducing him at an event this week."

"Why would he back Welles?" Sam asked.

Burt put the menu aside and took a drink of rye. "You're going to have to ask him that. He's out on the course."

"I will ask him."

"Don't say you heard it from me," Burt said.

When Paul Sinclair came in a half hour later, Sam called him over and bought him a beer.

"How was your game?" Sam asked.

"The front was bad," Paul said. "The back was okay."

"What did you shoot?"

"Eighty-five. You?"

"Seventy-seven." Sam saw Burt's eyes widen at the lie but Sam ignored him, leaning forward for the rock glass of liquor. "You didn't

31

happen to see Ben Rourke out on the course?"

Paul shook his head slightly, not happy with the question, it seemed.

"But you obviously know Ben," Sam said. "You both have been members here forever. You know each other."

Paul nodded.

Sam settled back, his drink in both hands. "Burt here tells me you're supporting this yahoo Welles for Congress."

Burt shook his head, pissed at the betrayal. Sam smiled at him. Don't roll your fucking eyes at my score.

"I am supporting him," Paul said. He'd ordered a light beer and now he took a drink. His hand shook slightly as he raised the glass. He looked thinner than Sam remembered. Something frail about him these days. "But I don't consider him a yahoo."

"Do you consider him a liberal?"

"I consider him a capable man, Sam. I'm not interested in labels. That's more your game."

Sam sat looking at the older man for a moment, his head cocked. "Why would you suddenly decide to back a young, black, liberal candidate who doesn't know his ass from a hole in the ground? You've been a die-hard party man all your life."

"Your research is faulty, Sam. I was a registered Democrat in my twenties."

"Sure. But then you smartened up." Sam smiled at Burt before turning back to Paul. "And now you're dumbing down. But you're not a stupid person, Paul. Why are you pretending to be?"

Paul bristled. "Anybody who disagrees with you qualifies as a stupid person, Sam. Isn't that right? If we all just acquiesced to your greater intellectual capacities, the world would be a better place. Isn't that how it is?"

"Pretty much," Sam said. "That doesn't explain why you'd endorse this—whatever the hell he is. Community organizer—isn't that what they call them? That's what they called the one from Chicago and he became president. Took us eight long years to send him packing."

"The two-term limit sent him packing."

"Whatever did it, he's gone. And now you're backing another one."

"Careful," Paul said. "Is that what this is about?"

"This is about you switching sides, Paul," Sam told him. "Tell you the truth, I'm just interested in this on a human nature scale. Why are you doing this? You feeling guilty about being old and rich, like Buffett?"

"I'm not as rich as Buffett," Paul said. "Even you are not as rich as Buffett. And I'm not particularly guilty about anything. I pay my taxes, I give to charity. I don't even lie about my golf score."

"You're a fucking saint," Sam said.

"And I don't curse for shock value," Paul added.

"What are you going to say to Ben Rourke when you see him?" Sam asked. "He could walk in here any minute. How long have you known Ben—thirty years? How you going to tell him you're backing his opponent? Or do you and Ben have a problem?" Sam hesitated, watching Paul. "Sonofabitch, that's it. You and Ben have a problem."

Paul stood up. "I would thank you for the drink but that might suggest that I enjoyed it."

Sam sat there drinking for a couple hours, thinking that Ben Rourke might come in. He played a round most Sundays when he wasn't down in Washington and the fact was that he wasn't in Washington all that much these days. After a half-dozen single malts, Sam gave up. However, as he walked out of the clubhouse heading for the parking lot, he spotted the Congressman himself on the putting green, standing over some alignment gizmo with arrows pointed toward the target hole. Ben was wearing bright red pants and a black Callaway shirt. His broad face was ruddy, the face of a man who spent time outdoors. Or drank a lot.

"That thing will be tucked away in the corner of your garage in a week," Sam said as he approached.

Ben smiled without looking up. "With all the others." He putted the ball and missed then glanced at Sam. "One of these days I'll put it all in a yard sale. Everything must go."

Sam was drunk enough to dispense with the small talk. "What's going on with Sinclair?"

"What do you mean?" Another stroke, another miss.

"He's supporting this Welles kid."

"So I hear." Ben missed again and gave up.

"Do you know why?"

Ben regarded the face of his putter a moment, as if it might be the source of his woes. "Officially I have no idea why Paul Sinclair would turn on me. But off the record, between you and me, Sam?"

"Yeah."

Ben shook his head. "Well, shit. Helen and I had a little thing once, twenty odd years ago. And I mean little. We fucked in their pool a couple of times when Paul was gone on business. She thought there was more to it than that. Women, right? I think she saw herself down in Washington, rubbing shoulders. She was pretty upset when I told her that wasn't happening. But she got over it."

"And now Paul finds out."

"That's it."

"How?"

"How do you think? She told him. She went into rehab, you knew that?"

"No. I don't know the woman. I've seen her around here a few times, that's all. She always looks like she has a stick up her ass."

"She's fun in a swimming pool," Ben said. "Or was anyway. But now she's in AA and you know how they got that thing about making amends."

"She spills to Paul and he decides he's going to help get you voted out of office."

"Apparently so." Ben tossed a ball onto the green and addressed it, ready to try again. "He could just wait. One more term and I'm packing it in anyway. Why wouldn't he just wait?"

"Because there's no revenge in waiting," Sam said.

"True." Ben drained the putt, dead center.

"There you go," Sam told him. "You worried about Welles?"

"Ten years ago, I wouldn't have been. Things have changed though. The district is thirty-eight per cent minority now. Black and

Hispanic. Those people are voting these days." He gestured toward the clubhouse, the bastion of rich white folks. "Whereas sometimes these people forget to. I'd like one more term, Sam. Take my pension and ride off into the sunset."

"You'll be okay," Sam told him. "As long as you don't figure on making any money playing golf."

EIGHT

There were just three of them in the boardroom downtown, the headquarters of the American Broadcast Network. Neil Nesmith was standing by an old-fashioned white board, on which he'd just written a half-dozen names in red marker. Nesmith in his wrinkled dress pants and short-sleeved shirt, his lank brown hair worn long and looking somewhat greasy, as if he washed it once a week. Jack McGuire was at the table, leaning back in his chair, one hand on the cup of coffee resting on his stomach. He'd finally given up on the comb-over a couple of years ago and now his hair, what was left of it, was cropped close. Bobby Holmes stood by the windows, looking down onto West Fifth forty floors below. Traffic was stopped dead, not an unusual occurrence. Bobby was waiting for Jack to take the lead. In fact, Bobby had been waiting on Jack, in a more general sense, for a few years now. But Jack was hanging in; he'd be eighty in December.

"What's the consensus, Neil?" Jack said. His voice was hoarse; as he spoke he reached into his pocket for a lozenge.

"Well," Neil said in his reticent manner. "That depends on whether we're talking about a big shake-up or a small shake-up."

"Give it to us both ways."

Neil stepped to the board and began rewriting the names there, moving each to a time slot. "If we want to make a small move, we shift Reynolds and Ramirez from the morning show to eight o'clock. Keep Michaels at nine and bump Jackson to ten. Or—we could leave the morning show where they are and try Ron Rivera at eight, see how he does there. Nobody's watching him at noon. People like him a lot, especially women, but it's noon, right? The question is—is he ready for prime time?"

Jack glanced at Bobby, who walked over to look at the white board for a moment, like a punter examining the totes at the racetrack. He turned to Jack but he spoke to Neil.

"We're getting killed at eight o'clock. Why is that?"

"A number of reasons," Neil said. "Trump's approval ratings are worse than ever and when that happens, it seems that more people watch CNN and MSNBC and the like. Which in turn helps keep his numbers down. Plus, it's summer. People don't watch TV as much in the summer months, that's a hard fact. At eight o'clock, they're still outside, doing sports or whatever."

Doing sports, Bobby said to himself. Who talked like that? Neil did, but then Bobby was pretty sure Neil couldn't throw a baseball across the room, or even ride a bicycle. It seemed as if he never went outside; his skin was the color of putty.

"Anything else?" Bobby asked. "Because I see that everybody—left and right—has better numbers than us at eight."

"Sam Jackson is treading water," Neil replied. "He still fawns over Trump but not quite as much as he used to. Lot of that going around. He's floundering, especially with young viewers. Twenty-one to thirty-five, he does poorly." Neil paused. "I'm not sure why."

"It's because he doesn't shock anybody anymore," Bobby said. "He just aggravates them. And he won't let anybody talk. Would you go on a show where the host keeps yelling that you're a traitor to your country and then doesn't let you respond? I'm amazed somebody hasn't punched his fucking lights out."

Neil nodded. "Rumor is, he wanted a job in Trump's cabinet. Never happened and he's been pissed about it ever since. Takes it out on everybody around him."

Bobby snorted. "Delusions of grandeur."

Jack nodded. "But we loved him when he was doing three-point-eight every night, didn't we?" He looked at the board a moment. "What's the big shake-up?"

"The big shake-up." Neil started erasing and rewriting the names. "We take a leap and slide Amy Reynolds and Chuck Ramsey into eight o'clock. Michaels stays at nine and we try Rivera at ten. A good spot to get him some recognition. Jackson would be gone."

Jack nodded, sucking on the lozenge, the wattle at his neck rising and falling with the effort. "What would that cost us—dumping Jackson?"

"Terms of his contract, around twelve million."

"Cheaper than keeping him on at eight," Jack said. He glanced again at Bobby. "What do you think?"

"I think," Bobby said slowly, "that we need to make some noise. This isn't the time to build something slow. Big election coming up, we need a bounce now. Give Amy Reynolds eight o'clock by herself."

"By herself," Jack repeated.

"Yeah," Bobby said. "She's ready. The woman is whip smart and let's face it, she looks like a fucking swimsuit model. So you get the people who want hard news and you get the mouth breathers, even if they watch with the sound off. And she's hungry. Put her there with Ramirez and she's going to be on the sidelines half the time. Give Ramsey ten o'clock and slide Rivera into the morning show. He'll need a co-host. Bring whatersname back from London. She's been doing some good work. And she fills the babe quotient we lose with Reynolds moving."

"Who?" Jack said.

"Sally Brown," Neil said. "She covered the subway bombing. She got the interview with the cop who shot the bomber?"

"Right," Jack said.

Bobby could tell that Jack had no clue who Sally Brown was. It didn't matter. Neil erased the board again and set it up the way Bobby had suggested. He stood back to look at it, a young Rembrandt admiring his own work. Bobby half expected him to sign the thing.

"All right?" Bobby asked.

Jack nodded. "How quick can we do this?"

"Like tearing off a Band-Aid," Bobby said. "Quicker the better. We need to talk contract with Amy. Hers runs until spring and we need to tie her up. We don't want her making a splash and then bolting to Fox. The others are signed so that's not a worry."

"When do we tell Sam?"

"The night before," Bobby said. "We don't need him venting for a week on air about what a bunch of chickenshits we are."

"Um…who will be telling him?" Neil asked.

"You," Bobby said. He knew that Neil would rather wrestle a live alligator than tell Sam Jackson he was history.

Neil swallowed, presumably anticipating the meeting. "I don't know that that is my job," he said after a moment.

Bobby laughed. "Just fucking with you, Neil old boy. I'll tell him."

"Too bad Trump didn't toss him a bone," Jack said.

Bobby laughed. "Trump's running out of bones to toss. But can you imagine the two of them in a room together? There wouldn't be enough oxygen left to keep a mouse alive."

"You would have to assume he's seen this coming," Jack said. "The man gets the numbers."

"Guys like that never see shit like this coming," Bobby said. "But he'll be all right. He can go back to teaching college, or just retire. God knows he's made lots of money."

"He doesn't care about the money," Jack said. "He cares about the pulpit. He started believing his own press a long time ago."

"Too bad for him," Bobby said.

NINE

They took both vehicles to the Carsonville market, as Jo was going from there directly to the town hall meeting in Monticello. She drove the Explorer and Henry the GMC. The drive took the better part of an hour and they left before dawn, drinking coffee on the way. There was a threat of rain and so they set up beneath the awnings provided by the market. The precipitation, virtually guaranteed by the TV weatherman and various internet sites, quite typically never arrived.

Business was slow, as it usually was on a Monday. Carsonville was not a tourist town to speak of, and that factored in too. However, there were a number of good restaurants within thirty miles or so, eateries that catered to diners looking for grass-fed beef, antibiotic-free chickens, organic vegetables and such. They usually sent buyers to the local markets and Jo ended up selling all of her tomatoes and most of the potatoes to a few of them.

Leaving Henry with the truck, she headed for Monticello shortly before noon. The meeting was being held at the request of the Catskill Honey Association. Local councilors had been invited, as had the larger farmers in the area, the ones responsible for the spreading of neonicotinoids on their crops. The ones who showed up did so with the firm intentions of telling all and sundry that the chemicals had nothing to do with the diminishing bee population.

The meeting was a mishmash from the start. A beekeeper from a few miles north of the town took the podium and began to berate the large-scale farmers present, demanding that they cease and desist—in his words—using GMO seeds, and calling out companies like Monsanto for being disciples of the devil. The beekeeper was bug-eyed and evangelistic in presentation and he spoke as if his opinion was the only one worth considering.

This did not go over well with the farmers, most of who had come to the meeting hoping to make their cases in a reasonable manner. As it was things disintegrated quickly; there was much yelling back and forth and nothing resembling a constructive dialogue ever developed. Neither of the two councilors present said a single word and when the assembly finally broke up they were out the door like they'd been shot from a cannon.

Jo, sitting in the back, soon wished she had stayed at the market with Henry. The meeting pretty much ended when the farmers walked out, although the beekeeper continued to rant for a few minutes longer. The rest of the association was left to review what had happened, even though most of them would agree that what had happened was that the beekeeper had sabotaged the entire affair.

Driving home, listening to Emmylou Harris, Jo wondered how the association had ever gotten involved with the man. More than that, she wondered how they would manage to get rid of him before he brought the whole thing crashing down around them.

Henry was already home when she got there. Driving into the laneway, she could see the GMC parked by the produce shed. And then she saw Henry. He was sitting on the ground beside the truck, in the dirt. He was crying.

He was on the ground and he was crying so hard it seemed he would never stand up again.

TEN

Jason Welles was shorter than Renata had expected. She'd seen his picture online, of course, and watched a video of him being interviewed on some local news show, but for some reason she'd imagined him to be a big man. He was maybe five-foot seven, but he was built like a middleweight boxer, which is what he was at one time, according to Wikipedia.

At this moment he was in a different ring, sitting across from Sam Jackson in the studio. They were taping the show in the morning because Sam had to fly to Texas that afternoon to receive an award for something or other, Renata couldn't recall just what. He was always being feted by one right-wing group or another and he nearly always showed up, if a first-class ticket was provided.

The first segment was innocuous and predictable, with Sam going out of his way to welcome the newcomer to the political scene. To someone tuning in for the first time, someone who didn't know better, he was acting like a kindly mentor to the young politician. Of course Renata knew better. They were just back from commercial now and the gloves were about to come off. Renata wondered if young Welles knew what was coming.

"You've hit the ground running, haven't you?" Sam said to start.

Welles nodded. "Lot of people to reach."

"So you grew up in Bed Stuy?" Sam asked.

"I did."

"Interested in politics growing up?"

"Not at all." Welles was relaxed and loose. He wore a dress shirt and gray slacks. No tie. His hair was clipped close to his skull and he wore thin, stylish glasses. He was a good-looking guy.

"What were you interested in?"

"You know. The usual things."

"I don't know," Sam said. "I didn't grow up in a black neighborhood in the nineties. You played sports?"

"Yeah."

"What about drugs?"

"What about drugs?"

Sam smiled. "These economical replies won't serve you well on the hill, sir. Didn't anybody ever tell you that politicians are long-winded? Let's try it this way—did you do drugs growing up?"

"Yes."

"Sell them?"

No hesitation. "Yes. I was convicted in 1999 of selling an ounce of grass to an undercover agent."

Sam feigned surprise. "You were convicted of selling marijuana?"

Welles laughed out loud. "Come on now. You're going to tell me this is news to you? What—nobody around here knows how to Google?"

"I'm sure somebody does," Sam told him. "I just sign the checks."

"Right," Welles said, "I was twenty years old and made a mistake."

"You've been very critical of the President's health-care policies," Sam said. "Why is that?"

"The President doesn't have a health-care policy," Welles replied. "Obamacare needed tweaking, not gutting."

"It was too damn expensive."

"I know it was expensive but that's the nature of the beast. If you look at the Canadian system, the Norwegian example, it's all the same. It costs a lot of money to insure people. But it's an investment that needs to be made."

"You don't think that it smacks of socialism?"

"It smacks of progression," Welles said. "We owe it to our citizens. We owe it to our children. People need to know that if they get sick, they don't have to worry about going bankrupt on top of everything else."

Renata straightened. He'd just opened the door.

"You say we owe it to our children," Sam repeated. "Do you have children?"

"Two."

"How old?"

"I have a daughter, eight, and a son who's five."

"Don't you have a teenager as well?"

"No."

"You have a son with a woman named Juanita Sanchez," Sam persisted. His tone never changed. "Born in 2004."

"That's not true."

"What's going on here?" Sam said. "I'm told it is true. Do you know a Juanita Sanchez?"

"I used to know her."

"Ex-girlfriend?"

"Yes." Welles waited but Sam didn't say anything. Not a word, not a gesture. Twenty seconds seemed like an hour. Welles was compelled to go on. "She suggested a few years ago that I was the father to this boy. The one you're talking about. She later recanted."

"So you took a DNA test?"

"There was no need to," Welles said. "She recanted. I'm not the father."

"But she claimed you were at one point?"

Welles was growing hesitant now. Defensive. "We had a bitter break-up. She was upset."

"She's not still upset?"

"I would hope not. I haven't spoken to her in more than ten years."

Sam nodded. "I spoke to her. Yesterday, in fact. She doesn't seem upset...but she says you're the father. She says she never pursued the matter because you refused to show any interest in your son. She also says you've never paid a nickel of support."

"He's not my son," Welles said. "And she admitted that years ago."

"She's singing a different tune today," Sam said. "And she'll be singing it on this show later in the week. Let's leave it until we hear her side of things, shall we? It might come down to the DNA after all."

"I'll take the test," Welles said. "This is ludicrous."

"Maybe it is and maybe it isn't," Sam said. "All that concerns me is the truth. I know that you've only been living in district eight for a year and a half. Did you leave Bed Stuy because of these potential paternity problems? Are there any other children out there we should worry about?"

"No, and I resent the implication."

"You come on *my* show singing the praises of a health-care system that will allegedly protect our children's future and then you're offended when I ask if you know who *your* children are? The people of district eight deserve a little more transparency than that, Mr. Welles. You can't pick and choose your responsibilities the way you pick a district to run in."

The segment deteriorated from there, with Sam lending all he could to the rot. Welles kept his composure but he was out the door the moment they went to commercial. When Sam came back for the end piece he made a speech about the need for our elected officials to be truthful in all things. He never actually called Jason Welles a liar, but he came close enough that Renata knew that there was going to be significant outrage coming their way, both from the black community and the DNC.

She was wrong about that. Before the credits rolled, the news of the shooting came in.

ELEVEN

Sam cancelled his Texas trip. They all remained at the station for the rest of the day, following the news as it slowly arrived. The network's affiliate in Pittsburgh had two reporters on the scene within an hour of the shots being fired. Hays was identified by one of the local cops. They found his mother's body shortly thereafter. The beagles too.

By six o'clock the media scrum on the scene was enormous. Reporters, knowing that the police wouldn't be releasing much information this early on, had taken to canvassing the neighborhood, looking for stories about the shooter Hays. Anybody within five miles who wanted to be on TV that night got their wish. All they had to say is that they'd once had a conversation with Arthur William Hays, or knew him in passing. If they'd had a confrontation with the man, that was even better. Or if they knew his mother, they were in. If they had a corresponding anecdote, not matter how benign or irrelevant, they were going to get airtime. The bartender at McPhee's Country BBQ was portrayed by one interviewer as a folk hero and by another as the elitist catalyst who set things in motion. A man who had purchased a beagle pup from Hays eight years earlier got to tell his tale, as inconsequential as it was. The networks were going to run with the story almost non-stop for the next couple of days, if not longer, and there were only so many ways to say that twenty-two children and two teachers were murdered in a small Pennsylvania town. This time, the devil truly was in the details.

Renata sat with the crew at the station, watching the monitors on the wall. She was shocked and angry and nearly immobile with grief. Her daughter, Amy, was still in Australia and Renata found herself texting her every half hour, gripped by an irrational fear that the insanity in Pennsylvania might suddenly spread itself across the globe.

Sam had been in and out since the news had arrived, and now had been gone for lunch for ninety minutes, apparently the only one in the building with any appetite. It was mid-afternoon when he returned, just as Matt Shepherd from the network arrived at the school with a camera crew. Shepherd stood on the street, with the blanket-covered bodies as a backdrop, and repeated what everybody else had been saying for hours now. Twenty-two children. Two teachers. One madman.

Sam watched the monitor for a moment. "Isn't that Shepherd a handsome man," he said. "Like a movie star."

Renata glanced at him briefly and looked away. He'd been drinking and he had the aura about him, the way he got when things weren't going his way. When the spotlight was elsewhere.

"Looks like we're going to have to shelve the Welles piece," he said after a bit. "We have months to hoist that little bastard on his petard." He laughed. "Let's hope he doesn't get cleared by a DNA test in the meantime."

Renata indicated the monitor. "This is a fucking tragedy, Sam. This is Biblical."

"Oh, I know," he said. "And we're going to have to run with it tonight. We're going to need somebody from the NRA because you know where the left's going to go with this. Anti-gun editorials are being written as we speak. Outraged liberals are bawling like newborns. We can get the movie star there on for a segment. He can look pretty and tell us what we already know. His stock in trade."

"We're pre-empted," Renata told him.

"What?"

"The national news team will be on all night," she said. "I assume all the other networks will do the same."

"I don't get pre-empted."

"We just did. So let's try to figure out what we'll do tomorrow."

He fell silent then, pissed off and internalizing it. Twenty-two children lying dead in a Pennsylvania schoolyard and all he was thinking about was how he'd gotten shafted by the network.

"I should have the lead on this," he said after watching the coverage a while longer. His voice was calm. Not necessarily a good sign.

"I know," Renata said.

"There was a time," he said. "There was a time when it would have been automatic."

Renata watched him as he shifted his weight from one foot to another, a man who fervently needed to do something. But had nothing to do.

"Let's get ready for tomorrow night," she said. "We'll kick ass on this. Come in twenty-four hours later and show them what we could have done tonight. What they should have allowed us to do."

He nodded silently.

"Okay," she pressed. "Make a list. Who do we want?"

"No lists," he said.

"What do you mean?"

"I'm going there," he said. "This calls for boots on the ground. Get me on a plane. Tell the Pittsburgh affiliate I'll be using their crew."

"What are you going to do in Pittsburgh?"

"I'm not going to Pittsburgh," he said. "I'm going to Laureltown."

TWELVE

Jo stood in the family room, looking out the French doors to the back yard. Her eyes went to the gazebo, where four days earlier she'd sat with a little girl just turned eight, the two of them looking at a book of their adventures together. There had been pizza and cake and ice cream. Children squealing with delight, joyful about of everything and nothing at the same time. Adults joking and drinking and talking of vacations taken, vacations to come. It had been fun and mundane and wonderful, all at once. Four days earlier.

Jo knew she would never sit in the gazebo again.

Behind her Susan was sleeping on the couch, or at least lying there with her eyes closed. Jo doubted she'd really slept at all in the past twenty-four hours. The TV was off, although she could hear another one downstairs, where Dave was, continually flipping from one channel to the next, as if some tidbit of information might somehow turn back the clock. Or maybe explain that which could never be explained. He hadn't cried and Jo was concerned.

As for herself, she felt as if she were a clustered assembly of clichés. She was in a state of shock. Of disbelief. She was outraged. She was cried-out. She was numb. All of those things were true but the truest seemed to be the last. She *was* numb, frozen with grief, and she couldn't imagine a time when she would be anything but that. She looked at Susan, at her eyes fluttering beneath the lids, and Jo knew that none of them would ever be the same again, none of them would be the same together because the thing that they loved together, the thing that they loved more than any single thing in their lives, was gone.

She heard Dave cursing loudly downstairs and she turned toward the sound. Susan shifted on the couch and opened her eyes. Jo attempted to smile at her but found she couldn't manage even that. Frozen people don't smile. Susan sat up. She looked at Jo for a moment, blinking, then glanced away to stare out the window. Maybe for the briefest moment, upon awakening, she had forgotten. Doubtful that. Outside it was sunny, a brilliant September day. Somewhere a lawnmower was running. Jo watched Susan and knew that she saw nothing of the day, heard nothing of the mower. How was she ever going to survive this? How could any of them?

"We should eat," Jo said after a moment.

Susan nodded slowly, as if the words came to her in slow motion. There was plenty to eat. With tragedy comes food. Friends and neighbors who couldn't put into words that which was indescribable could at least put together a casserole, or roast a chicken, and make huge quantities of lasagna. It had started arriving last night and continued all day.

"I could nuke something," Jo suggested.

Susan crossed her arms and hugged herself, as if she was cold, even though it was overly warm in the house. "Sure."

The family room was open to the kitchen and as Jo started for the fridge Dave came thumping up the stairs, in a hurry.

"Fucking asshole!"

He walked past Jo and grabbed the remote from the end table and turned the TV on. He stood six feet from the set mounted on the wall and began clicking through the channels. "Motherfucking asshole."

Jo looked at Susan, who got to her feet. She touched him on the arm.

"What is it?"

"Wait until I find it."

He continued to race through the stations and then, seeing Sam Jackson's face on the screen, he stopped. It was the local NBC affiliate but an anchor was talking from New York.

"Earlier today right-wing TV pundit Sam Jackson caused a stir when he showed up at the Laureltown school and made some rather shocking statements."

They cut to the footage. Sam Jackson stood in front of the school, dressed in cargo pants and a leather bomber jacket, like a reporter in a war zone. His fists were clenched, his eyes bright, his voice lifted like that of an evangelist.

"This time the chickens really have come home to roost. This is the wake-up call this country so desperately needs. For generations we've been sliding backwards. We used to be tough. We used to fight our own battles. We used to protect our own. But we've slowly become a nation of milquetoasts, a nation of pussyfooters. We allowed this deranged fiend to walk in here and kill our children. Because, oh, we're afraid of guns, we're afraid of violence. So we cower, we cringe, we hide our heads in the sand and allow this to happen. The parents of these children should be ashamed. You did not protect your children. You did not! Cowards, the whole lot of you. If any of you have any guts, you'll know that this changes everything. From here on in, all bets are off. This is a great day for America! This is a great day for America!"

Jo watched Susan, staring at the TV, her mouth slack, her eyes filling, her breath growing quicker. On the screen, the anchor was saying how the comments had outraged "many across the nation." Jo looked at Dave.

"Turn it off, Dave."

"This fucking guy—" Dave said.

Jo took the remote from him and clicked it off. She turned to Susan.

"None of that made any sense. You're not going to listen to that jerk. None of it made sense. Not one word."

Susan sat down and looked at Dave. He was livid with anger; it was as if he'd found a place to dock his grief.

53

"Dave," Jo said and he looked toward her. "You know I'm right. A week ago, would you have cared what that asshole had to say about anything? A week ago, would you have watched his show for even a minute? You wouldn't have."

"But how could he say that, Jo? How could he say *that*?"

"I don't know," Jo admitted. "You can't stop him. All you can do is ignore him."

"Somebody should stop him," Susan said. "Where's the decency?"

Jo looked at both of them and then away. Outside the wind had come up and was blowing through the trees behind the gazebo. Jo watched the pine boughs bending in the breeze and thought about tomorrow and the day after that and the day after that. How would any of them get through this?

It was ten o'clock when she got to the hotel. Susan's parents had arrived and then Dave's right behind them. Susan wanted Jo to stay but Jo decided that the family needed to be alone together for an evening. She took a room at the Radisson again. After checking in, she lay down on the bed for half an hour. She would not turn the TV on and she had nothing to read. She tried to nap but found that she couldn't.

She decided to have a drink in the lounge. There was a dozen or so people there, a group sitting at a big table, some couples scattered about, a single guy at the bar drinking draft. He was a few pounds overweight and had a crew cut; he turned to look openly at Jo as she entered. She avoided eye contact and kept walking to a table in the corner. She ordered vodka and tonic.

He came over a few minutes later, approaching cautiously, a deer entering an orchard. He called her by name.

"Daniel," she said after a moment. "I didn't recognize you."

He patted his stomach. "I've grown." He waited, shifting his weight from one foot to the other, like an over-anxious suitor.

After a moment's hesitation she asked him to sit down. She certainly wasn't looking for company but she was only having one drink anyway.

He put his glass of beer on the table and sat. "I haven't seen you...I don't know...ten years?"

"Probably more," Jo said.

"You look the same," he said. "Your hair's shorter."

Jo nodded, trying to think of something. He had a sadness about him, a resignation. She didn't remember that, not from high school. Were people in high school sad though, or was it too early for that? She realized that it didn't matter; today everybody was sad.

"You're a cop, right?" It seemed it was up to her to carry the conversation.

He took a drink. He hadn't shaved in a couple of days and he'd grown jowly over the decade or so, the added weight emphasizing the stubble on his cheeks. Jo remembered him being a jock—football, basketball, track, all that.

"Was," he said.

She tried to remember who he married. It wasn't all that long ago. He would be a year or two older than her—thirty-three, thirty-four maybe. She recalled him joining the force and marrying young. She wondered if he was still married. Here he was, drinking in a half-deserted lounge on Saturday night. She doubted it.

"You're not still in town?" he asked.

"No." She didn't say anything more for a time. "My goddaughter was killed at the school."

"Oh, Jesus."

"Yeah."

"That's rough," he said after a moment. "How old?"

"Eight."

"Oh, man. I have no idea what to say."

"Nobody does," Jo told him.

They sat quietly for a while. It hadn't been a good idea, him joining her, but now it was done, two almost strangers sitting there under the weight of what had happened. Where did they go from here?

He sighed heavily. "So...where do you live?"

"Upstate New York.'

He had more beer, wiped his mouth, thinking of another question, thinking of moving on. "What do you do there?"

"I'm a farmer."

"No shit?"

"No shit." Jo took a sip of vodka. "So what happened with you—you quit the force?"

"Yeah," he said. "Well, not really. The force quit me." He looked around, then back at her. "I got in some shit. Domestic problems."

"Remind me who you married."

"Beth Monroe."

Now Jo remembered. Beth Monroe was the only daughter of the local state assemblyman. He was a pretentious asshole and she was cut from precisely the same cloth. Jo had hated her in high school. She had a little group of hangers-on she lorded it over—the cheerleaders and high fashion types—and was an expert in excluding most everybody else. She was of the strange opinion that being the daughter of a slime-ball politician elevated her somehow. Jo remembered now that she'd been surprised when Beth and Daniel had married. But back then he'd been the athlete, good-looking and popular. Maybe she had plans for him—public office or something along those lines. Sounded as if things hadn't worked out. Maybe she hadn't liked him becoming a cop. It wouldn't be much of a stepping stone, at least to someone like Beth.

"Should I ask what happened with the police department?" Jo was thinking that she probably shouldn't. Maybe she needed a diversion for her mind, something else to think about, even if that something was the soap opera details of someone else's life.

"I got the boot," he said. "She had me up on assault charges. The department suspended me pending the trial so I said the hell with it. I just wanted out."

Jo took another drink. "Did you assault her?"

"I did," he said. "After she hit me. It was kind of a habit with her."

"Chewing your fingernails is a habit."

"Oh, I know," he said. "Just how things were though. There was a lot of drinking, the both of us. One night she hit me in the face and I pushed her. She fell over a chair and got up and called the cops. Then the lawyers."

"No kids?"

"No kids." He had a drink. "Geez, I didn't walk over to tell you my dumb story. What kind of farming do you do?"

"Organic and free-range," Jo said. "Market vegetables, a lot of heirloom stuff. We sell to local grocery stores, a few restaurants. Farmers markets."

"Who's we? You have a family?"

"Yeah, goats and chickens," she said. "My grandfather and I run the place. The farm's actually been in his family since 1879. I've been there five, well, almost six years now. I was engaged to a guy, living in Boston, and then it fell apart and I went back to the farm."

"How did it fall apart?"

Jo shook her head. "In more ways than I can count. After we'd been together for two years, I found out that virtually everything he'd told me about himself was false. He had an ex-wife and a kid he never mentioned, he never worked where he said he worked, he was up to his ears in debt. What else—oh, he was running some lame Ponzi scheme that was about to get him arrested."

"No wonder you headed for the hills."

"Yeah," Jo said. "I thought for a while that my heart had been broken but it wasn't true. I know that now, because now it really is broken. There's no comparison. I feel like I'm a heartbeat away from falling to pieces."

He looked around the dingy bar, as if her reply made him uncomfortable. Or maybe it was just that he couldn't find a way to respond. She needed to get off the subject; talking to him had made her stop thinking about Grace, if even for just a few minutes.

"So what do you do now?"

He had a sip of beer. The glass was nearly empty and it occurred to Jo that he was nursing it, extending the conversation. Why not? It was Saturday night and he was alone in a bar.

"This and that," he said. "I work event security in the city. A little investigative work for some insurance companies. I put up drywall. I even do roofing if the money's right."

"Renaissance man."

"Hardly. I'm basically a bum."

"Why are you so hard on yourself?" Jo couldn't stop. "She do that to you?"

"You remember Beth?"

"I remember her. We didn't travel in the same circles."

He shook his head. "Fuck it, I'm not going to badmouth her. We should never have gotten together. She had her good points."

"Yeah?"

"I can't remember any right this minute."

Jo smiled. "She still in town?"

"Philly. She's with some guy."

"What does he do?"

"No idea." He laughed. "I guarantee you he's not a cop. I hope he's got money. She took all of mine and I didn't even have any."

"That why you work all the jobs?"

He nodded slowly, as if deciding what to tell her. How much to tell her. "We got into this real estate deal. Her father was involved. Bought eight acres out by Johnstown and were going to develop it and get rich. Put it in my name because he couldn't have it in his, the political thing, right? Paid a lot of planners to get things off the ground— sewers and streets and surveys, all that jazz. Turned out we couldn't get the zoning we needed." He laughed. "It was right around then that Beth decided she didn't want to be married to me anymore. So I lost the property and ended up owing about eight hundred grand to boot."

"Ouch."

He dismissed the matter with a flick of his hand. "I should be debt free by the time I'm a hundred and four."

"At least you can laugh about it."

"On the outside," he smiled.

"But wouldn't half the debt belong to her?"

"I wasn't about to take her and her father on in court. I might end up owing more than I do."

"I remember meeting him once," Jo said. "He came to school to talk to us. Career day or something like that."

"Nice role model for the kids," Daniel laughed. "The guy's a bully and a crook."

"I don't recall anybody being too impressed. I think he did a lot of name-dropping."

"That's his style. He was one of the first to come out for Trump." Jo finished her vodka.

"I'll buy you a drink," he said.

"I have to go," she said, standing. "I've been walking around in a daze for two days. I need to try to sleep."

She was glad that he didn't press her on the drink. He stood as well. "Good seeing you, Jo. I wish it wasn't under such sad circumstances."

She didn't know what to do so she extended her hand.

"So do I," she said and she headed for her room, where she would spend most of the night vainly seeking sleep, thinking about Grace, and of how her heart would ever get past its shattered state.

THIRTEEN

Upon arriving in Laureltown Sam had convinced ABN to him give him a commentary on their noon update, which meant that his rant went out live. There was, in fact, a standard delay in the broadcast, but the crew didn't cut him off. Presumably they couldn't have seen it coming and by the time it registered with them, it was out there in the world, impossible to retrieve. Renata watched it live from the studio, where she had been pulling together the usual second amendment proponents for that night's show. Afterward Sam's soliloquy there was stunned silence until Will finally spoke.

"I've been looking for an excuse to quit this shit show."

"You might as well hold on and get your severance," Renata told him. "They were close to cancelling us before. This will do the trick."

"What about tonight's show?"

"Carry on like it's going to air," she said after a moment. "We could last a day or two. The brass might want to play it out. They can make themselves look good as they pretend to respond to the country's moral outrage. Because there's going to be a lot of fucking moral outrage over this."

"What about the guy from the NRA tonight? He might bail now."

"He won't bail. He's probably the only person in the country who agrees with Sam. So get him in here. The show must go on."

"Not that anybody's going to be watching."

"Oh, they'll be watching tonight," Renata said. "That's one thing I do know. Tomorrow's another subject altogether…but tonight they'll be watching."

She was right that they'd be watching. What she couldn't have guessed was that it was the beginning of something both remarkable and reprehensible. Sam's numbers that first night were up considerably, as expected. Viewers who had never watched before tuned in to see the lunatic. And while the network was presumably trying to decide just exactly when to cancel him, the ratings continued to climb and the fact that as many people tuned in to hate him as to admire him didn't matter. When Sam saw what was happening he beat the drum even harder, urging the population to arm itself against "the thugs, fiends and miscreants" who threatened the safety of "our most precious commodity—our children." He continued to blame the parents of the kids who were killed. The network, seeing what was happening, backed off for the time being, waiting to see just how long the surge lasted. They could always take the high ground down the road, when the ratings began to fall, as they inevitably would. Even a freak show gets stale after a while.

By the end of the first week Sam's ratings had doubled. The recalcitrant Will, the primary victim of Sam's bullying for seven years, promptly quit. Before he did, he told Sam that he wished that he—and not the children of Laureltown—had been in that schoolyard when Hays showed up. Even a worm will turn, trodden upon.

By the end of the second week, Sam won his time slot.

"Tell me the truth," Renata said. "When did you know what you were going to say in Laureltown?"

"When I said it," Sam replied.

They were having lunch in midtown, at an alehouse that served fish and chips and corned beef sandwiches on rye. Sam liked the corned beef.

"You couldn't begin to count the number of reporters there," Sam continued. "Lined up all along the road in front of the school like they were there to cover the Santa Claus parade. And every fucking one of them saying the same thing. It would have made great satire if it wasn't so pathetic." He had a drink of ale. "So it wasn't exactly a stroke of genius, changing the dialogue."

"Maybe it was," Renata said. "I mean—the numbers."

"Fuck the numbers."

"I can't believe you just said that."

"I didn't do it for the numbers," Sam said. "I did it to get fired. I fully expected to get the news when I got back to New York that night. I even had my farewell address ready." He smiled. "I was going to call the network out. Go down in a blaze of glory. And look what happened."

"Yeah, look what happened."

He took a drink. "This just proves my point. It's all theater and the actor with the brightest nose and the loudest horn gets the attention. What—the network suddenly loves me again? How am I different than I was a week ago? Two weeks ago?"

Renata lifted her glass and sat back to have a drink, thinking how odd it was that he should ask her that particular question. Because he *was* different than a week or two ago. He was looser. He was relaxed and that was something he hadn't been for some time.

"All right, what's going on?"

He shrugged. "You don't know? I got what I want. Now I can leave. First, I'm going to make them ask me to stay, and then I'm going to leave. My terms."

"When is all this going to happen?"

"I'll ride the wave as long as it's peaking," he said. "Then I'll tell the network to kiss my ass. I've just now realized that the only reason I wanted this was because I was afraid they were going to take it away. But I don't want it anymore. It's fucking exhausting, pulling on a persona every morning."

"So what will you do—just write?"

"No," he said. "Mikey does all the heavy lifting there anyway. Don't tell me you didn't know that."

She smiled. "I had my suspicions."

"You were afraid to ask?"

"You intimidate people, Sam."

He smiled, pleased with that, and drank more ale. "I don't know what I'm going to do. But it's time for a change."

FOURTEEN

She worked. She got up when it was daylight and sometimes before, and she worked until dark, until she made herself so physically tired that she could shut her brain down enough for sleep. Otherwise it was impossible. Someone once sang that he needed a dump truck to unload his head. There wasn't a truck big enough to handle Jo's tangled menagerie of thoughts and regrets and anger and guilt.

So she worked. It was an unconscious and futile effort to forget something she wouldn't forget if she lived a thousand years. There was nothing she could do about that and so she worked. She was fortunate that it was fall, the busiest time for the farm. She and Henry harvested every afternoon and drove to one farmers market or another nearly every morning. Sometimes she sent Henry on his own while she remained in the fields. She preferred not to see people if she could avoid it, especially happy people, trolling the market stalls, sometimes with little kids in tow.

Henry didn't talk much anymore. He'd never been the most gregarious man, except around certain people, and now he grew even quieter. He did his work and at night either went to bed early or retreated to his woodworking shop, where he did little but sit there by the cold wood stove, drinking his wine and smoking his home-grown weed.

A week after the shooting, he went by himself to the livestock auction in Britnell and came home that night with a brown and white pony, the animal tethered in a trailer he'd borrowed from a neighbor. Jo was tearing down a sagging wooden chicken coop when he unloaded the animal and he'd looked at her defiantly, as if expecting some sort of confrontation, or at least a demand for an explanation as to why he would buy a pony *now*. She said nothing. That evening, after dinner, he began to train the animal to pull an old cart that had been tucked away in the corner of the barn for decades. He kept at it nightly and was usually out there when Jo came in, finished for the day. Henry talked to the animal constantly, reassuring it, even joking with it. Jo had heard the tone before. It was the voice he had used when talking to Grace.

Jo borrowed money from the bank and hired a local contractor to put up a building where the chicken coop had been, where she planned to make goat cheese. One end would house the stalls for milking and the other the equipment for the cheese production. She wanted it up and running by spring. In truth, she couldn't afford the building or the equipment right now, but she did it anyway. She had no interest in reticence, in playing anything safe.

In the evenings she ate in the living room in front of the TV, flipping from one news station to the other. The coverage from Laureltown continued for weeks, long after there was anything new to tell. The gun debate roared and then sputtered and then faded away, as it always did. Experts were adamant in their various theories of how the tragedy could have been avoided, and not one of them knew—as Henry would say—shit from wild honey. How could they? The mental state of Arthur William Hays was dissected and analyzed and poked and prodded. To what avail? None of it would change what had happened and Jo doubted that any of it would stop it from happening again.

For a while she had called Susan every night. They couldn't bring themselves to talk about the shooting, so Jo fell into a habit of telling Susan about her day. What she'd harvested, cut, sold, dug up, built, fixed or planted. After a while, she came to realize that Susan wasn't paying all that much attention. Jo was a radio playing endlessly in a back room somewhere. Of course Susan wasn't listening. She wasn't listening to anything. How could she? The phone calls tailed off.

In spite of herself, Jo began to tune in to Sam Jackson's show, if only for a few minutes, almost every night. During the day she told herself not to do it and then did it anyway. She was like an alcoholic, waking up every morning vowing to quit the sauce, only to reach for the bottle at end of day.

He had expanded his rant incrementally. Ridiculously. He was like a character out of Monty Python, a cruel and colossal joke. He called for ten-year-olds to be trained in firearms. He wanted teachers carrying weapons. He became revered by a legion of marginal louts who believed that a pistol-packing citizenry was the solution to all the country's problems. And the louts were all tuning in, seeking direction from Sam Jackson, who was now signing off every night with the words, lifted from his tirade at Laureltown—"All bets are off!"

Jo, as she was watching, could imagine his disciples across the country, hurling the catch phrase back at the screen. A drooling mob. They believed what he was telling them. But did he believe it? Jo doubted it.

Each time she turned the show off, she vowed never to return to it. And yet she did. It was as if she wanted something from him, something to show that he didn't believe it. Contrition or regret, something that made him human. Or maybe she wanted to nurture her hatred for the man. That part was easy.

One day in October she was filling hamper baskets with acorn squash, in readiness for the market in Middleton the next day, when she looked up to see Susan pulling into the laneway in her Honda SUV. She got out, a canvas tote slung over her shoulder. She'd lost considerable weight in the weeks since the shooting. Her jeans hung on her.

"What are you doing here?" Jo said as they hugged.

"I don't know," Susan replied. "Woke up this morning and felt like a drive."

"A long drive."

"Well, Dave's back to work and I'm—well, I'm not ready to go back yet. I cannot be around those well-meaning people all day long."

"So you came here?"

Susan laughed. "You see? I needed that. Yeah, I thought I'd come and see you. You can put me to work if you want."

"I will absolutely put you to work."

Susan hesitated. There was something else. "And I brought you this." She reached into the bag and brought out the book. "You should have this, Jo."

"No," Jo said at once, pushing it away. "You should keep it. I couldn't take it."

Susan's held the book forward again; her hand was shaking slightly. "You don't understand. I can't have this in my house. I can't." She began to cry. "Every time I see it, it tears me to fucking pieces."

Jo took the book from her and hugged her again. "Okay," she said. "Okay."

They worked all afternoon, crating pumpkins and melons and squash. They shoveled out the goats' stall and Jo showed Susan how to drive the Ford tractor to spread the manure over the bean field. Henry came home from market and showed off the pony, unabashedly calling it Grace's, which made Susan tear up and smile at the same time. They had chicken for dinner and a bottle of Henry's wine, the quality somewhat suspect.

"There's stuff floating in there," Jo said, looking at the bottle.

"What the hell, it's still wine," he told her.

After they opened the second bottle it was agreed that Susan would spend the night. By ten o'clock Henry was gone to bed. Jo and Susan took their glasses outside to sit on the old porch. They could hear the frogs in the pond, and the goats and the chickens as they settled in for the night, the hens clucking softly, deep in their throats.

"So Dave's back to work," Jo said.

"Yeah."

"Is he okay?" She put her hand up to deflect any reply. "I'm sorry, that's an incredibly stupid question."

Susan dismissed the apology. "He's doing all right. Better than me, I'm afraid. He devotes a portion of his day to firing off nasty emails to ABN about Sam Jackson."

"He does?"

Susan nodded. "He's become obsessed with the guy. He wants him banned from the air. It's his mission, as if that would make things... better somehow."

"It would make the world better."

Susan nodded. "But apparently he's more popular than ever. Explain that to me. What does that say about us? What does that say about the country?"

"Not much," Jo said. "Or maybe it says too much."

"Do you ever turn it on?" Susan asked.

"No way," Jo lied. She indicated the barns. "I have plenty of manure right here. What do I need him for?"

"Dave watches sometimes. He only lasts a couple minutes though. Then he's yelling at the TV." Susan took a drink of the bad wine. "Dave knows some people in Pittsburgh, network guys. They say this saved Jackson's show. He was about to get cancelled."

"Good for him. I hope he can sleep at night. Oh shit, he probably sleeps like a baby."

Susan fell quiet. After a while she appeared to shrink in her chair and her breathing became ragged. Jo watched for a moment.

"What is it?"

"It's just...I keep wondering," Susan said. "I know I shouldn't. But what if he's right? What if it is our fault?" She began to cry now, the tears rising like a pot boiling over. "I didn't protect my baby. If I did, she'd still be alive. He's right, you know."

Jo stood quickly and went over to kneel in front of Susan. She took her friend's face in her hands, felt the warm tears on her fingers. "Don't you do that! Don't you fucking do *that*. That sonofabitch is a lot of things. But right isn't one of them."

She held Susan in her arms for a long time, until the sobbing subsided. They drank more wine and talked for another hour about things of no consequence.

When they went to bed, Jo lay awake in her room, thinking about it all. Susan in a grief so blinding she could actually consider that what happened was her fault. Dave writing angry and futile emails to a TV network that couldn't care less about him. Henry talking to a pony he'd purchased for a little girl gone away forever. That same little girl in the gazebo, the wonder in her eyes seeing a book about herself. And Sam Jackson. His hatred and his horseshit and his rhetoric, how pervasive it could be. And Jo still tuning in to the program, in spite of her overwhelming contempt for a man who was in every way an abomination. A man whose only function in life was to hurt people, to tear things down.

Somebody needed to tear him down.

FIFTEEN

It was assistant producer Kevin who took credit for persuading Senator Tom Harrison to come on the show. A few days after the Laureltown shooting Harrison had sponsored a bill banning assault weapons and had been appearing all over the map ever since, pushing it. But his office had turned down Renata several times, and even suggested that he stop asking. But then Sam ran into Harrison at a charity event with Rachel in the city. It was no coincidence. Sam never attended such things and Rachel was more than content with that. However, when he heard from Kevin that Harrison was going to be there, Sam insisted on coming along. Rachel tried to dissuade him; she knew that he was capable of changing the tone and the dialogue of any occasion, even one whose purpose was to raise money for medical research. He was adamant; he put on a tuxedo and drank scotch for an hour in his den while he waited for her to get ready.

At the event, Sam wasted no time in tracking down Harrison. The senator was standing with his wife, Martha, and both were talking to a TV actor and a columnist from the *Post*. Harrison, a glass of wine in his hand, stood ramrod straight, like the Marine he'd once been. He retained the crew cut from his military days. His wife was short and heavyset, with a helmet of blonde hair. She looked older than her husband, although she wasn't.

71

"Senator," Sam called out as he approached. He'd left Rachel when they'd arrived, grabbed a drink at the bar and gone looking for Harrison.

They'd never met before. Harrison's eyes flicked over Sam and then he accepted the extended hand, smiling but just slightly. Introductions were made but Sam paid scant attention to the actor or the columnist. Or Martha either, for that matter. He had the focus of a bird dog; he was there for one reason only and it wasn't to drink warm wine and schmooze with people he didn't care about.

"I've followed your career for years," Sam said. "I feel like I know who you are. So I have trouble believing it when I hear that you're afraid to come on my show. Guy like you."

Harrison nodded, as if to say—so this is how it's going to be. "A guy like me," he repeated slowly. "A guy like me is afraid of a lot of things. Your show would not be on that list."

"Then somebody should tell your office that," Sam said.

"I appreciate the advice."

"So you're saying you'll come on," Sam persisted.

"Isn't this a conversation for business hours?" Martha Harrison asked lightly. "We're here to support a cause."

"I can't get a reply during business hours," Sam said.

"A smart man knows when to take a hint," she told him.

Sam held up his hands. "You're right." He turned to Harrison. "I apologize, Senator. I wasn't aware that the wife was making these decisions for you. Duly noted."

Harrison was pissed now. He stepped close to Sam. "Are you saying that you and I are going to have a two-way conversation about gun control? Because if that's the case, tell me what day you want me there."

Renata had allowed Kevin to set it up and Harrison was now in the studio, sitting across from Sam, wearing a navy-blue suit with a white shirt and red tie. Sam had in recent weeks taken to wearing khakis and a blue cotton shirt, the sleeves rolled up. The pose of a working man, even though he'd never done a day's physical labor in his life. Displayed on the bookshelf behind him was the 1885 single-action Colt revolver that he had placed there immediately after Laureltown, telling the audience that the gun had belonged to his great-grandfather, who had served under Teddy Roosevelt. None of it was true; needing a prop, Sam had bought the weapon from an online auction house a few days after the shooting. Actually, he'd had Kevin buy it, to obscure the chain of ownership.

Harrison's appearance was a small coup for the show. They'd had trouble of late booking anybody from the Democrat side of the aisle. Kevin boasted to the network brass that he had scored the booking, not mentioning that said credit rested solely on the fact that he'd shown Sam a tiny item in the *Post*, which said that Harrison would be at the charity event.

Harrison had shown up with an aide and a jovial manner. He'd even brought a jar of honey from his home state of New Hampshire, which he'd presented to Sam before they'd gone into the studio.

"A little history, Senator," Sam said to begin. "Correct me if any of this rings false. You grew up on a farm outside of Concord. Started shooting guns when you were twelve years old. Hunted and fished growing up. Joined the Marines and did two tours in Vietnam, where we must assume that weapons were a part of your daily existence. You came home and have now represented the great state of New Hampshire for twenty-eight years. Never have you shown any interest in gun control." Sam paused for effect. "And now—all of a sudden— you, a decorated marine, have decided that you want to scuttle the Second Amendment. You, a war hero, are going to turn in your guns and are asking every citizen in this country to do the same."

"This is where I start to correct you," Harrison said. "First off, nobody has ever referred to me as a war hero. That is patently untrue. Secondly, I have never and will never advocate any *scuttling* of our Second Amendment rights. I defy you or your staff to find a single piece of evidence backing that claim. And I'm not turning my guns over to anybody, or asking anybody else to. I shot an eight-point buck last week with a 30.30 Winchester that's been in my family for decades."

"Then tell me what this bill of yours proposes to do," Sam said.

"You haven't read it?" Harrison asked. "I find that interesting, given that you've been badmouthing it on a nightly basis. You should have asked—I'd have sent you over a copy."

"Why don't you just tell me about it?"

Harrison leaned forward to take a drink of water. "It's a pretty comprehensive piece of legislation so I'll keep to the bare bones of things. First off, it calls for mandatory background checks for gun purchases. Over ninety per cent of Americans want this. Why can't it get through the Senate? Secondly, it calls for a ban on assault weapons, except in the hands of the military or law enforcement, and it also calls for a ban on bump stocks and on ammunition clips of thirty rounds. I told you I shot a buck last week? I was in a group of five men, most of whom I've known all my life. None of us felt the need to carry thirty rounds in our rifles when stalking a deer. And neither should anybody else."

"Here's the problem, Senator," Sam said. "It's not the *deer* we're worried about. We're worried about the criminal element, both from within and without this country. I'm talking about the drug dealers and pimps and terrorists and psychopaths and rapists and bandits and thugs. Any of whom might be armed with assault weapons. Any of whom might be carrying thirty round clips. You fight fire with fire, Senator."

"Which is why the military and the police should have those weapons."

"So you do want to deny the average Joe his Second Amendment rights."

"I do not. Have you ever read the amendment?"

"I can't believe you would ask me that," Sam scoffed. "I know my country. Have you watched this show? Have you read any of my books?"

"I haven't had the pleasure of either," Harrison said. "But I will tell you that the Second Amendment does not guarantee the right for your average Joe to bear arms. What it says—"

"You're going to dredge up the militia thing," Sam interrupted. "That's just semantics, Senator. Our founding fathers intended this nation to be armed. And we will be armed. We've been backsliding for too long. And you should trust me when I tell you there are millions of Americans who agree with me. Millions. A smart politician would take note of those numbers."

"This isn't about numbers. It's about common sense."

"You're tilting at windmills anyway," Sam said dismissively. "Who are we trying to kid? Obama couldn't get any traction on this so what makes you think it will happen now, with the Senate four-square against you, not to mention the guy in the Oval Office? Your party is trying to make political hay out of the tragedy in Laureltown. I get that. It's the way it works over there. But seriously—this dog won't hunt."

"I'm not so sure about that. This is an important bill, and more than that, it's an urgent issue."

"You've never been interested in gun control."

"Well, I am now," Harrison told him. "But what about you, Sam? Let me pose a question here. Do you believe in gun control of any kind?"

"No."

"You brought up Laureltown," Harrison continued. "Where a man named Arthur William Hays killed twenty-two children and two schoolteachers. He used a Bushmaster .223 with a thirty-round clip and a semi-automatic handgun. Tell me—were you okay with Arthur William Hays having those weapons that day? In that schoolyard?"

"Of course not."

"Then you believe in gun control."

Sam was caught, a rare event. "I believe in a well-armed citizenry!" he snapped after a moment. "That's what was required that day in Laureltown. One citizen with a gun. He would have stopped Hays cold. He'd have shot him down in the road like the mad cur that he was. But where was that citizen? He's not welcome here anymore. He's not welcome in this namby-pamby nation where people cower behind their doors at night and allow their children to be murdered in our playgrounds."

"You need to lose that thread," Harrison said. "The parents of those children are in no way responsible. You do them a great disservice."

"They're in every way responsible," Sam replied. "They didn't protect their kids. I have a daughter. If someone ever comes after her, he'd better cede his soul to Jesus because his ass is gonna belong to me." With his thumb he indicated the revolver on the shelf behind him. "Me and my friend Sam Colt."

"More guns is not the answer," Harrison said. "Control is the answer."

"You're on the wrong side of history, Senator," Sam told him. "When you outlaw guns, the only people with guns will be outlaws. We're going to take a break."

For a change, Sam didn't leave the studio between segments. He waited until they were clear and smiled at Harrison. "Come on now. Off the record. The party's got you out here tub thumping on this, don't they?"

"No," Harrison said. "This is about Laureltown, Sam. If nothing else, you and I agree on one thing. That man Hays should not have been in possession of a slingshot, let alone a firearm. We have to address that. When we're back, I'd like to talk about background checks."

Sam hesitated before glancing through the glass. "Kevin, how are we on time?"

Renata had been staying out of the way up until now and before she could say anything Kevin responded. He knew Sam's look, and he knew what the question meant. "Tight. But I think we've got what we need. Good job, Senator."

Harrison regarded Kevin darkly before turning to Sam. "There's more to talk about here."

"We'll have you back."

Harrison had been in the game long enough that he knew when he'd been snookered. He got to his feet. "I wouldn't count on it."

After the break Sam wrapped with a standard commentary. Gun control and creeping socialism. Not on Sam's watch. All bets are off.

When Sam walked into the booth afterward, most of the crew was watching one of the monitors.

"What's going on?" he asked.

"Harry Peakes died," Renata said. "About an hour ago."

"We're surprised?" Sam asked. "He was a hundred years old."

"Eighty-four."

Sam shrugged. Renata's phone rang and he stepped away. Sam walked over to stand behind the director.

"Run that bit when he told me I was in favor of gun control, when I hesitated before answering."

The director found the footage.

"Right there," Sam said. "Stop it. Right there, I'm back on my heels for just a second. We need to cut that. Stay with camera one on Harrison, let him finish and bang, I come right back with the line about armed citizens, or whatever I said. No hesitation. You can do that?"

"Not a problem, Sam."

"Good man," Sam said.

Renata approached, holding out her phone. "Bill Ford wants to talk to you."

SIXTEEN

The brothers Ford were waiting for him at a corner table in Shakespeare's Steak and Chop House on West 53rd. Sam had met them both before, on numerous occasions, but had never spoken to either man for more than a minute or so. They were in the news a lot these days, with the election approaching. Other than the fact that they were both tall and seventy-something, they didn't look like brothers. Bill was balding and dark, while the younger Ken was fair, with curly red hair. Ken had a reputation for not saying much. Bill wore a polo shirt while Ken was old school shirt and tie.

"We haven't ordered," Bill said when Sam sat down. "We were waiting on you."

"If I'm in Shakespeare's I'm having a steak," Sam said. The waiter was standing a few feet away. "And a Macallan to start. You might as well make it a double, save the wear and tear on your shoes, son."

Sam was aware that neither of the Fords drank and were in fact openly critical of it. Sam didn't give a shit.

"So what's going on, boys?"

"You heard the news about Harry Peakes," Bill said.

Sam nodded. "Another of the old guard gone. He was a good one."

"He lost his fastball years ago, but he'll be missed nonetheless," Bill said. "However, there's a bigger concern here. Peakes was up for re-election in November. The Dems have a pretty strong candidate in this man Barton. They're already making noise about the age issue."

"And now he's not just old, he's dead," Sam said. The waiter set the scotch down and Sam had a drink. "So who are you going to plug in there? And how can I help?"

Bill looked at Ken, who cleared his throat. "You're extremely popular in Wyoming, Sam."

Sam took a moment, wondering why he was being told this. "Well, that's my demographic."

"There was a time we wouldn't have thought this possible," Bill said.

Sam looked from one brother to the other. "You wouldn't have thought what was possible?"

"All of this, to be frank," Bill told him. "We didn't think that Trump was possible and look where we are. As for yourself, you're riding a wave. You're Huey Long right now."

Sam laughed. "Show me the demographic that knows who that is these days."

"They might not recognize the name but they know what appeals to them. We've been watching, and we've been talking about you. We think you could win that seat."

Sam had another drink. He hadn't known what to expect being summoned here, but it sure as hell wasn't this. "Is it wise—to be parachuting somebody in?"

"It is a risk, yeah," Bill said. "But either way, we have to introduce somebody brand new. We need a candidate with a familiar face. I have a house outside of Laramie. It could be in your name by tomorrow morning."

Sam laughed. "Well, shit. What the hell am I going to do in Congress? A good place for a man to get lost in the shuffle."

"Some men maybe," Bill said. "But the President likes you. I know for a fact that he wanted you part of his team but it was a numbers game. You know—take one from Row A, one from Row B, that sort of thing. You got lost in the shuffle. But he has not forgotten you, Sam, and what you did for him in '16. If you won the seat, you'd be looking at a cabinet post."

Sam's eyebrows rose at this. "What kind of post would a congressman from Wyoming rate? I'm not looking to become secretary of horse troughs."

"A significant post," Bill said. "Listen, the way it stands right now, the Democrats have a good chance to take that seat."

"What about the widow?" Sam asked. "Couldn't she win on the name alone?"

"She's the same age as Harry," Bill said. "If they were iffy on him because of that, they won't vote for her, with no experience. And she's not interested anyway. Look, we've been watching this situation for a couple of months. Harry was sick. We were hoping he'd make it to November but, if he didn't, we've been considering contingency plans. We thought we had a young state senator warming in the bullpen but he forgot to tell us about some Me Too issues."

Sam laughed. "Even movie stars aren't getting away with that these days."

"We've done some polling out there, Sam," Ken went on. "You're a bit of a folk hero with this all bets are off stuff. This is doable."

"It is?" Sam asked. "How does it work timewise? How soon do you need to announce?"

"Soon," Bill said. "Election day is six weeks away."

"We're going to be honest with you," Ken said. "All of these trends are fleeting. In spite of this alleged information age, your average citizen has the attention span of a gnat. At this moment in time, you're the cat's pajamas, Sam. Two years from now might be a different story but right now we see you as our best bet." He paused. "We're ready to commit five million dollars today to your campaign."

Sam had been waiting for the number. He'd known it was coming. From the moment they'd broached the subject he'd known. They wouldn't be suggesting it if they weren't going to pick up the tab. Five million seemed like a reasonable figure. Wyoming was a small state; TV time could be purchased there for a fraction of what it cost in New York or California. Not that Sam would have a snowball's chance of getting elected in those states. But Wyoming was another matter. Not only that, but he was pretty sure that the brothers would pony up even more if it was needed. To them it was Monopoly money.

But Congress?

"We do realize," Ken said, "that we're basically asking you to leave a very successful career."

"That's exactly what you're doing," Sam said.

"And we assume you weren't looking to leave the world of broadcasting at this time," Bill added.

Guess again, Sam thought. He had another drink. "I'm going to need to think about this."

"Absolutely," Bill agreed. "What do you need—a couple days?"

Sam drank off the scotch. "One day."

"Good," Bill said, clearly surprised. "Now what about those steaks?"

SEVENTEEN

It was the first time Jo had been to the Williamsburg market. She'd booked a stall a few days earlier, by phone, lucking out due to a cancellation. The market was usually booked solid, the woman who answered the phone told her. She came in alone, driving the seven-ton GMC, loaded with pumpkins and squash and potatoes and various melons, as well as a few hampers of late tomatoes and some of early apples. She drove into the city on Route 9, crossed over on the George Washington Bridge and took secondary streets to the market.

She'd left the farm an hour before sunrise, and was at the concrete slab that was the market shortly after six o'clock. Half the vendors were already there and set up. Jo found her stall, tucked in a corner between a guy selling huge salamis and blood sausage out of the back of a converted milk truck, and a woman who had eggs and cheese and jams and a dozen or so oil paintings displayed on a table made from two sawhorses and a sheet of plywood. The paintings were of flowers in vases, red roses and white lilies and crocuses of all colors, and a few landscapes.

Jo parked the truck and went to find the office to pay for her space. The woman she'd talked to on the phone had asked for a credit card number to hold the booking but Jo had told her that her card had just been compromised and she was waiting for a new one to arrive.

She would pay cash when she got there, which is what she did now. She had to fill out a form, given to her by the cashier or manager, or whatever her title was, a skinny woman with trailing red hair and a tattoo of a leaping dolphin on her upper arm. Jo registered as Pine Ridge Farms, a name that popped into her head. The form requested the license plate number of her truck, and she hesitated before making one up, hoping that the woman wouldn't walk over to check on it. Jo paid the stall fee and went to set up.

It was a warm autumn day and she sold a lot of produce. In the rare times that business was slow she was obliged to chat with her neighbors to each side. The salami guy had a thick accent Jo couldn't identify, other than it was European of some description. His name was André, which didn't help with the nationality.

The woman with the eggs and the artwork said her name was Lily. She was middle-aged, with dyed black hair and dangling gypsy earrings. When she wasn't dealing with customers, she was constantly taking pictures of everything around her—the customers, the vendors, the merchandise. She said she used the snapshots for her painting. Jo had to keep a watch out, ducking her head or turning away whenever the woman pointed the camera in her direction.

"Is good stuff you have," André told her at one point, palming a pumpkin like a basketball player with a ball. He was short, maybe five seven, with a large gut that stretched his dirty white T-shirt. "Never I see you here before. Where are coming from?"

Jo lifted another hamper of tomatoes from the truck while she considered what to say. "New Jersey."

"Oh?" he said. "But you are having New York license plates."

"My brother's truck," she told him. "I borrowed it for the day."

"Where is it in New Jersey you are?"

Jo thought about that. "Newton."

"My aunt lives in Newton." This from the woman called Lily. "Are you close to town?"

Just my luck, Jo thought. "No, up north a bit."

"Near Frankford then?"

"Not really." Jo needed to get off the subject. "Where are you from?"

"Up near West Point," Lily told her. "I have an old farmhouse."

Jo turned. "And you, André? Where's home?"

"I am here in city."

Jo indicated the meats, hanging like so many neckties from racks fastened to the back of the truck. "You make all your own stuff?"

"Of course. I am making sausage and salami for forty-three years, since I am ten years age."

Jo believed it. André actually smelled like smoked meat, as if the process had permeated his pores over four decades. The man was a walking salami. "Where are you from originally?

"I am of Greek and French both," he said. "Born in Montpelier, France. So you have farm in New Jersey?"

"Yes."

"It has how many acres?"

"Small," Jo said. She was saved from further interrogation when a customer walked up and asked a question about her tomatoes. She went into a lengthier discourse about heirlooms that she normally would.

Both André and Lily packed up and left by mid-afternoon. At around five Jo loaded what was left of the produce in the truck and locked it, then went for a walk toward the river. Most of the area was gentrified but there were still some old buildings along the waterfront. She found an abandoned covered parking lot by one, with a padlocked chain across the entrance and a number of KEEP OUT signs on the walls. She stepped over the chain and walked through the lot. The exit at the far end emptied on to Gage Street, heading north toward the bridge. She turned and went back to the entrance and stood there for a moment, looking toward the market a few blocks away.

Then she walked back to the truck and headed for home.

EIGHTEEN

He told Renata over the phone on Saturday afternoon. She immediately suggested that he come to her place to talk it over but Sam wasn't interested in talking it over.

"They don't actually think you can win?" There was an edge to her voice.

"Who?"

"The Fords," she said. "Who do you think?"

"Thanks for the vote of confidence." Sam was sitting in his car near the river. The wind was up; there were whitecaps on the water.

"You're not a politician," she said.

"Neither was Ronald Reagan," Sam reminded her. "What is your problem with this?"

She didn't say anything for a moment. "It's just that I thought you were going to stick it out until after the elections."

"Now I don't have to."

"Christ," she said and then she didn't say anything for a time. He could hear her breathing. He imagined her trying to control it. Out on the river, a tugboat was coming toward him, angling into the waves.

"I have to do this," he said. "It's my out."

"The Fords are actually buying into this? They can't see that it's a fucking act?"

"I'm not sure they're buying it, but apparently they think they can sell it," Sam said. "Besides, it's no more of an act than everybody else in the game. You going to tell me that Trump isn't an act? He's a circus clown who became fucking president. You think Bill Clinton wasn't an act. George Dubya—acting like a tough guy when we all know where he was during Vietnam. Under a bar stool in Texas somewhere, snorting cocaine."

"What are you going to tell the network?"

"Same thing I was going to tell them a month from now. Goodbye."

"Never mind the fucking network," she said. "What are you going to tell me?"

"Other than what I've just told you?"

"Yeah," she said. "Other than what you've just told me. This changes our dynamic somewhat, wouldn't you say?"

He'd almost never seen her angry but he'd known it was coming. Which is why he'd called her and not dropped by. "Well, yeah, it does. At least temporarily."

"Any chance you can elaborate on that?"

"We're not going to be able to see each other. Rachel and Vanessa are going to have to be part of this. You understand that?"

"Wow…you actually said their names."

He paused. "You do understand that part?"

"Stop pretending there are parts I don't understand, Sam. I get it all. What's Rachel think about this? Does she want to go to Washington?"

"I haven't told her yet."

"Well, I'll get off the phone," Renata said. "You know—so you can *call* her and ask."

"I'm not going to Washington," Rachel told him.

"You said that," Sam replied. "Three times now. Did I say anything about you moving to Washington?"

"Well, I'm not moving to fucking Wyoming either."

"Neither am I."

They were in the kitchen. Sam was sitting at the island drinking scotch and Rachel was at the counter in the kitchen, opening a bottle of chardonnay. She'd arrived home a half-hour earlier, saying she'd come from dinner with friends. Vanessa was in bed, the housekeeper gone for the day. It was just after ten o'clock.

"How are you going to manage that?" She poured the wine into a glass. "After you've been ranting against parachute candidates all these years? Does the name Hillary Clinton ring a bell?"

"The election's a month away. I'll spend a few days there, shake some hands, talk about the alfalfa or whatever. How much time do you think the average congressman spends in his home state?"

"So you'll buy a house there?" she asked. "Hey—you could buy a ranch and tell the voters it belonged to your great-grandfather. The one who rode up the hill with Teddy Roosevelt."

"Sounds to me as if you girls had lots to drink at dinner." Sam took a drink. "Bill Ford has a place in Laramie."

Rachel scoffed. "Bill Ford probably has fifty houses, one in each state, just for situations like this." She had more wine. "Why are you even considering this, when your ratings are through the roof? I might understand if it was a couple of months ago. Well, maybe not the Wyoming part."

"I've been looking for an excuse to leave the show. This fills the bill. And even if I get beat, I can still say I did it for my love of country. Fact is, a couple of months ago the Fords wouldn't have had any interest in me. And neither would the voters of Wyoming."

"I suppose not." She leaned back against the kitchen counter and drank the wine, watching him. She wanted a cigarette but she never smoked in the house. "Have you really thought about *being* a congressman? I mean, as opposed to just the idea of it. It's not the fucking senate. There's, like, four hundred congressmen, aren't there?"

"Four hundred and thirty-five."

"You're willing to be part of the pack? In the back row somewhere, little Sam Jackson from the little state of Wyoming? Is that how you see yourself?"

"The Ford brothers have considerably more foresight than you," Sam told her. "I won't be one of the pack. They've guaranteed me a cabinet post."

"I'm sure that's their standard sales pitch."

"Are you trying to piss me off? I know exactly what's going on here. I have a bully pulpit and there are people who think I should use it. They have the money but I have the pulpit. They need me as much as I need them. You don't have to like it, Rachel. But I'm not asking you to live in Washington or Wyoming or anyplace other than this beautiful house that I paid for and allow you to completely renovate every other year on my dime. So if I decide to do this—"

"You've decided," she interrupted him.

He hesitated. "I guess I have. What I started to say is that you will be required to show up for a few public events. Smile and look pretty, which you do well. You come up with a story that you're not in Wyoming because of your charitable work here. But that you're looking forward to living there, even though you never will. What else? You'll have to do a couple of photo ops. Nessa too."

Rachel sighed in resignation. She had never in eighteen years changed his mind about anything. And in truth, she didn't care if he went to Wyoming, or Washington either. She wasn't going anywhere. "Let's keep her out of it. Politicians manage to do that."

Sam shrugged. "We'll see." He poured more scotch. She was always amazed at how much liquor he could put away without showing it. "Speaking of Nessa, what's going on with the mick driver?"

"He was late again. I gave him two weeks' notice. Enough."

"We need to hire somebody then."

"The agency's sending over some resumes."

"You take care of it," he said.

"Who did you think would take care of it, Sam?"

"Quit pouting," he told her. "We're talking about a few weeks here. I'm not asking you to change your life. But I need you to be committed to this. You need to show up and show up with a smile. You do understand that part, right?"

"Yeah," she said. "I do."

"How do you know you won't like being a congressman's wife?" he asked. "What do they do anyway? They have lunch and organize charity events so they can salve their consciences over the fact that they don't accomplish anything of substance. Sound familiar, Rachel?"

"Fuck you," she said.

She'd had enough of the conversation. They rarely talked about anything and now, when they did, he was telling her that she'd be required to jump through hoops for him for the next month and a half. Not asking her, telling. She started for the stairs before stopping to look back at him. He was watching her with a shitty cast to his eye, as if he'd just won something and he was reveling in it.

"You realize what the other side is going to say, don't you? They're going to say that you're using those dead kids in Pennsylvania to try to get yourself elected to office. *You* understand that part, right?"

"Let 'em say it. I don't give a shit what the left says about me."

"You know, when most people say they don't give a shit, it's bogus, because they really do and they don't want to admit it. But with you, it's true." She smiled then, but there was no humor in it. "So let me tell you what I think about this notion of you running for Congress. I really don't give a shit."

NINETEEN

Jack was in the Bahamas when they got the news that the host of the network's eight o'clock hour had decided to run for Congress. Typical of Sam, he gave no warning. He didn't even have the courtesy to deliver the news personally, leaving the job to his lickspittle Kevin.

Jack wasn't at all certain as to how he felt about the announcement. He decided to fly back to New York to talk to Bobby about it in person. They met at Callahan's on Broadway. It was nine o'clock and Bobby was already there when Jack arrived. The dinner crowd was thinning and they had a corner table to themselves. Jack ordered a Manhattan and another martini for Bobby.

"He's the gift that keeps on giving, isn't he?" he asked while he waited for his drink. "We want to fire the guy because his ratings are in the shithouse. We're a heartbeat away, he goes on a rant about dead children and his numbers go through the roof. He turns around and uses those numbers to try and get himself elected to Congress, while telling us to take a flying fuck. Send this over to the drama department; they could make a series out of it."

Bobby laughed. "But who would believe it?"

Jack shook his head. "I'm smack in the middle of it and I don't."

Bobby had a drink. "He's just one of those guys. He could fall into a barrel of shit and come up smelling like orange blossoms. Not that I consider a U.S. congressman to be all that aromatic."

"Where's he getting the money?" Jack asked. "Don't tell me he's financing his own campaign."

"Not a chance. He was seen supping with the Ford brothers a few nights ago."

"Of course he was," Jack said. "I should have known that."

The drinks arrived. Jack took a slug of the bourbon mix and wiped his mouth. "So Rivera—that's the move?"

Bobby nodded. "We're calling him an interim host. Although Sam, through his proxy snot Kevin, strongly recommended Jim Paisley."

"Who?"

"He's got a regional show out of Nashville, evangelical type. He and Sam are buddies or something. The guy's a bit of a dimwit. I said that we weren't going to give eight o'clock to some rural preacher we haven't vetted. The way our luck's been running on this, we'd put him on the air and then find out he fucks goats. Sam got a little pissy and then gave us permission to approach Rivera."

"He does realize it's none of his business."

"Apparently he does not."

"Jesus," Jack said shaking his head. "And this guy's running for office. So how's it going to play out? Can he win?"

"He's got a chance," Bobby said. "With the Ford money behind him, who knows? That basically gives him unlimited campaign funds. And he's very popular right now with a certain segment of the population. Pure serendipity that the Wyoming seat became available at this point in time. I don't think you'd want to run Sam Jackson for office out at Fire Island."

"Where does it leave us if he wins?"

"Without Sam Jackson," Bobby said smiling. He finished the first martini and reached for the second. "This spike in his ratings wasn't going to last. It was a direct result of his Laureltown rant and sooner or later people were going to get tired of it. He's always been a one-trick pony."

"So if he gets elected, our dreams are fulfilled," Jack said.

Bobby nodded. "Something like that. We were going to have to dump him sooner or later. And this way, we don't have to buy him off."

"And what if he loses? Is he going to want his spot back?"

"He might," Bobby said. "But he's not going to get it."

Jack had another sip of the Manhattan. Bobby had noticed in recent months that he usually restricted himself to one drink. It hadn't always been that way. "So we want him to win. That's the most painless scenario. Which means we should give him every access to the network during his campaign."

"I think that's a good idea," Bobby said. "He's been our problem long enough."

TWENTY

Laramie might have been a good idea back in the frontier days, when it was little more than a stop on the flat prairie for people headed for Oregon or California or some other supposed Eden on the western reaches of the continent. Someplace better than this, and better than wherever they'd come from. That had been the way of it back then and maybe that was one of the problems today. People had no place left to go to better themselves, to pull themselves up. When that happened, they turned on each other. Which pretty much explained the inner cities these days, Sam thought. And a good part of the country on the whole.

Laramie was just a depot back then and in Sam's eyes, it had never become anything more than that. It had been dark when he'd landed the night before so he couldn't see much of the city, just row on row of lights, and vehicles making their way in and out of town. By light of day the place was like the prairie itself—low and flat and featureless. Box stores and garages and car dealerships. The population hadn't grown in decades, suggesting that people were still just passing through. Whatever the banality of the place, Sam supposed that it was as good a town as any to pretend to be his new home.

He'd flown out with Bill Ford on the private jet and spent the night at Ford's house on the plains a few miles out of town. The place was a three-story stone ranch house, built in the 1920s by a Boston bootlegger who wanted to play cowboy. The acreage itself had been long since sold off, to a conglomerate that grew barley by the thousands of acres. The house was filled with western art and stuffed animals—bison and bears and mountain goats. There was a theater room inside and a helicopter pad outside. A large barn that had once housed quarter horses was now filled with antique cars—Stutz Bearcats and Rolls-Royces and REO Speedwagons. Not a Chevy or a Plymouth to be found.

They had announced Sam's candidacy two days earlier. Everyone on the Republican side, both on the state and national level, had professed to be delighted with the choice, whether they were or not. The left, as expected, had immediately begun sniping about the parachute factor, digging up endless footage of Sam decrying the practice over the span of his TV career. As an issue it was like a kid throwing a tantrum. Ignore it and it would stop on its own.

Bill Ford had concocted a tale of how Sam had visited the Laramie house many times over the years and had been trying to buy it during that period, having fallen in love with the property as well as the state and Wyomingites in general. Now Ford, out of friendship to Sam and loyalty to his party, had finally agreed to sell. Nobody paying attention was buying the story for a minute but—outside of Rachel Maddow or Chris Matthews—nobody was going to spend a lot of time disputing it. It wasn't the first time a candidate had taken up residency in a district in order to run for Congress, although it might have been the first time a candidate had done it just five weeks before an election.

Bill Ford had been up early and gone for a run on the narrow road than snaked through the barley fields. When Sam came downstairs he found coffee brewed in the kitchen and a note from Bill, saying where he had gone. Sam sat drinking the coffee for half an hour while reading about himself on his tablet. The house was quiet, eerily so, with only the sound of an occasional passing car to break the silence. There was a big screen TV in the high-ceilinged front room, positioned between the heads of a grizzly bear and a pronghorn antelope, but Sam couldn't locate a remote to turn it on.

When Bill came back, they had breakfast on a two-tiered deck at the back of the house, with the prairies stretching before them to the west, where the Grand Tetons could be seen under a hazy morning sky. A housekeeper who'd arrived at eight o'clock brought them eggs and ham and home-fried potatoes.

Bill indicated Sam's computer. "What are they saying?"

Sam lifted a forkful of scrambled eggs. "I'm either the biggest opportunist since John D. Rockefeller or a savior, sent from above to save Wyoming from a great socialist plague." He chewed the eggs before reaching for his coffee. "Sean Hannity says I'm a true American hero."

By the time breakfast was finished and the dishes cleared, a woman had arrived, walking around the outside of the house and climbing the steps as if she knew where she'd find the two men. Her name was Molly Esponda. She was maybe forty, tall and lanky, with dark hair and eyes. She wore a long skirt with cowboy boots, a white blouse. She was a native of Cheyenne, Bill Ford announced, and she was Sam's campaign manager. Molly Esponda poured coffee for herself and as she did Bill Ford said he needed to make a call. He got up and walked into the house.

"Well, this is exciting," Molly said, looking over at Sam, holding the coffee cup in both hands, waiting for it to cool.

"What is?" Sam asked. He was feeling chafed that the Fords had hired her without consulting him. How did they know that he himself didn't have someone in mind? And who the hell was this cowgirl sitting across from him anyway?

"Running for Congress," Molly replied. "A brand-new campaign, a chance to get your message out. All that good stuff."

Sam shrugged. "Maybe you and I get excited about different things."

She smiled slightly and turned away. "Look at that morning sky." She gestured toward the foothills in the distance. "I bet you don't have a view like that in New York City."

"Expert on New York, are you?" Sam asked.

"I wouldn't say expert. I went to Columbia and worked in the city for a few years."

"Doing what?"

"I worked for Giuliani's office," she said. "I modeled a little."

"How does either of those qualify you to be my campaign manager?"

She had a drink, looking at him calmly over the cup as if she'd been expecting the question, or the attitude. Maybe both.

"Like Bill said, I'm from here." She leaned forward to place the cup on the table. "Given the circumstances of your candidacy, I think it was assumed you might not be up on the social intricacies or the history of the state. I can help with that. It might also be assumed that you don't know a lot of people here. Key Republicans. I can help with that too."

"If I were you, I wouldn't assume too much," Sam told her. "I know more about my country than ninety-nine per cent of the people out there. And what I don't know, I can learn pretty damn quick. We're talking about a state with a population I could cram in a New York City block." He glanced toward the house for a moment, thinking that Bill Ford's phone call had been awfully convenient. Leaving the two of them alone. He turned back to her. "Here's the thing. I don't like being told to what to do or where to go. Especially by someone who brags that she was a lingerie model or that she used to answer emails for that fucking lapdog Giuliani."

He was trying to piss her off and she wasn't going for it. She sat smiling to herself, looking past him, toward the barn full of old cars, the relentless plains beyond.

"Well?" he said after a moment. "Are you going to tell me why I need you?"

"You obviously don't." She turned to him. "I was persuaded to take this on, and I have to say I was reluctant to do so. I have a busy consulting business back home and two teenagers to boot. Literally, sometimes. This was going to be a full-out, five-week commitment that I really didn't need. I was doing it as a favor to the Fords. My impression of you was that you're a fucking know-it-all egotist who doesn't listen to anyone around him. But I thought it was an act.

Apparently, it's not. So I'll just finish my coffee and head quite happily on back to Cheyenne."

Sam forced a laugh. "You're awful touchy."

"No," she said. "I'm a pragmatist. I had a husband who was a lot like you. Fool me once." She stood up. "If you're interested, I have your day's itinerary drawn up. I'll email it to Bill and he can give it to you before he leaves. He's flying to Dallas this morning, in case you were under the impression he was going to babysit you personally for the next month or so. You're not nearly as precious as you think. But I'm sure you'll do fine out there all by yourself, independent man that you are."

She went down the steps and was gone. Sam had to follow her around the house to the driveway out front. When he got there, she was sitting behind the wheel of a white Yukon, typing something on her iPhone. Sending his itinerary, Sam guessed. Her window was down as he approached.

"Slow down," he said.

"What do you want?"

He paused. "I do need a campaign manager." He was looking to save face now. Unfamiliar territory for him. "Come on. You were right, that was an act back there. A little test, to see if you had cojones."

"Sorry," she said. "Ovaries."

"Whatever. I think we can work together. You're obviously an intelligent woman. And if Bill Ford recommends you—"

"Isn't this the conversation we should have had from the get-go?"

"You're right. I don't know why I was being an asshole."

"I've seen your show," she said. "You are an asshole."

At ten o'clock that evening they were in the lounge of the Plains Hotel in Cheyenne. Molly sat, half listening, while Sam gave an interview to a reporter from the *Dispatch*. They'd been on the move all day, starting with a radio interview in Laramie, a lunchtime stop at the Elk Lodge and a photo op in a gun store. Then they'd driven to Cheyenne and spent the rest of the day doing media interviews there. Molly had cherry-picked the agenda; every venue was pro-Republican and NRA-friendly. Eventually Sam would have to be made marginally available to the other side but for the time being, fresh out of the gate, they were preaching to the choir. Like most TV talking heads these days, Sam was a celebrity of sorts and his presence was causing more commotion than Molly had anticipated. A young redneck in a pickup truck actually shouted "All bets are off!" as he walked down the street.

Sam Jackson had never campaigned before and he had a lot to learn. Molly recognized right away the difficulties of teaching anything to a man who was convinced he already knew everything. Still, it was part of her job to try. When they stopped at the Elk Lodge in Laramie, Sam had refused the offer of lunch.

"You can't turn down food," Molly told him afterward. They were driving through traffic. "You're going to eat a lot of chicken-fried steak in the next five weeks. And beans and chili and beef jerky."

"The hell I am."

Pulling up to a red light, she gave him a look. "You're perceived as an outsider. Refusing the local cuisine just reaffirms that image. So suck it up and eat whatever they offer you, at least a bite or two. Are you familiar with prairie oysters?"

"They're bull's testicles."

"Correct."

"I'm not eating any testicles."

Molly hit the gas. "Suit yourself. If you don't eat 'em though, the locals are going to say you don't have 'em."

The reporter sitting with them now was a hack who had worked for a number of papers across the state for thirty years or more, a typical second-rate newsman with his best days behind him, posing as an ink-stained wretch from the days of yore. Wrinkled suit, shirt washed too many times, hair plastered down. He was stretching the interview out because he was drinking vodka tonics and, as long as it was official business, Molly was buying. It was more of an ass-kissing session than an interview anyway, with the wretch constantly referring to things Sam had said on his TV show, things that had nothing to do with Wyoming or the election but were easy to find on Google, which demonstrated the extent of his research. It was obvious he'd never read any of Sam's books, but then again, neither had Molly.

Like a drunken uncle, the man overstayed his welcome. When he was finally gone, Molly ordered bourbon for herself, her first drink of the day. Sam had been into the scotch since they'd stopped for dinner around seven. His drinking was something Bill Ford had warned Molly about. If the man was going to booze, they couldn't stop him but he needed to do it in private. Still, she was forced to admit that he'd handled himself well that day, not all that surprising for a man with a long career as an on-air personality who considered himself head and shoulders above the crowd anyway.

One day down and thirty-something to go.

"Esponda," he said when they were alone at the table. "How did you end up in Wyoming?"

"We've been here a long time," she told him. "My family is Basque. We came here at the turn of the last century. Sheep ranchers."

"Basque."

"That's right. Good thing we snuck in when we did. We showed up today, people like you would try to keep us out."

"I have no problem with Europeans coming here," Sam told her.

"See—that's the type of thing you can't say," Molly said. "It suggests that you do have a problem with non-Europeans coming here. And that just leads you down a slippery slope."

"Maybe I do have a problem with certain people from certain countries coming here. As does our President."

"Yeah—and he gets hammered for it," Molly reminded him. "Don't hand the opposition arrows to shoot back at you."

Sam shrugged. "You say your family's from Spain. So you're what—Roman Catholic?"

Sipping the bourbon, she nodded. She found she was somewhat fascinated by him, his narrow-minded confidence, his inability to focus on anything that didn't reflect directly on him. He would make a good case study for somebody. Not her though; she wasn't *that* fascinated.

"You're what this country needs," he told her. "God-fearing people. Hard-working, honest. Raising sheep and planting crops and taking care of their families."

"We got rid of the sheep a few generations ago."

"My point is," he went on, "we don't encourage that anymore. Immigrants nowadays want to run corner stores and car washes. They don't worship the way we do. They don't respect us or our constitution. So why do we welcome them? It should be pretty simple—if you're not going to make this country a better place, stay the fuck out."

"Quite a slogan," she said. "I'm thinking we won't put that one on a sign."

"You joke but you'd be surprised how many people would want one."

"I wouldn't be surprised in the least," Molly said. "Look at what happened in 2016."

"You saying you didn't vote for him? Staunch Republican that you are?"

Molly finished her drink and stood. "I'm going to hit it. We have an early start in the morning." She left him at the table with his drink, smiling as she walked away.

TWENTY-ONE

Jo loaded the truck Tuesday night. Henry was there to help but mostly he stood watching her while he made one last argument against what they were doing. He had been back and forth on the matter for a few days, ever since she told him her plan. Sometimes, when he was stoned or into the wine, he was four-square behind her, but then he would suddenly swing the other way and offer up dire predictions of where they would all end up if things went sour. Jo wasn't listening. She'd made up her mind.

She didn't sleep well. She told herself not to think about it, that the hardest part had been in the deciding. Now, it was all about the execution. Second-guessing wasn't going to help at this point.

She left the farm when it was still dark, rolling the GMC out of the driveway under the promise of a hazy dawn. She took the county roads, keeping off the thruway and away from the toll booths. Entering the city, she crossed the river on the George Washington Bridge again. The sun was just showing as she drove into the market area. She parked in the same stall and walked over to pay for her spot.

"Becoming a regular," the red-haired woman said. Her eyes were bloodshot and she smelled of pot.

"Maybe," Jo replied.

André the sausage maker was pulling in as she walked back to her stall. He greeted her like they had known each other for years. He wore the same blood-stained wife-beater as he had the previous time Jo had been there, a shirt that would have caused alarm had she not known what the man did for a living.

"Again you have your brother's truck."

Jo, unloading sweet potatoes, nodded.

"Mine own brother would not lend me the time of day," André said.

Lily arrived an hour later, after Jo had already set up her produce on the tables and was making some sales. André, not moving anything to speak of, was hanging around Jo's stall, making small talk. He had lots of questions about Jo's farm and she occupied herself inventing answers for him. Lily had some new watercolors she wanted to show off. Jo and André praised them, more than was justified. Jo had the uneasy feeling of family.

"I heard you had a big fire over your way," Lily said.

"Right." Jo hesitated. "I never heard many details though."

"The barn burned to the ground," Lily went on. "I thought you would have heard that. It was just north of Newton. Close to your place?"

"Not really."

"I thought it would have been."

Jo was saved by a young woman looking for plum tomatoes for canning. She sold her a hamper full, and then went into the truck for more. When she came back, André was on his cellphone.

"All right," he said into the phone before putting it away. He turned to Jo and Lily. "You will both come to my house for supper. My aunt will cook for us."

"Oh, I can't," Jo said at once.

"Of course you can," he told her.

"Not today," Jo said. "I have something on."

"What is this something? It cannot be that important."

"Actually, it is," she assured him.

TWENTY-TWO

They did the Fox morning show out of New York City at nine-thirty the next day, live from the network affiliate in Cheyenne. It was another lightweight interview. In four minutes, Sam managed to praise the Second Amendment, slam universal health care and even to slide in a few facts about Wyoming's coal and grain production. He'd obviously been reading some of the stuff Molly had been sending to his laptop. When the pert and bubbly host of the show somewhat reluctantly brought up the outsider issue, Sam told her that nobody complained when a certain Illinois outsider landed in Washington back in 1860.

"That's going to be my response to that nonsense from now on," he told Molly afterward. They were in her Yukon, heading for a lunch meeting with the head of the mineworkers' union.

"What is?"

"That little twinkie tried to nail me on the carpetbagger shit and I told her that nobody complained when another Republican, a guy named Abraham Lincoln, parachuted into Washington in 1860."

They were stopped at a light. Molly looked over. "You do recall that when Lincoln arrived in Washington half the country seceded from the Union?"

Sam was quiet for a long moment. "Fuck it. It's a good line. Your average citizen isn't sharp enough to pick up on that."

"We won't be putting that on a sign either."

By five o'clock they were back in Cheyenne. Molly drove through the city to an older neighborhood on the south side: a green and leafy enclave of large, somewhat garish, homes built in the days when people were still getting rich in the cattle business.

"What's here?" Sam asked as she slowed the Yukon down, approaching a brick Tudor three-story with wide porches on all sides.

"Rance Dunning is here."

"What's he want from me?"

"It's what you want from him," Molly said. "His endorsement."

"It has value?" Sam smirked. "I didn't realize it was 1988."

Senator Dunning was waiting for them on the west porch, alone, sitting in a large wicker armchair in the sun. His famously craggy eyebrows were as white as his mane and he wore brown cotton pants and a University of Wyoming sweatshirt, sneakers on his feet. There was a cane leaning against the wall, within reach. He stood up to give Molly a hug before shaking Sam's hand.

"Sit," he told them. "How was your day?"

The old man kept his eyes on Sam as Molly provided a condensed version of their recent itinerary. Sam returned the look for a few moments then glanced around the property, at the cottonwoods and white pines protecting the place from the wind, the gardens along-side the winding drive. The flowers suggested a woman's presence. It seemed to Sam that the old man's wife had died several years ago. Maybe there was a new wife in the picture, maybe even a young trophy type. Dunning had to be in his eighties; he'd been gone from the Senate for more than a decade.

"Sounds as if you've been sticking to the green pastures," Dunning said when Molly finished.

Molly smiled. "And where would you have started, Rance?"

"Those very fields," the old man told her.

Sam sat watching the two of them, sharing their little joke, and wondered if at some point he was going to be offered a drink. It didn't appear so. Dunning looked over.

"Aside from the predictable charges of parachuting into a state you've shown virtually no interest in until now," he said in his soft drawl, "what do you see as your biggest obstacle in getting elected?"

"I don't see any obstacles in getting myself elected," Sam replied.

The eyebrows went up. "No?"

"My message is clear. The country has responded to a similar message recently and I see no reason why they won't again."

"That's one note," Dunning said. "If you sound just one note, after a while people will stop listening. Not only that, but you're only preaching to one side of the congregation. You need to reach across that aisle, sir."

"I prefer to have them come to me," Sam said. "I'm not big on compromise. It smacks of weakness."

"You don't believe in compromise?" Dunning asked incredulously. "What if we took that position back in the '80s? What would we have accomplished without bipartisan support?"

"We'll never know," Sam said.

"But we know what we *did* accomplish," Dunning reminded him. "And, frankly, I see very little of that happening in Washington today."

Sam shrugged. "I'm sure you guys had fun joining hands and singing 'Kumbaya'. But things are different now. The other side doesn't want to listen. And I'm not inclined to beg them to."

"Then what do you intend to accomplish in Congress?"

"Plenty," Sam told him. "If we take back the House and hold the Senate, we should be able to do whatever the hell we want." He paused. "And I think we've already seen that the President is…somewhat easily influenced."

Dunning glanced at Molly a moment. "That's not the way I have ever approached things. I've never embraced the notion of excluding half of our population. I don't believe that's the way to govern."

Molly watched Sam's eyes narrow. It had been a mistake bringing him here.

"Times have changed," Sam told the old man. "What's the point of having a whip in your hand if you're not willing to use it?"

"That's a decidedly unfortunate metaphor, sir," Dunning said. "And one that would make a lot of people uncomfortable."

"Making people uncomfortable is what I do," Sam told him.

"And you take pride in that?"

"You're fucking right I take pride in it."

Molly didn't say much on the drive back into the city. She could have told Sam that he shouldn't expect an endorsement from the man who was probably the most respected elder statesman in Wyoming, but she was sure that Sam knew that, just as she was quite certain that Sam didn't give a shit. What Molly couldn't figure out was—why not?

Sam was set to appear at a fundraiser at the Emerald Greens Golf and Country Club at seven o'clock so they had an early dinner at a steak house downtown. Sam ordered a double scotch and a porterhouse. Molly asked for soda water and the grilled steelhead.

While they waited for their food, Sam pulled his phone from his pocket and began typing. Googling himself, Molly suspected. Who was saying what about Sam Jackson. Electronic devices had turned the world into one giant high school.

"You need to get me on *The Press Box*."

She gestured toward the phone. "Why?"

"Fucking Tim Rutherford," Sam said. "Snide little prick."

He handed Molly the phone so she could see what he was talking about. She managed not to smile as she read aloud what the TV host had said. "'There was quite an air show over Wyoming this past weekend, as Sam Jackson jumped out of a Boeing 747 and parachuted into the state, his very descent baffling the scientific community, which has maintained for centuries that hot air rises.'"

Molly shrugged as she handed the phone back. "At least the left has noticed you."

"Get me on his show."

"I can try," Molly said. "But he's pretty selective about who he offers a soapbox."

"He's afraid of me."

"Are you under the impression that everybody is afraid of you?"

Sam considered the question. "Pretty much. Guys like Tim Rutherford anyway."

Molly thought about that and then excused herself to go to the restroom. She washed her hands, then took out her cell and called Roxanne at New Age Polling.

"Molly. You get the weekend numbers?"

"Yeah," Roxanne said. "I was just going to email them over. They're not good."

"Where are we?"

"Thirty-five per cent. Barton's at forty-four."

Molly thought about it. "But we're early in."

"He's got a huge credibility problem, Molly."

They talked a bit longer and then Molly called Bill Ford. "I don't know that this is going to work, Bill."

"Why not?"

She told him the numbers.

"It's been two days," Bill said.

"It's not that so much," Molly said. "The people of Wyoming are not stupid. They see exactly what's going on here. Obviously there are people who will just vote the ticket, but we're getting a lot of 'he's not one of us' in the polling data. And that's from Republicans, Bill. You have to remember: Barton's born and bred here. Not only that, but Sam Jackson comes off as an arrogant elitist. That doesn't play well out in the hinterland."

"Come election day though, he's going to be the only guy running for the GOP," Bill said.

"So you're betting they'll hold their noses and vote for him," Molly said.

"I'm betting five million dollars they will."

She heard Bill then say something to somebody in the room with him, wherever he was. "Okay," he said when he came back. "We trust you on this. Let's run him out there every day for a week and see where we stand. If the dog can't hunt, we'll have another look at things."

When Molly got back to the table Sam was reading something on his phone and drinking scotch. Molly sat and considered the best way to approach him about the alcohol factor. He had enough problems without appearing to be a lush. She was still considering it when his cell rang. As soon as he replied Molly could hear the urgent tone at the other end. A woman's voice. Sam's expression never changed as he listened.

"Okay," he said. He listened some more, the voice on the other end growing louder. "I said okay," he told the woman again and hung up.

Molly wasn't going to ask. He didn't look at her, just sat there for a moment, glancing around the dark restaurant. He drained the scotch and raised the empty glass above his head to get the waiter's attention. Finally he looked over at Molly.

"I need to get on a plane for New York."

"What's going on?"

"My daughter's missing."

TWENTY-THREE

Jo hadn't seen Daniel since their encounter in the Laureltown bar several weeks earlier, although they had been talking on the phone quite frequently of late. When he pulled up in the black limousine, she was waiting in the covered parking lot near the river. She'd cut the padlock from the chain across the entrance with Henry's ancient bolt cutters and driven the GMC to the far corner of the lot. She opened the roll-up door as Daniel got out to open the back door of the limo. The girl looked scared when he took her from the back seat and led her to the truck. For a multi-millionaire's kid, she looked like any other. Pink runners, white jeans and a T-shirt with a cartoon figure on it. Her blonde hair in a ponytail. She had pierced ears, Jo noticed. Not unusual these days for her age.

"Where are you taking me?" she asked, her voice thin with fear.

"To meet your mother," Daniel said.

"I don't believe you."

Daniel didn't say anything else and neither did Jo. Inside the truck, bolted to the floor at the front of the box, amid the hampers of tomatoes and bags of potatoes, was a bucket seat, salvaged from a van Henry had once driven to market. They put the girl in the seat and fastened the seat belt. Both the seat and belt had been Henry's idea.

"You get her phone?" Jo asked.

Daniel nodded and took a slip of paper from his pocket and handed it over. There were two phone numbers there, one each for the girl's mother and father. Jo looked at the numbers and put the paper in her shirt pocket.

"Please let me go home," the little girl said. She was crying now, growing desperate. As she spoke she wiped the tears from her cheeks with her fingers.

"You'll be home in a couple of days," Jo told her. "Don't get out of that seat."

"Please," the girl said again.

"Be quiet," Jo said.

She closed the door and latched it. She stood looking at Daniel as he got into the limo and drove off across the lot. Jo walked around and got behind the wheel of the GMC. She listened for a moment for any sounds suggesting that the girl was moving around. She put the truck in gear and headed for home.

Henry was waiting when she got there, standing at the bottom of the steps to the porch, as if he'd been there for hours. He had a look of uncertainty as she pulled up, a look that suggested that he'd been holding out hope that Jo would return alone. Every time he'd wavered in the past week Jo had shown him the tape she'd made of Sam Jackson's rant, which was enough to make even an old hippie's blood rise.

Henry was reassuring the little girl as soon as Jo rolled up the door. She had remained in the seat, as she'd been told, but she was obviously frightened beyond words. Her breathing was shallow and rapid.

"You're going to be okay," Henry was telling her. "Nobody's gonna hurt you. You can unbuckle now."

"I want to go home," the girl said. But she did what she was told.

"You will," Henry promised. "In a few days. Now come on."

The girl got to her feet but held back. Jo watched from outside the truck. It was obvious that the little girl, so reluctant to enter the truck back in the city, was now just as nervous about leaving it. It had suddenly become her sanctuary.

"Let's go," Jo snapped.

They had a room ready for her at the rear of the farmhouse. There was a bed and a dresser and a table and chair, all that she would need for a couple of days, although Henry had been adding things to it for the past week—pictures of horses and other animals, a vase of petunias, books that had belonged to Jo and various other grandchildren from a couple of decades past. He'd even picked up a bar fridge in town at a second-hand place and stocked it with juice and snacks. There was a single window in the room, overlooking the old barn and the pasture where the goats grazed. Henry had nailed steel mesh over the outside of the window, and over the bathroom window next door.

Jo held back and allowed Henry to introduce the little girl to her cell, as he had been referring to the room in his frequent moments of doubt over what they were doing. Now he was explaining things that didn't require explaining.

"There's your bed. And there's a table there and a chair. And that's a little fridge, with juice and stuff."

The girl stood in the doorway, looking at the room. She turned and glanced back to Jo, in the hallway, then took a couple of steps toward Henry. "If you let me go now," she said softly, "I'll make sure you don't get into trouble. *Please.*"

From the hallway Jo saw Henry's resolve begin to crumble. The little girl was intuitive in choosing Henry. Jo had been thinking the kid might be a bit of a dullard, given her bloodlines, but apparently that wasn't the case. Jo walked into the room and the girl looked at her, eyes wary.

"Sit down and be quiet," Jo said.

Henry shot Jo a look but she ignored him. "Sit down," she said again.

The little girl sat in the chair. Henry walked to the bureau and picked up a brass cowbell that had been on a shelf in the old milk house for as long as Jo remembered. He brought it over to the girl and clanged it loudly a couple of times.

"If you need to use the bathroom, just ring this," he said. "We might be outside working, but we'll hear you. Do you know what this is?"

The girl shook her head.

"It's what they call a cowbell. A mother cow would wear this around her neck in the pioneer days so she wouldn't get lost. This bell here is over a hundred—"

"All right," Jo said. "She doesn't need a history lesson."

Henry gave Jo another look of reproach and, after putting the bell in the girl's hand, walked out of the room. The kid sat staring at Jo. She seemed a little less freaked out now. Maybe the bell did it.

"You're going to be here a couple of days," Jo said. "You need to keep quiet. You start screaming and nobody is going to hear you anyway. You understand that?"

The girl nodded.

"All right." Jo left, locking the door behind her.

Henry was waiting in the kitchen. "She's a child and she's frightened out of her mind. You need to be considerate of that."

"We knew she was going to be scared, Henry," Jo told him. "We're in it now. She'll figure it out that we're not going to hurt her."

"It might help if you weren't mean to her."

"This isn't Disneyland."

Henry fell silent and glanced out the kitchen window, his teeth worrying his bottom lip. Jo could tell that he wanted to complain further but couldn't think of a way to do it. After all, he was part of it. All he could do was repeat his words. "Can't you see she's scared?"

"How scared is she, Henry?" Jo demanded. "As scared as those kids in the schoolyard in Laureltown? Compared to those kids, how frightened is she? She's in a room with a bed and a fridge and a cowbell. How frightened is she?"

"It's not a contest," he said.

"It's not summer camp either," Jo said. "We've been through this. If this is going to work, I can't become her friend. I can't allow myself to care about her. Now I'm going to have something to eat and then we have to load the truck for morning."

She went into the fridge for some leftover chicken and began to make a sandwich on the cutting board. Behind her she felt Henry slip from the room. The hallway ran behind the kitchen and she could plainly hear him enter the kid's room to tell her again that she was going to be all right. He asked the little girl her name and she told him it was Vanessa but sometimes people called her Nessa. Then she asked Henry his name.

"Jesus, Henry," Jo muttered under her breath. "You're not going to tell her."

But he didn't. He asked her if she wanted a chicken sandwich and she declined. He reminded her about the food in the fridge and then Jo heard him leave and lock the door. He came back into the kitchen and poured himself a glass of his homemade wine. He drank it while Jo ate the sandwich and after they went out together to load the truck for the following day.

TWENTY-FOUR

"The kid's dead," Olson said.

Bell was driving, moving across town on 96th Street in heavy traffic. They'd gotten the call while they were at the station, just coming on shift. First they'd driven to the office of the car service to talk to the manager there and now they were heading for Sam Jackson's house on the Upper West Side. It was a few minutes to seven and the streets were moving at a glacial pace.

"You don't know that," Bell said.

"I know stats," Olson said. "Three hours in, ninety-nine per cent of the time the kid's dead. Sexually assaulted, strangled, tossed in a dumpster or the river. Or some variation of that scenario."

"You're a cheerful fucker."

"It's in my blood," Olson told him. "I'm Scandinavian."

Bell glanced over to see if he was making a joke. He and Olson had been partners for less than two weeks. Bell didn't know the man, aside from seeing him around the station, a tall heavyset scowler with a shaved head and rimless glasses. He was in his fifties, pushing retirement, Bell would have guessed.

"From where?" Bell asked.

"Sweden."

"But you were born here," Bell suggested. "You first generation?"

"Hell, no. My family came here in 1897."

"About time you cheered up, isn't it?"

Olson shrugged. "I'm just telling you that the girl's dead."

"I'm not so sure," Bell said. "If this was a random grab, sex thing, then I might agree with you. But this feels different."

"Why?"

"The celebrity angle for one. The money factor for another. And there's the disgruntled driver who'd been given notice."

"Maybe he's the perv."

"Maybe he is," Bell admitted.

There were a couple of uniforms at the Jackson house. The wife's name was Rachel. She was on her feet in a living room that opened into a huge kitchen, a tall good-looking blonde, early forties maybe. The place was nice, the furniture and fixtures expensive and tasteful, which surprised Bell somewhat. He'd seen Sam Jackson's show and he was expecting something garish—gold taps, nymphs in fountains. Like Trump. Presumably the wife was in charge of decorating.

She was understandably on edge, but dry-eyed. She had a friend there with her, a skinny brunette with puffy lips and artificially tanned skin. There for support. There was a pot of coffee on the island that separated the rooms and a box of pastries from Starbucks. Bell guessed that the friend had brought the food. Olson took the uniforms aside and talked to them before telling them they could go. Rachel Jackson watched them leave and turned to Bell.

"You guys are detectives then? What have you found out?"

"We talked to the manager of the car service. The car isn't back."

"It's him," Rachel said. "It's that fucking driver." She indicated the door just taken by the uniforms. "I told them that."

"Yeah, and they told us," Bell said. "We're checking him out. Sean McIlroy, right? You recently gave him notice?"

"That's what this is about," she said. "That vindictive bastard took my daughter."

"You might very well be right," Bell said.

"Then why isn't that man in custody?" the brunette demanded.

Bell looked at her, wondering if the Botox had seeped into her brain. "We don't know where Mr. McIlroy is at this time." He turned back to Rachel. "As of right now we don't have the car and we don't have McIlroy and we don't have your daughter. We do know that McIlroy was bonded, which means he doesn't have a record and that he's not a registered sex offender. If he did this, we should hope that he's just, you know—teaching you a lesson, in his mind anyway. And maybe after money."

"What kind of person would do that?" Rachel asked.

"What do you know about him?" Olson asked. "Did you interact with him at all?"

"Not really," Rachel said. "Just to say hello once in a while. My husband thinks he's a boozer."

Olson glanced at Bell; McIlroy's boss had suggested the same thing.

Rachel pulled a cellphone from her pocket and walked away as she punched in a number. She stood looking out a bay window for a moment before turning back to them. "Why doesn't she answer her phone?"

Olson walked over. "Your daughter has a phone with her?"

"Of course," Rachel said. "It goes right to voicemail. Which means he turned it off. Or maybe he destroyed it."

"Do you tell the officers she has a phone?" Olson asked.

"No. I didn't think to."

"They didn't ask?"

"No."

"All right," Bell said. "We need the phone number, we need the server and the account number. We can trace the phone."

"Even if it's turned off?"

"It might get turned on," Olson said. "Can you give us that information?"

While she went into another room Bell looked at the brunette. "Friend of the family?"

"Probably Rachel's *dearest* friend."

"Your name?"

"Lila DiMaggio."

"Related to the Clipper?"

"Clipper?" she asked. "You mean like a barber?"

"Never mind." Bell indicated their surroundings. "Where's the husband?"

"He's in Wyoming." The brunette was quite dramatic, in her body language, her manner of speech. "But on his way home as we speak. He's a very famous person, you know." She glanced toward the other room, then leaned close to Bell and whispered. "And they're very well off. That's what this is about, if you ask me. This driver wants money. Which is a good thing, right? I mean, as opposed to it being a sex crime or something like that."

Before Bell could respond Rachel returned with the paperwork on the daughter's phone. Olson took it from her and sat down at the island with his cell to call it in. Bell watched as he poured himself a cup of coffee and took a scone from the box while he waited for someone in the tech department. Bell turned to Rachel. Her lips were tight, her breathing measured; he could see that she was doing her utmost to keep it together.

"I want you to tell me what happened when you gave McIlroy his notice. What he said, how he acted. Anything you remember."

"He asked for another chance," she said. "And when I said no, he said I wasn't being fair."

"Was he pissed off?" Bell asked. "Raising his voice? Did you feel threatened?"

"He was more whiny than pissed off. Like the world was against him. One of those guys."

One of those guys, Bell thought. Those guys don't usually abduct children. They're more likely to be found on a barstool somewhere, telling their tale of woe to anybody who will listen. But Bell couldn't know about this guy Sean McIlroy. There were exceptions to every rule.

At the island Olson hung up his phone. He sat there with his coffee. Obviously he was okay with Bell doing the dirty work. Bell turned to Rachel again.

"All right, there's something we need to cover here," he said. "I apologize in advance but I have to ask. Is everything okay with you and your husband?"

"What are you talking about?"

"Is there a chance that your daughter might be with your husband?" Bell paused. "It happens sometimes, when couples aren't getting along."

"This isn't one of those times, detective," she said coldly. "Sam's in Wyoming. He announced three days ago he's running for the United States Congress. I'm not sure when he would find time to abduct our daughter, even if we were having problems, which we are *not*."

"Okay," Bell said.

Olson's phone rang and he picked it up.

"Yeah?" he said and then listened. "No shit? We're on our way."

He hung up and looked at Bell. "They found the car. Parking lot near the Williamsburg Bridge."

Rachel moved toward Olson, her bottom lip quivering. She wanted him to tell her more and when he didn't, she asked. "Vanessa?"

"No," Olson said. He looked at Bell. "But they found the driver. He's not our guy."

"Why not?"

"They found him in the trunk."

TWENTY-FIVE

Sean McIlroy sat in the back seat of the cruiser, looking like a whipped dog. He was dirty and ashamed and a little hungover. And he was genuinely worried about the kid, Bell could see. At least he had that going for him. Of course, there was still a chance he was in on it, but Bell was inclined to think otherwise. He and Olson were sitting up front. Forensics was over at the limo, fifty yards away, dusting for prints, looking for hairs, threads, blood. Anything and everything.

"Driscoll," Sean said, finally remembering the last name. "Bill Driscoll."

"Where'd you meet him?" Olson asked.

"Hamilton Tap House."

"On Sutherland?"

"Yeah."

"When?"

"Maybe two weeks ago," Sean said, thinking on it. "I stop at the Tap, every now and again, and one day—"

"You're there every day," Bell told him. "According to your boss."

"So I frequent the place. Never knew that to be a crime. Anyway, him and I started shooting pool one day. He's an electrician, in town working on some big renovation project on the waterfront. Working at night because there's, like, people there during the day. Office workers."

"You and this Driscoll became drinking buddies," Olson said.

"I wouldn't say we're buddies," McIlroy said. "I told you I just met the guy."

"Was he buying?" Bell asked.

"What?"

"Was he buying the beer?"

"I guess so," McIlroy said. "I mean, I guess he bought more than I did. He had lots of cash on him. Those tradesmen make a good fucking living, with the overtime and all that. So yeah, he liked to spend it."

"He tell you where he was from?"

"Buffalo. Big Bills fan, said he has season tickets."

Olson was writing everything down. Bell was going to be surprised to find out that a Bill Driscoll had season tickets for the Bills.

"What happened today, Sean?"

"Today," he began. "Well, I stopped in for a beer around lunch. And he comes in, maybe two o'clock or so, and we have a couple. Shooting the shit, you know. And he tells me he's got a package coming down from Buffalo, and could I give him a ride to get it? I'm kinda reluctant because it's the company's car and all but I say what the hell. Do a guy a favor, right?"

"What time is this?"

"Right around three. I know, cuz I pick the kid up at four and I was thinking I had time to get the car, take him across town and make it back in time."

"Three o'clock," Bell said. "How many beers did you have?"

"I don't know. Two or three."

"Bullshit," Bell said. "You were at the bar three hours. Three beers an hour; I'm going to say nine, minimum. And then you get behind the fucking wheel."

"I know my limits."

Bell glanced at Olson for a moment. This guy was less likely a suspect every minute. "All right, what happened?"

"I'm taking him down to the place to get his package. He says it's like a courier depot in Williamsburg. So we get there and he tells me to pull in beside this old warehouse, and there's nothing there. No sign or anything. So I'm, like, this is the place? And he sticks a gun in my face. Puts me in the trunk, wraps my hands and feet with duct tape and stuffs a rag in my mouth, tapes that too."

"What did he say?"

"Nothing," McIlroy said. "I asked him what the hell was going on and he told me to shut up. Then he stuffed the rag."

"Then what?"

"Then we're driving. He knows exactly where he's going because we stop and I hear the door open and I hear him talking to the kid."

"What did he say?"

"I couldn't hear too good from the trunk, but he says my name and something about me being sick and then he says something, I think, about they have to meet the kid's mother somewhere. I'm not sure about that part. I was kind of disoriented, locked in there."

"And drunk," Bell reminded him.

"I wasn't fucking drunk," McIlroy said.

"Keep going."

"So then we're driving again, and I can't hear nothing, and after a little while we stop, and I hear them get out and I hear them talking and she's, like, asking something and then I can't hear fuck all. Like they're too far away. And a few minutes later we drive away again, but not far, like maybe a hundred yards, two hundred yards. And then we park and that's it. He's gone and I'm there in the fucking trunk."

"But he's alone then," Bell said. "The last time he parked?"

"Seemed like it. I only heard the one door."

Now Olson turned in the seat. "What did you hear when he took her out of the car? Did he put her in another vehicle?"

"Not sure."

"What did you hear?"

"Something kinda weird, like one of those roller things in a factory, you know to move boxes and shit."

"Were you inside a building?"

"How the fuck would I know if I was inside a building? I was inside a trunk."

Olson glanced at Bell, shook his head. "What kind of gun was it?"

"I don't know. It was black."

"Revolver or automatic?"

"I don't know guns. It was big and it looked like it could put a big hole in my head."

Bell started the car. "Okay, we're taking you to the station. We need a description of this Driscoll character, and we'll need you to look at some pictures."

"Pictures of who?" McIlroy asked.

Bell shrugged. "Sex offenders, kidnappers, rogue electricians with tall tales. You'd better be telling the truth, Sean. And you'd better hope we find that girl alive."

TWENTY-SIX

Bell called the mother from the station and told her what he knew. He also told her they'd issued an amber alert. He didn't have anything encouraging to say to her, so he didn't try. He hung up and got a coffee from the machine. Sean McIlroy was downstairs with Olson and a sketch artist, conjuring up a portrait of the guy calling himself Bill Driscoll. After that they'd show him some mug shots but Bell wasn't holding out much hope there. He was going through the registry when Olson came up from below.

"How's our boy doing?"

"We have a sketch," Olson said. "Looks a little like Curly from the Three Stooges."

Bell shook his head.

"You think he's in on it?"

"McIlroy?" Bell said. "He couldn't plan a game of solitaire."

"Doesn't mean he wasn't an accomplice. A dupe."

"He's a dope, I don't know about dupe."

Olson indicated the laptop. "Anything?"

"A number of Driscolls, William," Bell said. "And a few sex offenders. One in New Mexico, seventy-two years old. Another in Florida but he's black. Other than that, we have some dealers, dopers, bikers, scammers. None of them fit. None of them look like Curly."

"Could be a first-timer," Olson said.

"Always that chance," Bell agreed. "Let's face it: the guy's name is not Bill Driscoll. He's not going to go to all this work and then tell McIlroy his real name. And I still say it's not a sex crime."

"What is it?"

"Given the principals, money or politics," Bell said. "Take your pick. Either way, I hope it means the girl is still alive." He looked up to see one of the techies crossing the room toward them, a short woman with red hair.

"We found the girl's phone," the techie said.

"Where is it?" Bell asked.

"That's the tricky part."

"Why is it tricky?" Olson asked.

"Because it's moving."

Vanessa Jackson's cellphone was indeed moving. Or at least it was moving again. It had gone from the city to Philadelphia and stalled there for an hour and for that time Bell had feared that it had been dumped somewhere, or that something worse had gone down. However, while the server was trying to pinpoint the location it started again and was now traveling steadily west. The FBI was involved now, and they were following the signal too, both in a cyber and literal manner. A half-dozen agents sat around a computer screen in the Philadelphia office, while a van with an additional four agents drove across the state of Pennsylvania, waiting for the phone to stop again. Right now they were on Route 30, twenty miles east of York. It was estimated that the phone was moving at about fifty miles an hour.

"The phone was off before," Bell said. "Now it's on or they couldn't track it. Why is it on?"

He was sitting in Captain Gardner's office, with Olson and the red-haired woman and the captain himself. The woman's name was Lynn. After nobody introduced her, Bell had finally asked.

"He turned it on?" Olson suggested.

"Why would he do that?"

"I don't know," Bell admitted. "Maybe she turned it on. Maybe he doesn't know she has it? How many ten-year-olds have cellphones?"

"A lot more that you might think," Lynn said.

"If she still has the phone, why isn't she using it?" Olson said.

"She could be tied up, or drugged, or otherwise incapacitated."

"Or dead," Olson suggested.

"God, but you're depressing," Bell said.

Olson indicated the laptop. "The FBI can't get a plate number?"

"The science isn't that precise," Lynn said. "We can't tell which car the phone is in. If it stops we can pinpoint it, at a house or whatever. But for now, it's very general. We know the area and we know it's moving so we assume it's in a vehicle."

The captain indicated the screen and looked at Bell. "No Driscolls in that area, with a record?"

Bell shook his head. "This guy isn't Driscoll anyway. No way he used his real name."

"That name," Lynn said. "Something about it, I don't know, sounds too familiar. Did you guys Google it?"

"No," Olson said. "We didn't try Facebook or Twitter either."

Ignoring his tone, Lynn opened another engine on the laptop and entered the name. After scrolling down a moment, she smiled. "You know O. Henry?"

"It's a chocolate bar," Olson said.

"Philistine," she said. "He was a short story writer. Gift of the Magi? Well, he wrote a story called The Ransom of Red Chief. About two guys in the nineteenth century who kidnap a boy. Kid turns out to be a holy terror and the kidnappers have to pay the parents to take him back. One of the kidnappers was Bill Driscoll."

"Well," the captain said. "We have a literary type on our hands."

"This Henry guy still alive?" Olson asked.

"No, he's not," Lynn replied. "Let's hope the girl is."

TWENTY-SEVEN

When Sam arrived in New York, he went straight to the Plaza, where Bill Ford was waiting. Bill had heard about the change in plans from Molly and called while Sam was still in the air, asking him to stop by.

"I need to get home," Sam had told him.

"Come by here first."

Bill was in the penthouse suite, sitting with his feet up, a platter of fruit on the table beside him, Rush Limbaugh on the TV calling Nancy Pelosi a liar over something. Bill wore wrinkled cotton pants and a golf shirt. Sam entered and looked around. Bill read his mind, not a tough chore in this case.

"There's booze over there." He turned the TV off. "If you need it."

Sam poured himself a healthy slug of single malt and came over to sit down. Taking a drink, he looked around. The place was massive, with twelve foot-ceilings and a view of the park. The furniture was chocolate brown, the carpet beige.

"That's tough news about your daughter," Bill said.

Sam had a drink and nodded. He was looking at a painting on the wall, a print of a Native American sitting on his pony on the plains somewhere. It might have been Wyoming. The man was looking off in the distance, where a locomotive was crossing the prairie, a long plume of white smoke trailing from the engine. The painting was meant to be allegorical, Sam supposed.

"What's the thinking on it?" Bill asked.

"If some sexual deviant grabbed her, the outlook is not good," Sam said, still considering the painting. "That's pretty much a given in these cases. But if it's about money, they'll keep her alive."

"What if it's neither?"

Now Sam turned to him. "What do you mean?"

"You have to look at the timing of this thing. You've just announced, and now this."

Sam took a moment. "You're saying it's political?"

Bill shrugged and put a piece of melon in his mouth.

"To what end?" Sam asked.

"To get you to suspend your campaign," Bill said. "You are going to suspend your campaign?"

"I have to."

"Of course."

Sam drank, watching the older man over the rim of the glass. "Are you saying I shouldn't?"

"Of course not. This is your daughter." Bill shrugged. "Besides, I doubt that somebody has done this in order to scare you out of the race. You don't strike me as a man who runs away from things."

"I'm not." Sam took another drink and realized he'd been practically gulping the whiskey. "Do you really think they're capable of something like this?"

"Who?"

"The other side."

"Depends who you're talking about when you say the other side," Bill said. "If you mean the man you're running against, I would say no. If you mean certain people who have an interest in his winning, well, that's another story. Politics is a dirty game. I hope that's not news to you."

Sam got to his feet and walked to the bar. After he poured, he turned back to Bill Ford. "Are you capable of this?"

"If you're asking me if I had your daughter kidnapped to draw attention to your campaign, the answer is no," Bill said. "But some-body kidnapped her, and it will draw attention to your campaign. Not necessarily in a negative way either. I'll be frank with you—we've done some early polling and your numbers stink. The whole parachute issue is proving to be a bigger obstacle than we anticipated. We need to change the dialogue and we haven't found a way to do that. Until now."

"You're saying I should use the fact that my daughter's been abducted."

"Our first concern is your daughter," Bill said. "You need to do everything in your power to get her back safe and sound. However, if you were to decide to stay in the race, the added publicity might make it less likely that the people holding her will hurt her. And the increased visibility might even help in finding her."

Sam considered this.

Bill continued. "Not only that, but this might give you an oppor-tunity to show people who you really are. Voters will empathize with a father in your position. Especially a father who's willing to stand up to these thugs. And while that's happening, the other side is going to be less eager to attack you, given the circumstances. Do you see what I mean?"

"Yeah," Sam said, downing the scotch. "I see what you mean."

When Doug Ryder got home, the kids were already in bed. Nancy was waiting dinner for him, although it was somewhat overcooked. He'd been in the city longer than he'd counted on and when he got back to Philly and gone to pick up the car at the dealership, it wasn't ready yet. Something about the brakes needing new rotors, which had to be sent over from another dealer. That's what they told him anyway. Doug knew nothing about cars and often suspected he was being taken advantage of. The Kia had less than thirty thousand miles on it. Why would it need new brakes?

He and Nancy ate together in the kitchen, tough roast beef and reheated potatoes and corn. He told her about his two days in New York, about the meetings he'd had. It had been worth the trip. He'd picked up two new accounts, which would mean that his year was already set. So much for his old partners who'd told him that he couldn't run a consulting business out of Seven Valleys, Pennsylvania. These days you could run anything out of anywhere. The house in Seven Valleys had cost them just two hundred and twelve thousand. The same place in Philly, the neighborhood they'd moved from eighteen months ago, would be at least twice that.

After dinner, they drank coffee while Nancy told him about Emily's soccer game that afternoon. She'd scored her first goal. She wanted to stay up to tell her dad about it but it had gotten too late. School tomorrow. Nancy suggested that Doug make a big deal about it in the morning.

The agents hit both doors, front and rear, at the same time, using some sort of battering device to smash them open, hinges ripping from the jams, glass shattering. Nancy screamed as the men barged into the kitchen, bulky guys in black flak jackets and heavy jackboots. They wore headgear too, with shields, FBI stenciled on the helmets. They held assault weapons and they were yelling for Doug and Nancy to get on the floor while they swept the house, waking the kids and causing all manner of panic.

Doug's overnight bag was inside the front door, where he'd dropped it coming in. The agents eventually found the phone they were looking for in a side compartment. Doug told them he had no idea how it got there and, after twelve hours detention and interrogation and background checks at an FBI office in Philadelphia, they finally seemed to believe him. One of the agents drove him home around noon the next day. When Doug asked why they'd been following the phone, the agent told him it was none of his business. The guy seemed a little pissed that he'd been chosen to drive Doug back to Seven Valleys. Doug wanted to tell the guy that he was a little pissed himself, with his front and back door smashed to pieces and his kids scared half to death, being dragged out of bed by strangers in riot gear. Not to mention the all-night grilling that followed. He decided to keep quiet though. He doubted there was an upside to aggravating the FBI.

TWENTY-EIGHT

Daniel left the limo in the underground parking lot, a couple hundred yards from where they made the switch. Walking up to street level, he peeled off the black latex gloves and stuck them in his coat pocket. He took the subway downtown and got out and walked the last six blocks to Grand Central Station, where he went down a level to wait for his train. It was five o'clock and the station was busy. He found an empty seat along the south wall and sat down. While he waited he took the girl's phone from his pocket and turned it on and went into the contacts again. He'd already written down the numbers for the two labeled Mom and Dad and given them to Jo. There were no others there that seemed to be worth noting but he took out his pad and wrote them out anyway, along with the names. Better to have them and not need them than the other way around.

While Daniel was scrolling through the phone, a man in a Phillies windbreaker sat down a couple of seats over, placing his overnight bag between them. The man took out his phone and checked for messages before sending out a couple of texts. When he finished, he glanced at his watch and leaned back to close his eyes. Daniel put the phone on mute and slipped the it into an open side pocket on the man's overnight bag. A little while later, they called his train and he left. He was back in Pittsburgh by midnight.

TWENTY-NINE

The market she'd chosen was in Greenfield, Massachusetts. It was a three-hour drive so she was up at three-thirty and on the road by four. She hadn't slept well, with a kidnap victim down the hall and Henry roaming through the house until all hours. When she'd left in the GMC, he was standing in the lane in his stocking feet, deciding what he would make the little girl for breakfast. He wondered if she ate eggs.

"City people worry about their cholesterol levels."

"She's ten, Henry," Jo said. "She doesn't have a cholesterol level."

Jo had vended at the Greenfield market the previous week, to get the lay of the town. She arrived a little past seven and spent half an hour setting up. The market was on Court Square downtown, beneath a high obelisk with an eagle atop. It was a rainy day and she didn't move a lot of produce. A number of vendors picked up and left before noon. Jo hung in until two o'clock and then loaded the truck and locked the doors.

She tucked her hair up under a Red Sox cap and walked along Main Street to the laundry she'd scouted the previous week. The pay phones were at the back, beyond a row of dryers. There were two people in the place, both young women sitting by the washing machines, chatting. They barely gave Jo a glance as she moved past them. She picked up the receiver and then stopped, realizing in that moment that this was her last chance to turn back. Once she made the call, the ball would be truly in motion. She looked at the two women by the dryers. They probably had kids in school today and if they did, they probably assumed the kids were safe there. There was a time when Jo would have assumed the same. Not anymore.

She pumped the coins into the phone and called the number.

She knew the voice that answered. She'd heard it too many times of late, coming from her TV.

"I've got your kid," she told him.

"Who is this?" he demanded.

"It's the person who has your kid."

"I want to talk to her. Put her on the phone."

Jo could hear someone in the background, a woman's voice, asking Sam Jackson who he was talking to. The voice was rising, frantic. The mother, no doubt.

"Shut up and listen," Jo said. "You're not in charge here. Do what you're told and you'll get your daughter back. Fuck up, and you'll never see her again. You got that?"

The woman's voice again, growing louder, demanding to know who was on the line.

"You are in a world of trouble, young lady," Sam said. "Are you familiar with the expression *in way over your head*? Because that is where you are."

"Are you familiar with shut up and listen?" Jo asked. "Cuz that's where *you* are. You're going to do three things. First of all, you're going to go to Laureltown and meet with the parents of the kids who were killed and you're going to tell them you were wrong and you're going to beg for a forgiveness you don't deserve. Second, you're going to go on your show and tell everybody watching the same thing. And you'd better fucking sell it too. There's ten million idiots out there who think you know what you're talking about when you say the parents are to blame for those kids' deaths and you're going to have to convince them otherwise."

"Jesus," Sam said. "Is that what this is about?"

"That's what this is about. Thirdly, you're going to deposit a million dollars in an offshore account. I'll give you the info when you have the money ready. When you've done all three, to my satisfaction, you'll get your daughter back."

There was an extended silence and then Jo heard the woman demanding to know what was going on. She heard Sam Jackson brush the woman off.

"I'll handle it." And then to Jo, "You've got a few problems, lady. One, I doubt very much that you have my daughter. You've been watching the news and decided in your addled state to try a little shakedown. Two, you're going to jail. If you don't have my daughter, you're going to jail for extortion. If you do, you're going to jail for extortion and kidnapping. So the best thing you can do right now is turn yourself in to the police and pray I'm in a forgiving mood when it comes to pressing charges."

"Give me the phone!" The woman's voice.

"You don't have my daughter," Sam told Jo again.

"I do though," Jo said. "I'll give you twenty-four hours to think about it. While you're at it, you can start thinking about what you're going to say to those parents. That's not negotiable, asshole. None of it is."

"I want proof," Sam said and Jo heard a cry, like someone in pain, and then the woman was on the phone.

"This is Rachel Jackson! Where's my baby?"

"Talk to your husband," Jo said and hung up.

THIRTY

The FBI had taken over. The case was federal now, with the little girl's phone having traveled to Pennsylvania, and now the call coming from Massachusetts. The agent in charge was named Dugan, a quick-moving whippet of a man, with too much product in his hair for a cop, to Bell's eyes anyway. It was seven o'clock, five hours after the phone call came in. They were in the Jackson house, both Bell and Dugan, with Sam and Rachel in the room where Sam had received the call. Dugan had arrived a few minutes earlier with an update. When he got there he suggested to Bell that he no longer concern himself with the investigation but Bell had disagreed. The girl had been kidnapped in New York City. It was still his case. Since then Dugan had been ignoring him.

They'd been waiting. A warrant was needed before they could request the call details from Sam Jackson's cellphone server. It had taken all afternoon to secure it and then serve it. Since then Dugan had been on and off his own cell constantly.

"A pay phone in a laundry in Greenfield, Massachusetts," he was saying now. "I've sent a couple of agents there from Boston. And we're talking to the local cops."

Rachel was on her feet, arms crossed as if in the act of holding herself together, desperate for news of any kind. Sam was sitting at the island, his laptop opened in front of him. He was as calm as she was not.

"Where is this place?" Rachel asked.

"Little town north of Springfield," Dugan told her.

"Security cameras in the laundry?" Bell asked.

"No," Dugan said after a moment. He turned slowly to give Bell an impatient look. "Why would there be? Somebody going to steal a box of Tide?"

Bell had already decided that Dugan was a snide little fucker, who was obviously under the impression that he was the smartest person in the room. Certainly the smartest cop in the room.

"This is downtown?" Bell asked. "Retail area? There must be cameras somewhere. One of them might have picked up something."

"The FBI is looking into that, Detective," Dugan said. "The FBI has done this before."

"Does this mean that Vanessa is close by?" Rachel asked. "I mean—is that what you think?"

"That would be a good bet," Dugan said. "Maybe outside of town, some rural area. They obviously don't want to use a land line, and they're too smart to use a cellphone."

"Too smart?" Sam repeated, laughing. He was typing an email and when he finished he closed the laptop before turning to Dugan. "You're under the impression that this woman has my daughter?"

"You're not?" Dugan asked.

"Anybody can make a phone call," Sam said.

"How did they get your phone number?" Rachel asked. "They got it from Nessa's phone."

"It's not hard to find a phone number," Sam said. "Why do you think I change mine every six months?"

Dugan regarded Sam for a moment, evaluating him. "Let's go over again exactly what she said."

"She said she had my daughter and she wanted a million dollars," Sam said.

"That was it?"

Sam looked the agent in the eye. "That was it."

"According to the server, you were on the phone for over two minutes," Bell said. "There was more conversation than just that."

"I told her I wanted proof," Sam said. "I advised her of her future if she didn't start using what few brains she has. That took a while. She said she would call back in twenty-four hours."

"What proof can they give?" Rachel demanded. "Do you want them to cut a finger off?"

"The woman's lying," Sam said. "Who says there's a woman even involved? It was a man who grabbed her, this so-called Driscoll. He's the one who took the cellphone and sent it on its way to Buttfuck, Pennsylvania. If anybody involved in this has my number, it would be him. So why isn't he the one making the call?"

Bell looked at Dugan, who seemed to be considering the question. It had no merit, though. Who was to say who else was involved?

"While we're at it," Sam went on, "where does our boy Sean the dimwitted driver fit in here? How can we be sure that he isn't up to his eyeballs in this? You guys just kicked him loose?"

"Don't worry, we have him under surveillance," Dugan said. "Night and day. He makes a phone call and we're going to know about it. He meets somebody in a bar, in the park, and we're there."

"What do we do next?" Rachel asked.

"Let's see what my guys in Massachusetts come up with," Dugan said. "Maybe the woman's a local and somebody saw her at the phone. We do have to consider the possibility that she's lying. But she did make contact and she did say she's going to call back tomorrow. Nobody else has attempted to contact you."

"What if she has Vanessa?" Rachel asked.

"You guys will have to decide whether or not to pay the money," Dugan said. "It's not up to us to influence you."

"There will be no ransom paid," Sam said. He put his coat on.

"Where are you going?" Rachel asked.

"To the station. I'm doing an interview on the show about this. I have a million requests coming in and I don't feel like answering the same questions over and over again. I do one interview and that's done. No more until I get my daughter back. I have an election campaign to run."

"I suggest you don't mention the phone call," Dugan said. "It could encourage copycats and we don't need that at this point."

"I have no intention of mentioning the phone call. And just so you know, Agent Dugan, I can come to those decisions on my own. What you need to do is find my daughter."

He walked out. Bell looked over at Rachel, who was staring at the floor, her breath coming in short bursts. Dugan, clearly not happy with Sam Jackson's parting shot, made a show of calling one of the agents in Massachusetts, asking for an update. He walked into the other room as he talked on his cell, his voice growing louder as he queried somebody about whatever he was being told.

Rachel looked up at Bell now. "Would you like some coffee?"

"Sure."

There was a pot already made. Bell moved to the island and she sat across from him. She looked different than when they'd first met, Bell thought, and he realized she wasn't wearing makeup. She had faint lines beneath her eyes and her lips were pale. She actually looked better this way, to Bell anyway. He wasn't a fan of heavy makeup, all that gunk around the eyes, blush on the cheeks.

"Would you pay the money?" she asked after a moment. "I mean, if it was your daughter—would you pay them?"

"If it was my daughter," Bell replied. "Yes."

"Do you have a daughter?"

Bell shook his head. "Two boys. Both in college."

"That's nice," Rachel said. "Are you guys close?"

Bell shrugged. "Comes and goes. They live with their mother half the time and me the rest." He smiled. "They play us one against the other. I tell them they can't do something and their mother says they can, and vice versa. Typical stuff."

"I haven't been a very good mother," Rachel said suddenly. She'd been staring at the countertop and now she looked defiantly at Bell. "But that's going to change. When I get my baby back, I'm going to try harder. I'm going to spend a lot more time with her. I swear I'm going to change. I just need you guys to find her and bring her home. Okay?"

"We're going to do everything we can."

Rachel wiped her eyes with her fingertips. "Okay."

Bell drank the coffee. "You know, I thought that your husband might suspend his campaign because of this."

She looked at him a moment. "I didn't."

THIRTY-ONE

Ron Rivera had taken over Sam Jackson's show a week before and it had not been a gratifying experience so far. He knew that the audience he'd inherited wasn't his. They were used to a certain something from Sam Jackson and even if Rivera wanted to accommodate them, which he did not, he didn't have the bombast and tone to pull it off. So he'd been mostly concentrating on the election, hauling in whatever candidates they could find, Fox pass-overs for the most part, but he was aware that many of the pieces they'd done had been lightweight at best, standard exchanges of vague promises and typical partisan sniping. The numbers had fallen significantly day by day. Bobby Holmes had told him to anticipate that and not to let it worry him. That didn't stop it from worrying him.

At least tonight was different. Instead of taping five hours earlier they were going live and Rivera had Sam Jackson sitting across from him. Not only that, but he had a story. A genuine story, one that was being talked about across the country, and even the world.

"You're not used to sitting on that side of the table," he said to begin. "And I can't say how sorry I am that you are, under these trying circumstances."

Sam nodded but made no reply. He hadn't shaken Rivera's hand when he arrived, just spoken to Kevin, his old producer, as if Kevin was the one who'd be asking the questions. Rivera wasn't overly surprised; he'd been in Sam's presence before and been treated the same way. It could have been a racial thing, but Rivera wasn't so sure that it was true. It seemed to him that Sam Jackson was truly democratic. He lorded his superiority over everyone.

"Let's begin with an update. What's the latest on the investigation?"

"Ongoing," Sam said curtly.

Thanks for elaborating, Rivera thought. It's only live TV. "Do we know anything further regarding your daughter's whereabouts at this time?"

"We do not."

"Have you heard anything from the kidnappers?"

"No."

Rivera nodded. It was like pulling teeth. "Do you have any theories on who might be behind this?"

"I don't need any theories," Sam told him. "I know who's behind it."

"You do?"

"Terrorists."

"Terrorists?" Rivera repeated, surprised at the word. "Who specifically?"

"I can't answer that," Sam said. "I'm a lightning rod. I piss off a lot of people. On the international level—Iran doesn't like me, China hates me, Kim Jong-un would like to gut me like a fish. At home, I'm despised by the anti-gun faction, the pro-choice people, the idiots who supported Obamacare. So, it would be a futile exercise to try to identify here tonight the cowards who choose to attack me by abducting a ten-year-old girl. And even if I could, I would not speak their names in public. I don't give cowards recognition."

"But what would they be trying to accomplish by abducting your daughter?" Rivera asked.

"They want publicity, I assume. And I suppose money too. They're not going to get either from me."

"So you don't intend to negotiate?"

"With terrorists? No."

Rivera looked at the notes he'd made. None of them were going to help. "Let's get back to the investigation. We know that the FBI is involved. What can you tell us about the incident itself? Is it true that the car used to pick up Vanessa from school was hijacked?"

"That's true."

"The driver tied up and put in the trunk?"

"That's true too," Sam said. "The man's name is Sean McIlroy. He's a drunk who I should have fired months ago. Apparently the kidnapper cozied up to him in a bar and bought him a few beers and the next thing I know; my daughter is missing. A few beers—today's version of thirty pieces of silver."

Rivera decided to change the subject before Sam announced McIlroy's home address and phone number. "How is your wife holding up? I'm sure she's beside herself."

"She's fine," Sam said. "She has no interest in surrendering to terrorists either."

"Is there anything else you can tell us about the investigation? Are there any leads at all?"

"Even if they were, I wouldn't tell you," Sam said. "I'm a hundred per cent certain that the people responsible for this are watching me right now. I just hope they realize who they're dealing with."

"Do you have a message for them?"

"Yes. My message is—no surrender."

Rivera got a prompt from the booth. "I want to thank you for coming here under these difficult circumstances. We'll be back."

"What are you doing?" Sam asked when they were clear.

"What do you mean?"

"You just gave me the bum's rush, pal. We're doing another segment."

Rivera was confused. "Was there something else you wanted to say? I mean, you haven't revealed a hell of a lot so far. Although I'm thinking your limo driver's going to have a tough time finding a new job."

Sam ignored the slam. "We haven't talked about my campaign. We need to do that."

Kevin walked into the studio. He'd obviously been listening. "We'll do another segment, Ron. Touch on the Wyoming race, get an update."

Rivera, with no say in the matter, said nothing.

THIRTY-TWO

From the studio, Sam had the driver take him over to the Plaza, where Bill Ford was again waiting. He was drinking cola and watching the weather channel when Sam entered. This time Sam went to the bar without waiting for an invite.

"You were right," he said as he poured the single malt.

Ford reached for the remote and muted the sound. "How so?"

"It's political. Some woman called me today and said she has Vanessa. She had terms."

"Well, well."

Sam crossed the room to sit down opposite Ford.

"What kind of terms?" Bill asked.

"She wants me to eat shit," Sam said. "In front of the cameras, and in front of the parents of Laureltown. Oh, and she wants a million dollars."

"Is that right?" Bill said, considering the information. "That's a new twist. Kind of a hail Mary, coming from the left, isn't it?"

"I thought so."

"How do you know she even has her?"

"She's got her," Sam said. "I don't have any doubts about that. The way she talked to me, she's got her. She thinks she can make me jump through hoops. Some bleeding heart trying to act tough. On a certain level, it's entertaining."

"And she never said anything about you leaving the campaign?"

"No. I was waiting for that. Expecting it, in fact. Seems as if she has a different agenda altogether."

Bill had a drink of soda. "What are you going to do?"

"Nothing."

"What do you mean when you say nothing?"

Sam looked at the painting on the wall again. The sad Indian, watching the train, his fate and his people's fate about to be decided beneath the wheels of the locomotive.

"I've been thinking about what you said. If I give in to this woman, then I'm finished. I'd be like that fucking Indian up there on the wall. It's antithetical to what I've been preaching. I can forget about my base and when that happens, I can forget about Wyoming too. But— if I stand pat, not only do I maintain my maverick image, but I get unlimited coverage every day that this continues. Free coverage. And, believe me, this will play like a brass fucking band in Wyoming. Me telling these people to go to hell."

"What about your daughter?"

"These people are amateurs," Sam said. "The FBI will track them down within a week. And think of the photo op when I get my little girl back, Bill. I tell you—we couldn't script this."

"Jesus Christ," Bill said after long consideration. "*You* didn't do this?"

Sam had the glass halfway to his mouth. "I seem to recall asking *you* that question," he laughed. "Hell, no. But wouldn't it be something if I did?"

"It would be something that you wouldn't want discovered."

"Relax," Sam said. "The kidnapping is legit. And, given this broad's demands, it's somehow connected to Laureltown."

"What's the FBI saying about that?"

"I didn't tell them that part."

It took Bill Ford a moment to get it. "Because we want the voters to think this is about your campaign, somebody attempting to intimidate you, not about Laureltown. Or anything else, for that matter."

"That's right."

Bill Ford sat quietly, looking at Sam, sprawled in the chair, scotch in hand. "What if it backfires? What if they harm her?"

"They harm my daughter and they will have the wrath of God—and me—upon them." Sam smiled. "How's that for a sound bite?"

THIRTY-THREE

Pay phones were becoming dinosaurs. There were just eleven in the town of Greenfield. Dugan decided to put a body close to each of them, calling in a half-dozen state police to help out. It seemed unlikely that the woman would return to the laundry but Dugan put a Massachusetts trooper there anyway, a fifty-year-old woman wearing sweat pants and sandals, reading *People* magazine by one of the machines, her badge and her Glock tucked beneath some towels in a clothes hamper at her feet.

In the smaller towns outside of Greenfield—places like Deerfield and Bernardston and Ashfield—he had patrol cars on the move, watching for a woman who might be searching for a phone, or a woman looking out of place in general. Strangers were conspicuous in the boonies. Dugan was quite certain that the woman, if she called, would use a pay phone again. She thought she was being clever, avoiding new age technology.

In that, Dugan was right. When the woman called Sam Jackson for the second time, at one o'clock the following afternoon, it was indeed from a pay phone. However, the call didn't come from Greenfield or Deerfield, or Ashfield either. It came from a phone located roughly two hundred miles west of where the trooper sat in the laundry, with her semi-automatic and her magazine and her neatly folded towels.

Sam was at home with Rachel when the call came in, and Dugan was there as well, anticipating it. An FBI tech guy was also present, a stocky agent named Heyward, with his computer tapped into Sam's cellphone provider. The call was, in effect, on speaker through the man's laptop. Sam wasn't happy with the development; he preferred keeping the conversation private. He couldn't tell that to the FBI though.

"How are you making out?" Jo asked when he answered.

"Well, for one thing, I'm not going to jail," Sam told her.

"Never mind your bullshit. How are you making out with my terms?"

"When are you going to prove to me that you have my daughter?" Sam countered. He was watching the tech guy as he spoke. The guy was shaking his head; the call wasn't coming from Greenfield. "Where are you anyway?"

"You don't need to ask me that," Jo replied. "Ask one of those guys you have there with you. The FBI or NYPD, whoever it is. Ask the guy who's hooked into your server and is monitoring this call. He knows where I am."

As she was talking the tech guy wrote something on a pad and handed it to Dugan, who read it and then showed it to Sam and Rachel, who was standing anxiously by Sam's side. Sam nodded and walked away, the phone to his ear, as if he was moving out of earshot, which of course he couldn't do, with the computer connected to the call.

"So how are things in Elmira?"

"They're okay," Jo replied. "Now what about my terms?"

"So you're just driving randomly around the country, pretending to have my daughter?"

"I have her," Jo said.

"Prove it."

"You need to stop fucking around," Jo said. "Or are you really that much of a jackass? I always assumed it was an act, to suck up to the morons who watch you on TV."

Rachel moved to Sam and tried to take the phone from him. "Let me talk to her."

Sam held her off with a straight arm. "I don't know that you have my daughter."

"I have her," Jo said. "Do what I tell you and you'll get her back. Three things…"

"I want proof!" Sam shouted and hung up.

Nobody in the room said anything for maybe thirty seconds. Rachel stood staring at Sam, her mouth half open, before turning to Heyward.

"Call her back!" she said. "Do you have the number? Call her."

Heyward looked at Dugan, who shook his head. "She's gone. She knows we have the location. She's gone."

Rachel turned on Sam. She was livid. "What did you do? What the fuck is wrong with you?"

"You need to settle down," he told her. "Getting hysterical doesn't accomplish anything."

She looked for a moment as if she might strike him, but then turned and walked over to sit on the couch, where she put her face in her hands and began to cry, her shoulders heaving. Dugan watched her for a moment before turning to Heyward, who was typing quickly on the laptop.

"The phone's at a place called Earl's Gas & Go," Heyward said after a moment. "I'm bringing it up on Google Earth." He paused, enlarging the image. "Looks like one of those combination gas station and restaurant deals. County road on the edge of town. Elmira, New York."

"If they pump gas, they'll have cameras," Dugan said.

"Too bad all your men are in Massachusetts," Sam said. "With their heads up their asses."

"I beg your pardon," Dugan said.

"You heard me."

"Why did you hang up on her?" Dugan demanded.

"Because I don't believe she has my daughter," Sam said. "She's wasting my time. If she has Vanessa, why isn't she willing to show proof? She's running a scam."

"Then you keep her on the phone," Dugan told him. "Either way, you keep her on the phone."

"Like I said, she was wasting my time," Sam replied. "She doesn't have her."

"You don't know that!" Rachel snapped. She was still sitting on the couch, her face wet with tears, glaring at Sam. He didn't favor her with a look.

"You don't think this woman has your daughter," Dugan said. "But you don't seem overly concerned just who does."

"Maybe I keep thinking you're going to do your job and find her," Sam said. "Where's this Driscoll guy anyway? Apparently he just disappeared into thin air."

"We have agents on that," Dugan said.

"You don't have shit on the guy." Sam indicated Heyward and his laptop. "In this day and age, you haven't turned up a single credible lead at this point."

"We had a lead," Dugan said. "You just hung up on her."

Sam shook his head, denying it. Dugan dismissed him with a wave of his hand and turned back to Heyward.

"All right—what do we have? We know they were here in the city on Tuesday. Wednesday afternoon they were in Greenfield, and right now in Elmira. Maybe they took the thruway. Maybe. We need somebody checking the videotapes at the toll booths. We're talking, what, Interstate 87 to 90 to get to Greenfield? And then 90 back west heading toward Elmira. We're looking for a common denominator here—the vehicle they're using."

"Jesus," Heyward said. "Do you have any idea how many cars you're talking about?"

"No, I don't. But we're about to find out."

"They could be taking secondary roads."

Dugan nodded. "But we don't know that. We have a citizen here who's under the impression that we're not doing our job. Another thing—get a tape of the call to voice analysis. Find out if this woman is from Brooklyn or Boston or Timbuktu."

"You mean the con artist?" Sam asked. He had his own laptop open now and he was reading something as he spoke.

Dugan turned on him. "She said three things. Yesterday she wanted a million dollars. But today she said three things. What are the other two?"

"No idea."

"No idea," Dugan repeated in disgust. "Well, I have an idea."

"What's that?"

"Next time she calls, keep her on the line."

THIRTY-FOUR

Jo left the restaurant the same way she entered, through the back door, on the far side of the building from the gas pumps where the security cameras were located. The restaurant had been nearly full, the lunch crowd, when she got there. The pay phone was tucked in a corner by the restrooms. The only camera in the restaurant was in the front, trained on the cashier's location.

It was a quarter-mile walk back to the Elmira farmers market. She'd already packed up whatever she hadn't sold that morning. As she walked she removed the Mets cap and sunglasses and shook her hair loose. When she got to the market there were a few vendors still on site, with a dozen or so customers wandering about. Jo checked the latch on the rear door of the GMC and was walking around the truck when she heard the voice.

"Hold on there."

She turned to see a state trooper walking toward her. His hat was pulled low; she couldn't see his eyes. Jo's heart began to pound and she actually looked behind her, hoping he was speaking to someone else. He wasn't. For a split second she considered leaping into the truck and driving off. Maybe his cruiser wasn't close and she could get away. Urging her brain to work, she told herself that flight wasn't an option. He would have the truck's description out there within minutes.

She decided to turn and keep walking, off into the market, just another customer. As she moved past the front of the truck, he spoke again.

"Hold on!"

She stopped and looked back. His pace had quickened.

"Is this your vehicle?"

Jo looked at the cop and then the truck. She had nowhere to go now.

"I saw you latching the door," the cop said. "This is your truck?"

She was caught. "Yes."

The trooper crooked his finger. "Come here, I want to show you something."

With no choice, Jo followed him as he walked over to the side of the GMC and knelt down, in front of the rear wheels.

"You have a fuel leak, ma'am." He pointed underneath the chassis. "I smelled it when I walked by earlier."

Jo, the relief washing over her, knelt beside the man and had a look. The fuel line was wet where he had indicated. It was not dripping though.

"It's not real bad," the trooper said. "But it needs to be repaired. I suggest you see to it ASAP."

"Absolutely. I'll have it done today."

The cop straightened up. "I thought I should tell you."

"I really do appreciate it, sir."

She watched as the trooper walked away, swinging his arms out from his side in the manner that cops sometimes had, as if they were patrolling the streets of Dodge City in the days of yore. She waited until he was gone, got into the truck, and headed south.

She took county roads and two-lane blacktops and met Daniel at a Red Lobster just outside of Milton, Pennsylvania. He was there before her, sitting in a corner booth with a coffee and a brown envelope on the table before him. It was mid-afternoon and the place was nearly empty. Jo ordered coffee for herself and while she waited for it, she filled him in.

"*He* hung up," Daniel repeated in disbelief. "Why would he do that?"

"I've been asking myself that," Jo said.

"Did they have your location by then?"

"Yeah." Jo took a drink of coffee. It was pretty bad, leftover from the lunch crowd, she suspected.

"And he hangs up," Daniel said, more to himself this time, his eyes narrowing as he considered the act. "What the hell is that about? Standard procedure, they do everything in their power to keep you on the line." He paused. "But for some reason he didn't want to talk to you."

"That was obvious."

Daniel had a drink of coffee. "Or—he didn't want to talk to you with the FBI standing there. Why wouldn't he want to talk to you with them listening in?"

Jo shook her head.

"What were you talking about when he hung up?" Daniel asked. "Specifically."

"I was just about to repeat the terms when he cut me off. He hung up quick."

"All right," Daniel said slowly. "That's it then. He never told them. He's not telling them your demands. Why not?"

"Because he doesn't want to do it," Jo said, realizing. "Apologize, that is. He probably doesn't care about the million dollars. But he doesn't want to admit he was wrong. Not in public. He's never wrong."

"*And* he's running for Congress now," Daniel said. "That was something we hadn't counted on. When was the last time a candidate for office admitted he was wrong about anything? So he didn't tell the FBI about the terms. Did he tell his anybody? His wife?"

"Maybe not."

The waitress, probably bored with the empty restaurant, came over with the coffee pot to ask whether they needed refills. Daniel did. When she was gone, Jo indicated the envelope.

"That's the account info?"

Daniel handed it over. "Pretty simple. The bank and the account number. He can do it by wire."

"And how's it going to get you out of debt?" Jo asked. "I mean how do you access it?"

"I'm still working on that," Daniel admitted. "Not my area of expertise. And it's not as if I can ask anybody." He slowly rotated the coffee cup on the table.

"What's with your hands?" Jo asked.

He looked at them. His fingernails were rimmed with white powder, the skin nicked here and there. "Putting up drywall for a guy."

"Tough to pay off eight hundred grand doing that." She had a drink and put the cup aside, done with it. "This is pretty risky business. You know, compared to drywall."

"It's not just the money, Jo. Those kids were killed in my hometown. You think you're the only one who hates the guy?"

"I would hope not."

He nodded. "The kid all right?"

"A little freaked out," Jo said, not looking at him. She didn't want to talk about it because she was having trouble thinking about it. "Henry's looking after her like she's a baby bird."

"Let's hope it goes down quick."

"Let's hope that," Jo said. "He keeps saying he wants proof. Which is his way of avoiding the issue. I guess we're going to have to give it to him."

"What are you thinking?"

"Maybe a picture of her holding a newspaper. Like in the movies."

"It would have to be a Polaroid and you'd have to send it snail mail and untraceable." Daniel removed his notebook from his pocket. "I might have a better idea."

THIRTY-FIVE

Molly flew in from Cheyenne that night, at Bill Ford's request. He put her up at the Plaza, the floor below him, a suite not nearly as lavish as his but still much nicer than she would have booked on her own dime. The two of them met there with Sam Jackson at ten o'clock. Molly wasn't particularly happy, having been summoned cross-country on short notice to help out a man she didn't have much regard for. But it was part of the job. She'd been hoping to talk to Bill Ford privately before the three of them met but she hadn't been able to reach him on the phone since she landed at LaGuardia. And when he showed up at her door in the hotel, he had Sam Jackson in tow.

Sam moved to the bar and poured himself a drink. When he offered the bottle toward Molly, she hesitated and then asked for bourbon. To hell with Bill Ford and his prohibition pose, dragging her out of Wyoming at his whim.

Sam sprawled into a chair with his scotch and produced a slip of paper from his pocket, which he handed to Molly. "Use this phone number from now on. The FBI is monitoring the calls on the other one. They don't need to be privy to the campaign stuff. Last time I looked, this is still America."

"It's still America," Molly said. "But is there still a campaign?"

"What's that supposed to mean?"

"Jesus, man," Molly said. "How can you even think about anything other than your daughter?"

"Oh, they'll find her," Sam said. "These people are idiots but they're not dangerous. Try to imagine a bunch of tree-huggers kidnapping your kid. Well, that's exactly what happened here. A bunch of tree-huggers kidnapped my daughter."

"How do you know that?" Molly asked. "How do you know it's not a sexual predator?"

"If it is, she's already dead." Sam took a drink.

Molly stared at him a moment before glancing over at Bill, who was standing by the large windows, looking at the park. Feeling her eyes on him, he turned.

"The kidnappers have been in touch," he said. "The media doesn't know it. But it seems that Sam's right. They want an apology for some of the things he's said. It's a political act, not a criminal act. Well, it's both actually, but it's politically driven."

"What kind of apology?" Molly asked.

Bill looked at Sam. He could answer this one himself.

"For my comments on the Laureltown shooting," Sam said after a moment. "Which suggests that it's the anti-gun lobby. Somebody smoking too much pot and watching too much MSNBC."

"Or somebody from Laureltown?" Molly said.

Sam shook his head. "No. You think a bunch of parents got together to kidnap a child because of a few comments made on a TV show? This is bigger than that and, given the timing, probably designed to drive me out of the race. Well, that's going to backfire on them."

"You're going to continue to campaign?" Molly asked. "For fuck sakes, they have your daughter."

"Yeah, and they're going to pay for that. But first of all, let's use this to our advantage."

Molly drank some bourbon and ran her fingers across her forehead as she tried to think of what to say to him. "Here's the thing— you can't run for a congressional seat in Wyoming without actually being in Wyoming. And you can't leave New York with your daughter still missing and possibly—I'm sorry—possibly dead. You *cannot* do either of those things. You cannot ignore the fact that your daughter has been abducted."

"I have no intention of ignoring it," Sam said. "I'm going to use it."

"You're going to use it." Molly looked toward Bill for help but he was looking out over the city again. If she didn't know better, she'd have thought he wasn't paying attention. She knew better.

"No surrender," Sam said then. "That's my new campaign slogan. No Surrender. It's a natural progression from all bets are off. These people think they're going to bring me to heel? They'd better think again. And the voters are going to sympathize with me. The reason I'm not in Wyoming is that I'm here in New York, standing my ground against some anonymous, cowardly urban terrorists. Are you going to tell me that's not a compelling story line?"

"People are going to want to know why you're out on the campaign trail at a time like this," Molly said. "They're going to ask what you're doing to get your daughter back."

"And we're going to tell them I'm doing everything in my power."

"Are you?" Molly asked.

"Of course I am. As of tomorrow morning, my house becomes campaign headquarters. I have both the FBI and NYPD following me around anyway, so I might as well move them into the house and tell them to go sit in the corner while they wait for another call to come in. We can do everything from there—whatever radio stuff you can generate from Wyoming, TV hook-ups, print media, whatever. And I can arrange for network time at least a couple of nights a week, under the guise of updating the investigation. This is a godsend. Keep in mind, that the people responsible are quite eager to maintain contact. Which is a positive thing in terms of exposure."

"But are you doing everything you can?" Molly persisted. "Because I have the sense that you'd be happy if your little girl remained missing until, say—election day? Would that work for you, Sam?"

She saw his eyes go flat and she felt Bill approaching rather quickly. "I don't think that's a fair assessment, Molly. We have to play the cards we've been dealt here. Sam Jackson is not going to run from a fight."

"No Surrender," Sam said again, still glaring at Molly, challenging her.

"Yeah, I got that," Molly told him. "I just don't know how this plays back home. It may be a compelling story but is it a Wyoming story? Barton's people are already referring to Sam as that carpetbagger from New York. Well, this keeps him in New York."

"It also keeps him on the news all over the country," Bill reminded her. "Frank Barton would kill for exposure like this."

Molly pulled back then. She had more to say but she would say it to Bill alone. She'd wait until Sam left the suite, which he did after finishing his drink. He was meeting with someone from the network, he said. Molly might have wondered why he wouldn't go home to his wife, the mother of their missing ten-year-old daughter, but she was already past wondering things like that about the man.

When he was gone she looked at Bill, who was now sitting on the couch, legs crossed. He'd taken a bottle of juice from the bar and was sipping it.

"What have you gotten me into?" she asked. "The guy just referred to the abduction of his daughter as a godsend."

Bill shook his head. "He didn't mean that."

"He fucking well said it. Please tell me he didn't take the girl himself. Because that's all I kept thinking about when he was sitting in that chair, swilling scotch and talking about losing his daughter like he lost his car keys and how he plans to use it to get himself elected. Tell me that he didn't take her."

"Hell, he thought maybe we did it." Bill drank more juice. "No, somebody has her. Somebody with a left-wing agenda. Which is why he's doing the right thing here and why we have to stick with him. You said it yourself, Molly—he doesn't have a platform. All he has is an image. But that's how people get elected nowadays. Sam Jackson is the No Surrender man. If he knuckles under to these—what did he call them—urban terrorists, then he's finished."

"Who do you think took her?" Molly asked. "That poor kid."

"They want an apology for the Laureltown rant," Bill said. "So I'm guessing it's some anti-gun group that's gone rogue. But the type of person who would abduct a child to protest some crass remarks about dead children in a schoolyard is not the type of person who's going to harm that child."

"I suppose not," Molly admitted. "I hope not. But I wouldn't want my kid's life hanging on that supposition, would you? Do you think that Sam has come to that conclusion? That's why he's acting like—" she hesitated, putting her hands in the air.

"Like what?"

"Like he lost his car keys."

"I have no idea what goes through the man's mind," Bill said. "And I don't care. Like I said, there's nothing to him other than an image built on sound bites and rants. But he can get elected because of that, not in spite of it. Besides, we pull him now and we'd be handing the seat to Barton. Four weeks to the election, Molly."

She took a drink. She knew it was true.

"We play the cards we're dealt," Bill reminded her.

"Whether we like them or not," she said.

Bill shrugged. "Whether we like them or not."

"What in God's name are you doing?" Renata asked as she handed him the drink.

They were sitting in the living room of her condo. He had called from the car, while idling outside, saying he'd just left Bill Ford at the Plaza and needed to talk. She'd considered telling him to go home and talk to his wife but had relented and buzzed him up. She poured a scotch for him out of habit and now he was sitting spread-legged on the couch, drinking it. She remained on her feet. She was wearing track pants and a hoodie; she was about to go for a run when he called. Another two minutes and she would have missed him. That would have been fine by her.

"What do you mean?"

"I mean what in the fuck are you doing?" she demanded. "Vanessa has been kidnapped and you're on TV talking shit? Am I missing something here? Did you invent a story about a kidnapping, Sam?"

"Of course not. Good Christ."

She came reluctantly over to sit down on the couch, away from him though. "So what's going on?"

He took a drink. "Why do you keep asking me that?"

"You showed up *here*," she reminded him.

He shook his head. "All right, you've always known what was best for me. I feel as if I've lost control of this. Tell me what you would have suggested."

"Don't you have new people advising you now?"

"How long do you intend to stick with that attitude?"

"You're the one who shunted me to the sidelines, Sam. Your memory going too, along with your judgment?"

He finished the scotch in one gulp and got to his feet. She thought he was leaving and she was going to let him. Instead, he walked to the sideboard and poured more liquor.

"You won't answer because you don't have an answer."

He hesitated, watching her. "Okay, here's the problem. I'm running for a seat in Congress as a man who doesn't give in and doesn't give up. How do I justify all of a sudden acquiescing to these people? You tell me how to do that."

She sat quietly, watching him. It was rare that he ever let down his guard. She had been regretting buzzing him up but now she softened, if just a little. "First of all, who are *these people*?" she asked.

He shrugged. "I don't know. The people who took her."

"Don't fucking do that," she snapped. "Don't come here looking for my advice and then hold out on what you know."

He walked over and sat down in a wingback chair across from her. "It's connected to Laureltown. They want an apology. They want money too, but I have a feeling that the apology is the deal breaker. You cannot repeat what I just told you."

"Jesus," Renata said.

"Yeah."

"Then apologize," she said.

"What?"

"Apologize," she repeated. "Give them what they want. She's your daughter, for Chrissakes." She watched him a moment, saw the defiant look cross his face. "Apologize because she's your daughter, and for that matter, because you were wrong in the first place. You know damn well you were. It was nothing more than theater and you're not going to let a piece of theater get in the way of Vanessa's safety."

He put the glass on the end table beside him and rubbed his eyes with his fingertips. "I don't know how I can do that. This fucking campaign has a life of its own. I don't know how I can do an about-face and maintain any momentum."

"All of a sudden, you sound like a man who really wants to go to Congress," Renata said. "I thought this was just a lark."

He looked at her darkly. "There are worse ambitions."

"I suppose," she said. "But to the matter at hand. You need to apologize. For once in your life."

He reached for the glass. "I can't."

That was his answer. He'd arrived there seeking her counsel but he'd already gotten himself to a place where he was only going to listen to her if she told him what he wanted to hear. He'd tried and failed. They both had, she realized.

"I'm tired," he said then. His eyes went to the hallway. The bedroom. "Why don't we go and lay down?"

"Go ahead," she told him. "I'm going for a run."

THIRTY-SIX

After leaving the Red Lobster, Jo stayed off the turnpike and drove the back roads home. It was early evening, still daylight, when she got there. Henry wasn't in the fields or the barn or the warehouse either when she backed up the truck to unload. As she lifted the rear door though, he came wandering out of the house. Jo gave him a look and began hauling the vegetables out of the truck. They had to refill hampers and bags and six-quart baskets for the next day, when she'd be heading for Hershey. She didn't say anything until they were finished. Then she indicated the house.

"What were you doing?"

"Oh, just talking." He flicked his hand toward the goats, pastured in the field behind the barn. "She can see the goats from her cell, and the pony too, and she was asking about them. She's a smart kid, you know."

"It's not a cell, Henry."

"Easy for you to say. You're not locked up."

Jo started for the house. "What a pain in the ass."

Henry was on her heels. "She's not a pain in the ass."

"I was talking about you, Henry."

In the kitchen, Jo got a beer and a wedge of cheese from the fridge. She sat down at the table and drank the beer from the bottle and ate the cheese with some crackers. Henry remained on his feet.

"She was asking about you," he said, his voice dropped to a whisper.

"Yeah?"

"Why you don't like her."

"Christ, Henry."

"Think about it." He came over to sit across from her now. "She's already terrified. She thinks she's going to be harmed and she's convinced you hate her. How's she supposed to feel?"

"She's working you, you know that."

"Kids that age don't think that way."

"When I was that age, I had you wrapped around my little finger," Jo told him. "We all did."

The old man gave her a slow look of reproach. "It's not her fault she's not Grace. You can't hate the child for that."

"I don't hate her. I just don't want to like her."

"I'm surprised at you," Henry said. "She's a child. And someday you'll have children of your own."

"No," Jo snapped. "That will never happen. This fucking world does not deserve children."

Henry leaned in, his voice low. "This girl did nothing to you."

"All right," Jo sighed after a moment. She took a drink of beer and put a piece of cheese in her mouth as she walked down the hallway. When she unlocked the door and went into the room, the girl was sitting on the bed, her back to the headboard. She had a book in her lap, one with a giraffe named Gerald on the cover. Jo remembered it from years ago.

"Hey," Jo said.

The girl looked at her and then back at the book.

"You doing okay?"

She put the book down. "I want to go home."

"It's going to be a couple days."

"That's what you said before."

Jo walked over to look out the window. From there she could see the side wall of the old wooden barn, and the goat pasture in behind.

The nannies were picking at the grass along the rail fence and the billy was standing on a little knoll in the center of the field. The pony was grazing alone, down toward the creek. From the window that was all that could be seen. Jo had chosen the room because the other buildings, particularly the warehouse where the produce was loaded and unloaded, were out of sight. She didn't want the girl to identify any vehicles afterward. Specifically, she didn't want to give her the chance to memorize any plate numbers. She'd seen the GMC van in Williamsburg, the rear of it anyway, but presumably she'd been too freaked out at the time to remember any details.

"Did you talk to my father?" the girl asked.

Jo didn't turn. "Why do you think that?"

"The old man with the ponytail said you were going to talk to my father and then I'd be going home."

The old man with the ponytail. At least Henry hadn't given her his name and social security number. Not yet anyway. Jo kept her eyes on the goats in the field. She hoped the man with the ponytail had remembered to milk them today, preoccupied as he was with their boarder.

"I have talked to your father and we're working things out." Jo turned to her now. "You're okay here. You have enough to eat and drink, right?"

"Did you ask my father for money?"

"You don't need to know any of this."

"Oh—because it doesn't concern me?"

Jo was right about the kid working Henry. She knew it because now the kid was working her. "Don't worry about it."

"Yeah, I'll try not to worry about things," the girl said. "What if my father won't give you money?"

Jo started for the door. "I said not to worry about it, okay?" She glanced back and realized that the girl had been wearing the same clothes for three days. Shit. "What size are you?"

The girl fell silent, petulant that Jo had changed the subject.

"What size are you?"

"Nine."

"Okay."

"You could call my mother," the girl said. "I can give you her number."

Jo hesitated in the doorway. "I have her number."

The next day was Hershey, Pennsylvania. Jo ran into a detour that hadn't been there the previous week, when she'd scouted the site, and she got lost taking it. She arrived at the market just past eight o'clock. Everyone else was set up and selling. She found her stall and went to work assembling the tables, keeping her head down, trying to avoid undue attention to herself. She'd vended there a week earlier and had kept her own counsel, but not to the point of being rude. That, too, would have been conspicuous. After Hershey, she had one more town on the list. She had assumed, going in, that she wouldn't need any more than four days to get things resolved.

Now she wasn't sure.

THIRTY-SEVEN

When Molly arrived at Sam Jackson's house by the park at ten the next morning, the place had already been transformed. The FBI was set up in a front room, with an intense and abrupt agent named Dugan running the show. There were computers and phones and various other electronic devices Molly couldn't identify. When she introduced herself to Dugan he merely nodded and kept talking to one of the other agents, a pudgy guy in his shirtsleeves, sitting at a laptop.

Sam Jackson was in a room that appeared to be an oversized den, giving orders to a young guy with fuzzy blond hair, apparently some sort of video technician. There were two digital cameras mounted on tripods, trained on Sam's desk from different angles and some lighting bounces on the wall behind them. The blond-haired man was doing something with microphones when Molly entered. Sam was behind the desk, stapling a banner to the bookshelves there. The banner read NO SURRENDER. No one bothered to introduce Molly to the guy fumbling with the mikes so she did it herself.

"Greg Chalmers," he responded, shaking her hand quickly before going back to his work. His palm was sweaty.

"All right," Sam said, stepping back to look at the banner. "We're going to be ready to roll here shortly. We'll use the land line for radio and press interviews. This video hook-up goes to the network feed so we can go live anywhere, anytime."

Molly glanced about the room, the room in New York City from where Sam Jackson intended to run for Congress for the state of Wyoming. She wanted nothing to do with this. Fucking Bill Ford and his deep pockets, luring her in. She could have said no though, and knowing that made her weary to the bone.

"What have we got lined up?" Sam asked.

"What do we have lined up," Molly said slowly, shaking herself from her malaise. "Well, everybody wants to talk to you. No surprise, you're a public figure whose daughter has been kidnapped. Do they want to talk to you about your campaign? That's another question."

"We'll talk about both," Sam said. "That's how it works. That's the beauty of it."

The beauty of it, Molly thought. The beauty of having your daughter abducted.

"What about *The Press Box*?" Sam asked.

"They turned us down. You know that."

"That was before. This is human interest now. Does that prick Rutherford have any kids?"

"It's a political show, Sam," Molly reminded him.

"Try him again."

"Okay." Molly pointed her chin toward the FBI presence in the other room. "And all that?"

"They need to be close, so they say," Sam said. "I'm sure as hell not going to spend my day at FBI headquarters so I told them to set up here. Let's get started. Just so you know—I'm doing my old show again tonight."

"You are?"

"I called there and offered an update on the kidnapping," Sam said. "I need to get No Surrender out there."

"They're okay with that? It smacks of political bias."

"Not when a man has lost his daughter to terrorists," Sam told her.

"You like that word."

"When the shoe fits," Sam said. "Now what do we have first?"

Molly took her phone from her pocket and scrolled through the itinerary. "Talk radio from Casper. I have to send them your land line."

"Let's do it."

Once the connection was made and Sam was talking to the radio host in Wyoming, Molly wandered back into the main room where she sat on the arm of a sofa and emailed a producer she knew from *The Press Box*. The reply came back in less than a minute. Tim Rutherford wasn't interested in sitting down with Sam Jackson. Everybody knew that by now. Everybody but Sam Jackson.

Molly put her phone away and looked up to see a woman, standing just inside the open kitchen with a cup of coffee in her hand, dressed in jeans and a faded blue T-shirt. She was around Molly's age, tall and blonde, and she looked like shit standing there, glancing back and forth to all of the activity around her. Her hair was lank and her face puffy. Molly knew at once who she was. She walked over and introduced herself.

"Hi," Rachel said. Nothing more. She was watching the FBI guys, huddled over their equipment.

"Quite a production here," Molly said.

"Yeah."

"I'm sorry about your daughter. I hope they find her soon."

Rachel looked at her. Pale blue eyes rimmed with red. Something defiant behind the sadness. Molly waited for her to say something but she wouldn't.

"We'll try to stay out of your way," Molly said. "I know this isn't ideal, running the campaign from here. Apparently there was no other way."

"There was one other way," Rachel said.

Molly took a moment. "You mean he could have dropped out."

"Yeah."

"I suggested that."

"My husband doesn't take suggestions well. Why would he— when he's always right?"

Molly wasn't sure what to think of the woman. Given Sam Jackson's pomposity, she'd been expecting somebody subservient or detached, maybe even dimwitted. This woman seemed angry and tired and hurting. But of course she was hurting.

"What do you think of No Surrender?" Molly asked.

Rachel exhaled, like a swimmer surfacing. "Do you have kids?"

"Yes."

"What do you think of it?"

"I think," Molly said slowly, "that I would try to find another way to address the situation. A more conciliatory tone, to begin with."

Rachel turned to her. Until now, she'd been standing stiffly to the side, her body language armored against Molly. Against anybody. "Why are you working for him?"

"For money," Molly said. "Bill Ford's paying me to try to get him elected."

"Whether you approve of his methods or not?"

"Nobody likes their job all the time," Molly said. "That's the nature of work. Politics is all about compromise. Nothing would ever get done otherwise."

"So you're a person who has learned to look the other way," Rachel said. "Is that what you're saying?"

"I suppose."

"And you're good at it?"

"We both are, I'm guessing."

THIRTY-EIGHT

Bell arrived at the Jackson house a little past noon. He'd been off the past two days and wasn't scheduled to work until the weekend but after the phone call from Rachel Jackson he'd driven over. He wasn't doing anything anyway, other than procrastinating. He had a gallon of stain by his back door, ready to refinish the deck outside. It had been sitting there all summer long, only moving when Bell tripped over it. After talking to Rachel he'd tried to get in touch with the FBI guy Dugan but it was obvious that the man was ignoring him. Bell left two messages, waited an hour for a return call that never came, and headed to the house.

The door was wide open when he got there so he walked in. Dugan, in the big open family area, gave him a look bordering somewhere between pointed disregard and pure contempt. Bell smiled at him and kept walking, toward the sound of Sam Jackson's voice. The man was in a large study that had been turned into an ersatz TV studio. He was doing a phone interview, leaning back in a swivel chair behind a large wooden desk, hands clasped behind his head as he held forth. The phone was on speaker; the person on the other end was a frustrated and stammering woman, bent on trying to squeeze a word in here and there. There were two other people in the room—a tall woman with dark eyes and black hair, wearing boots and a long skirt, and a blond guy who was changing the lens in a video camera. The ongoing interview spared Bell any introductions. The guy ignored him while the dark-haired woman gave him a look of blatant appraisal. Bell, in jeans and a sweatshirt, suspected that he looked nothing like a cop. He smiled at her and went looking for Rachel Jackson.

She was in an expansive rock garden behind the house on a swing, staring at a brick wall at the back of the property. She was sitting ramrod straight, motionless, zoned out, and she obviously didn't hear Bell as he came out onto the flagstone patio. He watched her for a moment; he had an urge to leave her there in her solitude. But then, she had called him. Which meant that the solitude wasn't working for her.

"Hey," he said.

She wasn't startled. She turned her head toward him and nodded, as if agreeing to something. Maybe she had seen him all along and was waiting for him to speak. Her silence but his to break.

"What's going on?"

She indicated an Adirondack chair, green with yellow flowers painted on the slats. The flowers looked as if they'd been done by a child. They probably had been, Bell realized.

"Do you want coffee or something?" she asked.

Bell shook his head as he walked over to sit down.

"Have you had lunch?"

"I'm good," he told her. "You wanted to talk to me."

She began to rub the fingers of one hand with the other, as if she had a sudden itch. She wore no rings today, Bell noticed. The first time he'd met her she'd had on a half-dozen, silver and turquoise. But no wedding band.

"I'm feeling kind of shut out," she said. "I turn on the TV and Vanessa's picture is everywhere. There's all these theories about what happened to her. Who did it and why they did it. Where do they get their information?"

"I wouldn't pay any attention to that if I were you," Bell said. "The media isn't any better-informed than the police. Less, in fact. They have a different agenda than we do. With them it's all about ratings and so they speculate. We don't."

"I know how TV works," Rachel said. "I'm all too familiar with it. I guess that's why I called you. I was hoping you had something new."

"If we did, I would have told you," Bell said.

"What about this Driscoll guy?"

"We have nothing on him," Bell said. "We have hair and fibers from the limo but nothing that matches anything in the DNA base. There were a lot of people in the car in the past month or so. Not just passengers. Other drivers, the mechanics who service it, car jockeys at the lot. We got nothing on Driscoll, or whatever his real name is."

"Somebody must have him on a camera somewhere," Rachel said. "What about the bar where he met McIlroy?"

"The bar has security cameras that haven't worked in months. We're still looking at different street videos, in and out of the city that day. But we're talking thousands of cars and we don't know what we're even looking for. Needle in a haystack."

"If I hear that phrase once more, I'm going to scream."

Bell nodded. "We've actually picked up the limo on a couple of cameras but the locations haven't helped us. One was near Vanessa's school. Well, we already knew that. We have a few frames of similar limos where we can't make out the plates. That doesn't do us any good. A lot of limos in the city."

"But she didn't leave the city in the limo," Rachel said.

"No," Bell agreed. "Like I said, we don't know what vehicle she left in. We were hoping to see the limo stopped somewhere. You know, meeting someone. The exchange."

"How do you even know she left the city?"

"We don't."

"I mean," Rachel said, considering it now for the first time, "the assumption was that she was around Greenfield. At first anyway. But then we got the call from Elmira. Maybe she's still here in the city and they're out there leading you guys on a wild goose chase. She might be a few blocks from here."

"We can't dismiss that possibility," Bell said. "That's why we need to keep in contact with them." He paused. "What happened yesterday?"

Her mouth tightened. "Sam says he doesn't believe this woman. Doesn't believe she has Vanessa. So he hung up on her."

"That's what I heard. I have to say, I had trouble believing it. How did the FBI like it?"

"They were pissed. And so was I."

"What are they saying now?"

"Not much of anything," Rachel said. "Not to me anyway. That's why I called you. I need to know that something is happening. I need to know that somebody is trying to find my baby. I think about her, locked up somewhere, or tied up, and she's all alone, and she's telling herself that we're out there looking for her, that's how she's holding it together, and yet it doesn't seem as if we are. We're sitting around, looking at computers and maps and waiting for phone calls. And my husband's in there with his stupid fucking campaign. If that's what you want to call it."

Bell was quiet for a time. When he felt her eyes on him, he glanced at her then indicated their surroundings. The garden. The house. All of it.

"What is this?" he asked.

"What is what?" she repeated, her voice sharp.

He looked at her steadily and she looked away. Bell thought that he'd overstepped his bounds. Her marriage was none of his business; it really didn't factor into the situation at hand. He was about to apologize when she spoke.

"It wasn't always this way," she said. "I met him when I was working at Pendleton Press. He was a history prof then at Duke and he'd written a book about the Revolutionary War. A good book. I was his publicist. He was a typical first-time author, green as grass. Very polite, always wanting to pick up the tab for lunch or dinner. Writers never pick up tabs. He wrote another book, about the relationship between Robert E. Lee and James Longstreet." She shook her head. "If he stayed with the writing, maybe things would have been different. But he started doing guest spots on Fox, and you know—voicing his opinions. Believe it or not, he was middle of the road, politically, back then. But he knew what Fox wanted, what worked for them, what kept them inviting him back. Then ABN offered him the show, and that was it. It was as if the exposure triggered something in his brain that had been lying dormant. He's been erupting ever since."

"And you have to live with it," Bell said.

"Don't feel sorry for me, detective."

"I don't," he said. "Not about that."

She nodded, not saying anything else. He suspected she felt she'd said too much already.

"I'm going to talk to Dugan," he said. "He should not be shutting you out. Who's in there with Sam?"

She'd been near tears and now she wiped her eyes. "Some woman from Wyoming and the guy with the cameras and stuff."

"Who's the woman?"

"Molly something, I forget. She's the campaign manager."

"Did you know her before?"

"No. She says that Bill Ford hired her. Do you know who he is?"

"I've read about him."

"Well, he's the reason that Sam's running," Rachel said. "Him and his brother, pair of fucking oligarchs. They never gave him a second glance until he started singing Trump's praises on a nightly basis. All of a sudden, they're big fans. And when he started raving about the school shooting, they came calling." She paused for a moment. "Those poor kids in Laureltown. How's that for irony? Those parents lost their babies and now I've lost mine."

"No, you haven't," Bell said. "Your daughter's still alive, Rachel."

She nodded quickly at that, wanting so badly to believe him. Bell noticed that she had a habit of referring to the little girl as *her* daughter. Not theirs.

"Okay, I'm going to talk to my colleague from the Bureau," he told her.

Inside the house the Bureau was collectively having lunch. A young agent, a black guy with bulging muscles and a shaved head, had arrived with a large pizza and a bag of hoagies from a local deli, the name of the establishment emblazoned on the box in fiery red lettering. Bell knew the place and he knew it didn't do much business because the food was lousy. He also knew that the proprietor had been busted a few times for selling grass and hash to college kids. Bell doubted that the FBI knew that.

He walked over to Dugan, who was sitting on a couch, legs spread, eating a slice of pizza, with a second slice on a coffee table in front of him. He glanced up at Bell, his mouth full, his look somewhat amused.

"Your guys get anything from the toll booth cameras?" Bell asked, stopping a few feet away to look down at Dugan.

Dugan chewed his food sloppily and at length, making Bell wait. Bell smiled at him, resisting the urge to tell him to shove the second slice up his ass. Dugan swallowed and took a drink of soda before he replied.

"We're still looking at a hundred thousand cars running through a dozen or so toll booths, hoping we find a few that did the New York City to Greenfield to Elmira route. Did you want to double-check our work? I'd be happy to send the tapes to your desk downtown."

"I'll defer to the Bureau's expertise," Bell said.

"You have no idea how much that means to us." Dugan reached for the second slice.

"No movement from the limo driver?"

"Yeah," Dugan said. "From his house to the bar and back again. Turns out he's got a girlfriend in Yonkers too, or a booty call anyway. We paid her a visit but she's almost as dumb as he is. But again, if you want to check it out…"

Bell ignored the jibe this time. He looked around at the equipment in the room. The young guy with the biceps had disappeared. Out in the yard doing push-ups, Bell guessed. The tech guy Heyward was leaned back in his chair beside his laptop, enthusiastically attacking a hoagie. Bell watched the assault for a moment before turning back to Dugan. "So we wait for another call."

"*We* wait for another call," Dugan said. "I'm not sure why you're here."

"Working a case, same as you."

"You're the definition of redundant," Dugan said. "You do realize that?"

Bell was looking past him now, at two maps on the wall there. He hadn't noticed them before and he walked over for a closer look. The first map showed the city, and the route that the limo had taken, at least as much of the route that they knew. The second map was of a much larger area, and it displayed the various ways to get from the city to the town of Greenfield, and from there to Elmira, with the locations circled in red. The secondary roads were countless, the potential routes that a person could take impossible to compute. Bell's gut told him that the woman—and whoever she had with her, if anybody—had stayed away from the thruway. And while it was true that she might be traveling on her own, with the little girl still in the city somewhere, Bell doubted it. The girl was stashed somewhere in a rural area, although it was very unlikely she'd been in Greenfield or Elmira either. Smoke and mirrors, he thought. Then he heard Heyward's voice, muffled by the hoagie.

"Shit!"

He was looking at the laptop screen, sauce from the hoagie dripping from his bottom lip. He set the messy sandwich aside and wiped his hands quickly before typing something. "They called," he said. "Three times."

Dugan was on his feet. "What do you mean they called?"

Heyward pointed. "Three times in the last four minutes."

Dugan looked at the info on the screen and turned and headed for the room where Sam Jackson was. Bell followed. They found Sam sitting at the desk, with the tall woman standing beside him, showing him something on her iPad.

"Where the hell's your phone?" Dugan barked.

Sam looked up, not happy with the agent's tone. "What?"

"Your phone—where is it?"

Sam glanced around the desk. "My phone is right here."

"They called," Dugan snapped.

"Oh," Sam said calmly, looking at the screen. "I must have turned it off."

THIRTY-NINE

The town of Hershey was a tourist location, with the famed chocolate factory and the vintage flea market and *ZooAmerica* wildlife park among the attractions, and so the farmers market there was larger than most, a clustered menagerie of stalls selling fruits and vegetables and meats and seafood and crafts, the whole venture sprawled out over a couple of acres east of the town's center, the site of an old fairgrounds. Jo had managed to secure a spot on the periphery, outside of the flow of the main market. With her location, and all the competition, she didn't do a lot of business. Not that it mattered.

Shortly before one she packed up, locked the truck and walked along the northern edge of the market to the street there. Once on the sidewalk, hidden from the market by a row of buildings, she removed her ball cap and pulled a straw fedora from her bag. She put the hat on, along with her shades. A few blocks farther along she went into a community center, a gray block building with a small swimming pool and some tennis courts in behind. Inside the front door of the building was a bank of three pay phones, separated by scarred Plexiglas shields. When she'd been there a week earlier, just one of the phones was in working order. That was still the case. She took the sheet of paper she'd gotten from Daniel from her pocket, then wrapped the receiver with a tissue and punched in the number with her knuckle. It rang once and went straight to voice mail.

"You got Sam Jackson. Leave a message. No surrender."

Jo hung up. She stood there for a full minute and then dialed again.

"You got Sam Jackson. Leave a message. No surrender."

She put the receiver back. "Shit," she said.

She walked outside and had a look around. It was a quiet street, with older homes across from the center, story-and-a-half carriage houses from sixty or seventy years ago, amid a few bungalows of newer construction. There was a corner store half a block away, run by a Korean couple. Jo had been inside the previous week; there was a pay phone out front but there were two cameras in the store, at least two that she'd seen.

From behind the building she could hear splashing and kids laughing in the pool. There was a lifeguard on duty, Jo knew, and a woman in an office that looked out over the pool. The entrance with the phones was blind to the office.

Jo stood in the shade of the building for a few moments, watching the afternoon traffic and wondering what to do. Straight to voice mail meant that the phone was turned off. Why the hell would he turn his phone off, under these circumstances? Maybe the battery was dead and he'd forgotten to charge it. Or maybe he was on the phone. If that was the case, he wouldn't stay on long, not if he was anticipating her call. She went back inside and called the number again.

"You got Sam Jackson. Leave a message. No surrender."

Jo hung up. No surrender. What was that? More of his nonsense, his maverick asshole shtick. She suddenly had a thought. The police knew that she was calling. The phone was turned off on purpose. Answered or not, the calls were going through the server, which meant they probably already had her location.

And then she heard sirens.

She hurried out the door again and started toward the market. She pulled the fedora down over her eyes and then at once decided to change direction, crossing the street to walk into the residential area, moving onto a narrow boulevard with leafy maple and oak trees overhead. The sirens got louder. Her pace and her heart rate accelerating rapidly, she told herself to calm down. It wasn't possible that they could have pinpointed the phone and contacted the local cops that quickly. Unless they knew she would be calling from Hershey, unless they'd figured out her movements. But how could they? Then again, Jo had no idea what they could do in this day and age. Homeland Security and all of that. It was Big Brother at last. Why did she think she could outsmart them?

She went nearly a block along the shaded street and then stopped to look back. The sirens were near now. She could see the corner of the community center, the tennis courts in behind. A few seconds later she saw the police car, lights flashing. It went straight past, never slowing. And then behind it, a fire truck.

She exhaled. Her heart was still racing and she was sweating beneath the cool shade of the trees. "All right," she said quietly.

Still they would have her location by now. She needed to get moving. She went back along the street, resisting the urge to hurry, to draw attention to herself from anybody watching from inside the cozy little homes. The cops might canvas the neighborhood later. When she reached Sullivan Street, she glanced toward the community center. All quiet for now. She could imagine the calls being made though, the local cops being notified. Cruisers on the way.

She made her way back to the market, removing the fedora as she walked and stuffing it in her bag. At the entrance to the fairgrounds she pulled on the ball cap she'd been wearing earlier while vending. She got into the truck and drove out the back gate. Five minutes later she was on a narrow country road, heading home.

FORTY

Bell leaned against the door jamb, watching. Sam hadn't bothered to get to his feet. He sat behind the desk, calmly looking at his wife, who had just come into the room. The campaign manager and the camera guy were standing to the side; neither had said anything since Dugan had stormed in.

"Why?" Rachel asked, her voice cracking. "Why would you do that?"

"As I have just explained to the agent here," Sam said, pointing his chin toward Dugan, "I was doing back-to-back radio interviews on the land line. I had to turn my cell off, quite obviously, for that. Why is everybody having such a hard time understanding that?"

"I can't do this," Rachel said softly. Bell stepped forward, almost involuntarily, thinking that she might collapse.

Sam held up his phone. "It's on now. She'll call back."

"She won't call back," Dugan said. "She knows we have the location. She's long gone. Like yesterday. You remember yesterday—when you hung up on her?"

"I remember yesterday," Sam said. "It was day three of the FBI's ongoing incompetence in this matter. And this would be day four of the same."

Dugan turned and walked out. Bell waited a moment, watching

Rachel Jackson. Sam seemed to notice Bell for the first time.

"What is the NYPD doing at this time?"

"Waiting for a break in the case," Bell told. "You know—like a phone call."

He left the room then as well, moving through the house to where Heyward, his cellphone to his ear, was in the process of updating the location map, while Dugan stood by watching. The call had come from Hershey, Pennsylvania. Heyward encircled the town in red before stepping away, still talking to somebody on the phone.

"It's a circle," Dugan said. "Closest thing we have to a pattern. They're moving counterclockwise around the city." Using his forefinger, he tapped the locations on the map. "New York to Greenfield, Greenfield to Elmira, Elmira to Hershey. Which means—they should continue moving south, toward Baltimore. Maybe back east to Newark. Definitely a pattern."

"A pattern signifying what?" Bell asked. "All we know is that so far she's been calling from small town pay phones. Clockwise, counter-clockwise, corkscrew—it doesn't tell us shit."

"It tells us that they're on the move, and we now know the direction."

"We don't even know it's *they*," Bell reminded him. "You're under the impression they're moving the little girl from town to town?"

"It would seem that way, wouldn't it?"

"No," Bell said. "Not to me."

"So you're with Sam Jackson on this," Dugan said. "You think this woman is just a scammer?"

"Oh, I think she has the girl," Bell said. "Or she's working with somebody who does. This is too well-orchestrated to be somebody just throwing darts at the wall. But I don't see them *moving* the girl. Her picture is on every website, every newspaper. The six o'clock news. What do they gain by moving her? They've got her stashed somewhere."

Dugan flicked the back of his hand toward the map. "Where?"

"If I knew that," Bell said, "I'd go and get her."

"Okay, hold on," Heyward said into the phone and he looked at

Dugan. "Pay phone's in a little community center, middle of town. I got one of the local cops on the line. He's at the scene now. Phone's in the entrance, no cameras. They're going to dust for prints."

"Good luck with that," Dugan said.

Heyward began talking into the phone again, telling whoever was on the other end to speak to anybody working at the center, and anybody who might have been in the area at the time the woman called.

Dugan was on his own phone then, instructing somebody to get their asses over to Hershey to do a door-to-door canvas of the neighborhood around the community center.

"Somebody saw this woman," he said into the phone. "Somebody at that building, somebody on the street. And somebody saw her get into a car. She's not invisible. You and Malone need to get over there. I don't want the local cops fucking this up."

Bell was looking at the map. The last remark was for his ears and he knew it. He smiled. Fuck you, Dugan. He considered the route again. Greenfield, Massachusetts. Elmira, New York. Hershey, Pennsylvania. Dugan was right—it was a circle moving counterclockwise around the city. But that didn't tell them anything, and it certainly didn't suggest where the woman would call from next. But why those towns? Bell was inclined to believe that they weren't random. And they hadn't been chosen because they all happened to have pay phones located in relatively private areas. There were thousands of towns that would qualify. There was a method to what she was doing, but Bell had no clue as to what it was. He took a step forward, closer to the map, looking again at the towns in question.

"You're assuming that the woman is traveling in a circle," he said over his shoulder.

Dugan was sending a text and he finished before looking up. "I'm not assuming anything. I *know* she's traveling in a circle. You've got eyes, don't you?"

Bell traced the route with his forefinger. "So you're saying she drove to Greenfield, then she drove to Elmira, then to Hershey."

"Yes," Dugan said impatiently. "She called from those three towns."

"If she's got the little girl, then that means she's dragged the kid across three states so far. I don't buy that. Why would she risk a routine traffic stop with the kid in the car?" Bell tapped his finger on the map, on a spot roughly in the center of Dugan's circle. "What if they're holed up here someplace? She drives to Greenfield, makes a call, and goes home. Drives to Elmira, makes the call, and goes home. And then Hershey, same thing. It's a circle, but she's not moving in a circle. She's operating from the hub."

Dugan shook his head. "Why would she be doing that?"

"To confuse us." Bell smiled. "And it's working. Right, Special Agent Dugan? The question remains though—why those towns? Is it random, simply because they're far apart? Is that all it is?"

"You're forgetting I'm not buying your fucking hub theory," Dugan told him.

Bell kept looking at the map. "You ever play Keep Away when you were a kid, Dugan? You're in the middle and your buddies are tossing the ball back and forth and they've got you running every which way. You ever play that?"

"No," Dugan said. He was looking at his phone again, not all that interested in the conversation. "I wasn't into playground games."

"Well, that's what she's doing with us," Bell said. "She's playing Keep Away."

FORTY-ONE

Jo was on the road for an hour before she could allow herself to relax. She'd been relatively calm, making the calls in Greenfield, and in Elmira, but Hershey had rattled her. She had never anticipated Sam Jackson not answering his phone. How could she? Who would anticipate a parent whose child had been abducted not bothering to take a call from the person responsible?

Her initial suspicion that the FBI was behind it didn't hold water, she realized now. How would they benefit from that? No, they wanted Jo on the phone, as often and for as long as possible. This was Sam Jackson, she knew. The notion that he wouldn't answer infuriated her. It would have lowered her opinion of him even further, if it were possible to go any lower.

She was on a two-lane highway, heading east, approaching the little town of East Stroudsburg when she remembered the clothes. On the edge of town, she came to a strip mall and pulled in, parking the GMC in the rear corner of the lot behind the stores.

She went into a Target and picked up two pairs of jeans, some tees and some underwear and socks, as well as a nightgown. Size nine. She grabbed whatever she saw first; she wouldn't allow herself to think about what would look good on the girl, what she might like, what was currently in fashion for ten-year-olds. She'd considered those things when shopping for Grace in the past—for Christmas or birthdays or just for fun—and she wouldn't consider them now. Or ever again.

Sam Jackson's refusal to answer his phone was still on her mind as she stood in line to pay. Things weren't progressing the way she had imagined. Looking at the bundle of clothes in her arms, she realized that things weren't progressing at all. It was a standoff and Sam Jackson was calling the shots.

She laid the clothes on the counter. The cashier was a heavy woman, with eyebrow piercings and a gregarious manner.

"Find everything you need for your little one?" she asked as she rang up the merchandise.

"Yeah," Jo replied absently.

"On your Target card?"

"Cash."

"Cash money," the woman said. "You the last of your breed, honey."

Jo paid and headed for the exit. There was a glassed-in foyer leading out, with pay phones along the wall. Jo pushed through the first door, hesitated, looking up. No cameras, not there in the foyer. She paused for maybe a three count then pulled the paper from her jacket pocket and dialed the number. She kept her back to the store and any cameras that might be inside. The phone rang twice and the woman answered, the voice somewhat familiar. They had talked before, briefly, two days ago.

"Rachel Jackson?" Jo asked. She pulled the second sheet of paper from her pocket.

"Yes. Who is this?"

"You know who it is," Jo told her. "So you guys think I don't have your daughter? I'm going to read you the numbers off her phone. The first number is for someone named Suzanne. Yours is next, I just dialed it. Her father's is third and you know I've dialed it. Next is Amanda." Jo read the number and kept going. Cecily. Amelia. Britney. Grandma. She read the names and she read the numbers, one by one.

"Okay!" Rachel Jackson blurted out. "I believe you. I've always believed you. Tell me where she is. Please.”

“She’s safe,” Jo said. “You tell me what the fuck happened today. Why didn’t he answer?”

“I don’t know.”

“That’s bullshit.”

“It’s not bullshit,” Rachel said. “He had his phone off. He was doing an interview, this stupid campaign.”

“So your campaign is more important than your daughter?”

“It’s not *my* campaign! And it’s not more important than Vanessa. Not to me.”

Jo heard shouting in the background. “Where are you?”

“I’m in the park. I had to get out of there. Is Vanessa with you? Can I talk to her, please? *Please?*”

“No, you can’t,” Jo said. “You want her back, tell your husband to meet my demands. Three things. No negotiating.”

“What things? Tell me!”

“Ask your husband,” Jo said and hung up.

She went out the door and walked around the building, her head down, the bag with her purchases held up, shielding the side of her face against whatever video surveillance the small-town mall might employ. It had been a stupid impulse, calling like that. When she got into the truck, she swung the vehicle in a wide circle and drove out the way she’d come in.

“Sonofabitch,” she realized when she was on the road. “He never told her either.”

FORTY-TWO

After the woman hung up, Rachel called Sam at once and told him what had happened. As she spoke to him she was hurrying through the park, dodging the rollerbladers, heading back home.

"She said three things again, Sam," she said sharply into the phone. "What are they?"

"I told you. I have no idea."

"Don't you lie to me," Rachel said, trying to remain calm. "Tell me what she wants. Tell me what we need to do."

"What who wants?" Sam asked. "You just got an anonymous phone call and you're all wound up about it. How do you know it was the same woman?"

"I just explained that part," Rachel said. "Why won't you tell me what she wants?"

"We'll talk when you get here." The phone in her hand went dead.

When she got home Dugan and Heyward were waiting for her, Heyward sitting by his computer, talking on his cell. Sam had changed into a suit and was standing in the kitchen with a cup of coffee. He had evidently given Rachel's cell number to the agents.

"Where did she call from?" Rachel asked.

Dugan indicated Heyward. "We're contacting your server. Tell me exactly what she said."

"She had the numbers from Vanessa's phone," Rachel said. "Mine, Sam's, my mother's. All her friends."

"What did she want?"

Rachel took a moment to gather herself. "Well, she wanted to tell me that. As proof that she actually has Vanessa. It does prove it, right? Nobody else could have those numbers."

"It doesn't prove anything," Sam said. "The phone was missing for hours before it turned up. Who knows who had access to it?"

"Why are you doing this?" Rachel demanded. "Why are you doing this, Sam? They've got Vanessa and they want to talk to us."

"I don't know that they have her," Sam said. "And even if they did—I don't negotiate with terrorists."

Rachel stared at him a moment before turning on Dugan. "She said three things. She wants three things. She said that the other day. Remember?"

Dugan looked at Sam, who shrugged his shoulders. "I can't tell you what that's about." He paused. "But I do have an idea. Why don't you guys track this woman down and bring her in? Why is that so difficult? You're holed up here while she's taking her little road show to half the towns in America."

Before Dugan could reply to that, Heyward got off the phone. "They want a warrant," he said.

"Who does?" Rachel demanded.

"Your server," Dugan said. "We expected that. We needed one for Sam's phone too."

"Why don't you already have it?" Rachel asked.

Dugan didn't say anything. After a moment Heyward did. "Well, she wasn't calling your phone."

"She just did," Rachel said.

FORTY-THREE

There was no market trip scheduled for the following day so when Jo got home she and Henry unloaded the produce she hadn't sold and carried it into the warehouse. As they worked she told the old man about what had happened in Hershey, and in East Stroudsburg afterwards.

"Did you tell the mother that she's okay?" was the first thing Henry asked.

"What?" Jo asked. "Yeah, I guess so." She hefted a bushel of red potatoes onto her knee and carried it inside.

"Either you did or you didn't," Henry said when she returned. He was leaning against the back of the truck. Listening to her, he hadn't been doing much work.

"She knows the kid's okay or I wouldn't be calling."

"How does she know that?" Henry asked. "Put yourself in her shoes. How could she know that?"

"I don't want to be in her shoes. I want to know why they're fucking us around. He doesn't have his phone on? What is that?"

Henry sighed. "I don't know."

"Well, I know one thing," Jo said. "It's not her doing this, it's him. She was desperate to talk; she wanted to know what I wanted."

"Did you tell her?"

205

"No."

"Why the hell not?"

"Because she can't give me what I want." Jo grabbed another basket.

"But she would."

"Probably," Jo said. "But he's running the show. So she's not helping much—and neither are you, Henry," she said over her shoulder as she went into the warehouse.

He pitched in then. When they were finished Jo nodded toward the house. "She okay?"

"What do you mean by that? Is she okay with her circumstances?"

"Stop that. I mean—she's eating and all that?"

"She eats."

"Good."

"I took that little TV in to her," Henry said. "With my VCR and a few movies."

"At least you didn't take her into town to the show," Jo said. "Oh, I bought some clothes for her. They're in the cab. You can give them to her."

"You can give them to her." Henry walked away, ending the discussion.

The girl was watching a movie when Jo unlocked the door and let herself into the room. Jo glanced at the set, propped atop the dresser. The movie was *The Man Who Shot Liberty Valance*. Well, the kid wasn't going to find any Harry Potter in Henry's collection. Jo would bet she'd never encountered a VCR before either.

"Hey," Jo said.

The little girl looked at her and then away. Jo tossed the bag with the clothes onto the bed.

"I got you some clothes. Jeans and stuff. Leave what you're wearing when you take a bath and I'll wash it."

The kid kept her eyes on the set. "Did you talk to my father again?"

"No," Jo said. She waited, deciding. "I talked to your Mom."

The girl's eyes lit up and she turned to Jo. "What did she say?"

"She didn't say anything. I just told her something and that was it."

The face fell. "She didn't ask about me?"

"Yeah, she asked about you."

"What did you tell her?"

"I told her you were okay."

The little girl was skeptical. "Did you for real? I'm worried about her. I don't know if she can handle something like this."

Well shit, Jo thought. It wasn't supposed to be this way. She looked at the TV, where Lee Marvin was menacing a gangly Jimmy Stewart. "You're not worried about your father?"

"No."

"All right." Jo turned to go but then stopped. "You want to have a bath?"

"I had one already. The guy makes me."

"Well, there's a nightgown there."

"Am I supposed to thank you?"

"No," Jo said. "I'd rather you didn't."

Jo stood in the open doorway and watched the girl, who was staring at the little screen, her attention rapt, as if a sixty-year-old western was the only thing in the world of interest to her. Ignoring Jo, just to show her she could.

"Who's Suzanne?" Jo asked.

The girl quickly looked over. It seemed the question had surprised her. "She's our nanny."

"Okay," Jo said and she left, locking the door behind her. She went into the kitchen and sat at the table. The mail was there and she went through it absently, without seeing what she was reading, thinking about a girl born into wealth and privilege, with everything life could offer before her. Thinking of why the first contact on the girl's phone would be her nanny.

FORTY-FOUR

When Sam went to the ABN studios to tape the Rivera show that afternoon, Dugan went with him. Heyward, with his laptop, tagged along. Dugan advised Sam to keep his phone turned on, his tone suggesting that he wasn't all that happy with the way the situation had played out earlier. Sam, little concerned with Dugan's happiness level, never responded.

Ron Rivera wasn't thrilled to have Sam hijack the show once again. He'd complained about it earlier in a phone call to Bobby Holmes.

"Since when are we his campaign tool?" he'd asked.

"The kidnapping is a huge story," Bobby had replied. "And Sam's not talking to NBC or ABC or CNN, just us and Fox so far. As long as the kid's missing, we give him the air time he wants."

"You're saying I don't have to let him babble on about running for Congress?"

Bobby had laughed. "If you can figure a way to shut him up, go for it."

The producer Kevin started kissing Sam's ass the moment he walked through the door, and never stopped. Sam was given the run of things, leaving Rivera once more with the feeling that he really didn't need to be there. They could have propped up a mannequin in his chair and had Kevin lob a few softball questions Sam's way from the booth. Rivera decided to stay out of the way, putting up with it until it was nearly time to roll. A couple of minutes before they went to tape, though, he leaned in toward Sam.

"Be nice if you could give us a little more on the situation with your daughter this time, Sam," he said. "That's the story here."

Sam started to say something and then stopped. "Okay, Ron," he said after a moment. "Say, is Ron really your name—or is it some bastardized version of the real thing?"

"It's a bastardized version of Ronald."

They rolled tape and Rivera asked for an update on Vanessa. "Have you heard anything at all from the kidnappers?"

"We've heard from people claiming to be the kidnappers," Sam replied. "Quite a number of them, in fact. Most of them, probably all of them, are pretenders, looking to take advantage of this situation to line their own pockets. I'm coordinating the investigation myself, working closely with the FBI, of course. Until such time that somebody can come up with proof that they have my daughter, there's very little we can do. I have neither the time nor the inclination to listen to pretenders. But we are vigilant, we are following every lead, and we will be successful. In a situation fraught with uncertainty, there is one thing I can guarantee—I will get my daughter back safely."

"Any theories on who might have taken her?"

"The good news is," Sam began slowly, "that we can assume that this isn't sexually motivated, nor is it the work of some deranged madman, as was the case in Laureltown last month. This is political through and through. Look at the timing. I'm known as a guy who calls a spade a spade. I'm known as a guy who isn't afraid to stand up and tell people that this country is going to hell in a handbasket, that we've become a nation of weaklings. Do you know who that scares? The weaklings, of course. And the cowards. And so—when I announce that I intend on November the third to take my message to Washington, that scares the hell out of the weaklings. That scares the hell out of the cowards. On TV, I'm just some guy flapping his gums. But in Washington, I'm somebody who can enact change, who can begin to move this country *back* to where it was."

Rivera jumped in now. "You're saying that your daughter has been abducted by a person or persons who disagree with your politics?"

"Isn't it obvious?"

"Not entirely," Rivera said. "So what do these people want?"

"To remove me from the political stage, of course."

"Someone has said that to you?"

"We're getting into an area of the investigation that I really can't comment on at this time," Sam said. "And to be clear I'm not saying that Frank Barton or anyone associated with his campaign has had anything to do with this."

"Hold on," Rivera said. "Your opponent Frank Barton? You're not suggesting that he is involved?"

"You're not listening, Ronald," Sam said. "I just told you that I do *not* think he's involved."

"Then why bring him up?"

"You brought him up." Sam smiled. "I know what was said. You need to remember that I sat in that chair for a good many years. *You* asked if I thought the people opposing my run for Congress were behind the abduction of my daughter."

"You're paraphrasing," Rivera told him. "And that's not what I meant."

"I don't know what you meant. I just know what you said."

Rivera, rattled now, retreated. "Let's get back to your daughter. You said you've been contacted by multiple people claiming to have her. Contacted how?"

"Different ways," Sam said. "Telephone, for one."

"Can you tell us about these conversations?"

"Yeah, they've been short," Sam said. "And they'll continue to be short until such time that I have proof that one of these—groups, I'll call them—has my daughter. Irrefutable proof, that's what I require. And until I have it, I won't be discussing anything with these terrorists. And even when I do have it, the only thing I'll be talking about is them giving themselves up. I want to make that clear."

"You won't negotiate?"

"Not with terrorists, no."

"This is your daughter's life we're talking about," Rivera said.

"They harm my daughter and there is no place on this earth where I won't find them," Sam said. "They harm my daughter and they will wish they were never born."

"You used the word 'groups'," Rivera said. "And earlier you brought up the possibility that this is politically motivated. If we accept that you are not suggesting that your opponent is involved, just who do you think is holding your daughter?"

Sam flipped his hand in the air. "Take your pick, Ronald. Proponents of a socialist health-care system, proponents of gun control, the anti-drilling lobby, the people who clamor for gay scout masters to take your sons camping in the woods. It's a long list if you look at it that way. But it's a short list if you look at it this way—it's people who are bound to destroy this country. Those people see me as an obstacle to their nefarious goals and they will do anything to get rid of me. However, on the other side of that rampart, I'm looked upon as a vanguard. I'm Davy Crockett at the Alamo. I'm Jim Bowie. I'm Travis. And what did those men say, Ronald? What did they say, standing atop that wall?"

Rivera shook his head. "You'll have to help me out."

"No surrender," Sam told him. "That's what they said."

FORTY-FIVE

Bill Ford called Molly in her room the minute Sam's interview was over. He was off again someplace; Molly couldn't recall where but she knew he'd left the city earlier that day. So many balls in the air, so little time until November. Sam had also called Molly as he was leaving the studio, reminding her to tune in. Molly had declined to go to the taping, coming back to the hotel to work on the next day's itinerary instead. She'd been in a skirt and heels all day and when she got back to the room she changed into track pants and a T-shirt.

"It's a masterful performance," Sam had told her.

"Well," she said now to Bill Ford. "Was it masterful?"

"I wouldn't have chosen that particular word." The cell connection wasn't good; maybe Bill was in the mountains or in his jet. "But it was effective. He's only got one note but he hits it every time. Doesn't he?"

"He does."

"What's this about several different people claiming to have the little girl?" Bill asked. "Is that true?"

"Not that I'm aware of. One woman has called, a couple of times." She told him about the incident earlier, Sam having his phone off.

"He doesn't want to talk to her because he doesn't want it resolved," Bill said after considering the information.

"But we knew that." Molly had ordered dinner from room service earlier and eaten half of it. Now she walked to the cart and poured herself a half cup of lukewarm coffee. "Christ, does he really think he can put this off until after the election? Like it's a trip to the dentist he doesn't have time for?"

"The only way he wants to resolve it now is if they give up and return the girl," Bill said. "That makes Sam the hero of the piece. He stood his ground."

"I can't see them doing that," Molly said. "Not when they've come this far. Keep in mind that the FBI is stumbling around in the dark on this. None of their high-tech investigative shit is working here and it is pissing them off royally. And it's not just the phone calls from the mystery woman. They haven't the slightest idea who the guy is who grabbed the girl to begin with. Add to that the fact that Sam has his cellphone turned off when the woman tries to call, and it's a real clusterfuck over there."

"So where are they now—sitting around, waiting for another call?"

"I didn't tell you. The woman called Sam's wife. A couple hours later."

"She did?"

"Yeah. And she rattled off all the contact numbers on the girl's cellphone. You know, as proof she has the kid. Sam said that doesn't prove anything."

"What was the wife's reaction?"

"She believes it," Molly said. "I mean, she wants to believe it so badly. Wouldn't you?"

"She can't be very happy with Sam then."

"I would call that an understatement." Molly had a sip of coffee. "So what does this do for us? You can bet that Barton's people are going to be screaming about his name being tossed around in a kidnapping investigation."

"Which means the clip is going to get played over and over. And keep in mind that Sam insisted that Barton is not involved."

"Well, after a fashion," Molly pointed out.

"I say we put the whole interview on the website," Bill said. "Let people decide what he said and what he didn't say."

Molly gave up on the coffee. "When Sam called after the taping, he claimed there were a bunch of young guys outside the studio, holding up No Surrender signs and chanting his name. You believe that?"

"Possibly," Bill said. "But if they had signs, I guarantee they got them from Sam, or somebody working for him."

"What good is that though? We're not after the New York vote. I have to admit he's got some momentum going over this abduction. Even you couldn't buy exposure like this, Bill. But we should be riding this wave back in Wyoming. How would it look if we went out there for a couple days, with the investigation ongoing? And would he go for it?"

"He might," Bill said. "It gets him away from the thing he's trying to avoid in the first place. As for how it would look, we'd have to finesse it. He'd have to make a statement, how he's in constant communication with the FBI, etc. It's doable." He paused. "We'll need some more graphics—signs, T-shirts, buttons. No Surrender, with Sam's image underneath, looking defiant."

"We could make up a poster," Molly said. "Put him on the wall at the Alamo, with Crockett and Bowie and Travis. Of course, that might lose us the Mexican vote."

"There's Mexicans in Wyoming?"

"That was a joke, Bill," Molly said.

As she ended the call, the phone rang in her hand. It was Sam, calling from the limo, wanting to know if she'd watched the interview. He was like a puppy, waiting to be praised for not pissing on the carpet. She skipped the expected kudos and told him about the plan to go back to Wyoming.

"I'm coming over," he said.

When he walked in the room fifteen minutes later, he went straight to the bar and poured himself a half a glass of scotch. For a man who presented himself as the ultimate maverick, he was as predictable as the sunrise. He plopped into a chair and indicated her wardrobe.

"Looking casual there, Molly." He sipped the drink. "Gotta

say, you can pull it off."

Molly had no interest in making small talk with him. "How would you square it with the FBI, heading back to Wyoming?"

"I wouldn't square anything. I'll just tell them and they can like it or lump it."

Molly sat down on the couch across from him. She would have liked a drink herself now, or a cold beer, but she decided against it. She didn't want him to get the impression they were socializing, especially after his remark about her clothes.

"It definitely opens up more media opportunities," she said, thinking out loud. "The people who'd rather not hear about your politics might be interested in your daughter's story." She paused. "Although you might have to temper your message."

"What's that mean?"

"The interview tonight was a tad fanciful, don't you think?" she asked.

Sam had a drink, smiling. "In what way?"

"You know the answer to that. Lincoln said that you can fool some of the people all of the time but you need to think about the rest. The *Washington Post* had Trump lying two thousand times during his first year in office alone. The number now is around fifteen thousand and his approval ratings are the lowest in history. You might keep that in mind."

"I don't lie."

Molly let it slide. She knew there was a very good possibility that Sam believed he didn't lie. Molly wasn't going to lose sleep over it either way.

"How soon can you be ready to go then?" she asked. "I can start setting things up."

"Why not tomorrow?"

"Tomorrow is good." Molly opened her iPad and made a point of checking the itinerary. She was quiet as she did and after a few moments Sam took the hint. Finishing his drink in a gulp, he got to his feet.

"I'll leave you to it," he said.

She stood and walked with him to the door. "I'll charter a plane for tomorrow afternoon, give you time to do whatever you need to on the home front."

"The home front can take care of itself," he said, smiling needlessly.

He stopped before opening the door, not looking at her at first, and then suddenly he turned and tried to kiss her, his right hand cupping her breast. Some instinct had warned her it was coming and she immediately struck him in the face with an open hand hard enough to send him backwards against the door.

"Don't ever fucking touch me," she said.

He covered by laughing. "Women nowadays. You don't know how to take a compliment."

The statement was so idiotic that Molly didn't bother to respond. She told him to get out and he did, still holding the smile, as if what had happened was no more than a prank gone awry. When he was gone, she drank a vodka and tonic and then another as she sat there, wondering what to do. At one point she dialed Bill Ford's number before hanging up.

By morning, she had decided not to quit. She was working for the Ford brothers, not Sam Jackson. She had taken the job and she would see it through. Whatever had happened was already in the past. She was quite certain it wouldn't happen again.

Not with her anyway.

FORTY-SIX

There was no reason for Molly to return to the Jackson house the next day but she went anyway. She woke with the image of Sam Jackson in her head, his face as he'd lunged at her, his hand on her breast. How strange was it that she was feeling guilty about the situation, when she was certain that he was not?

She arrived at the house, hoping to find the New York cop Bell there, but he wasn't on the premises. Sam Jackson was in the den-turned-studio with the cameraman Greg. Sam was texting on his phone while Greg was in the process of dismantling things. In the living room, the FBI was doing the same.

Molly was the fifth wheel. She was about to leave when Bell arrived. Molly watched as he asked Dugan what was going on and the agent ignored him as if he was not there. Moments later Rachel Jackson came downstairs. Molly assumed she had heard Bell's voice. Rachel nodded to Molly when she saw her and then addressed Bell.

"They're heading back to Wyoming," she said. "The show must go on."

"And the Bureau is going with them?" Bell asked, knowing full well that Dugan was within earshot.

"What the FBI does is none of your business," Dugan said.

Rachel stared Dugan down as she answered Bell. "Yes, the Bureau is tagging along on the campaign trail. It appears they are at the beck and call of my husband."

Dugan turned on his heel and walked away. He was smart enough that he wouldn't get into a pissing contest with the mother of a missing child. Bell watched him go before turning to Rachel.

"Did they get a trace on yesterday's call?"

Molly pretended to be busy on her iPad while Rachel gave Bell the update. It turned out that the call had come from a mall pay phone in a town called East Stroudsburg in Pennsylvania. The FBI had already determined that the entrance to the Target store, where the phone was located, had security cameras on timed loops, which erased every night at midnight. If the woman who had called had been caught on camera, or had been in the store itself, it wouldn't have mattered. The tape was gone.

"I assume the FBI sent agents to the store?" Bell asked.

"Jesus Christ," Dugan said from the other room.

Rachel nodded. "They didn't find anything. Or if they did, they didn't tell me."

Bell asked a few more questions, mainly just to further aggravate Dugan, and then left, telling Rachel that he would be in touch. Molly caught up with him outside as he was walking to his car.

"You're heading out?" she asked. "You just got here."

"Looks to me as if everybody's heading out," Bell said.

"What if the woman calls back?"

"The woman won't be calling back," Bell told her. "Not today anyway. She would have to be stupid to do that, and I have a feeling she's not."

Molly shrugged. "Yet one could say that a person, expecting a call like that, would have to be stupid to have his phone turned off."

"You might think that," Bell said. "But he's not stupid either. Is he?"

"No."

Bell waited for her to elaborate, or offer some theory on what had gone down the previous day. She did neither.

"You have time for a coffee?" she said instead.

"I suppose I do." He glanced toward the house and then back to her, just then realizing she'd been waiting to talk to him. "I thought you had a plane to catch."

"I have time."

They went to a place that Bell knew, a few blocks away, a diner that featured breakfast all day and comfort foods like meat loaf and fried chicken with dumplings. They both ordered coffee, carrying their cups to a booth near the rear of the place.

"Did you know his phone was off?" Bell asked.

Molly stirred milk into the coffee. "No. It would never have occurred to me that it was."

"Is it typical of him?"

"I've known the man five days," she said.

Bell was surprised. "Really? I just assumed the two of you went back a ways."

"Why would you assume that?"

Bell took a sip of the scalding coffee. "In the movies, the candidate always hires his most trusted friend to be his campaign manager. You know—Walter Brennan or Ralph Bellamy."

"I look like Walter Brennan?"

"You do not. Bellamy neither."

"Good to know," Molly said. "Technically Sam didn't hire me. Bill Ford did. I'm a fourth-generation Wyomingite. Yes, that's what we're called. I'm a registered Republican and I know a lot of people there, party-wise and media-wise. Sam does not. That's why I'm his campaign manager."

"But now you find yourself in the middle of all this," Bell said.

"No, I find myself on the periphery of all this. But you're right—it's not what I signed on for. And in case you're wondering, I believe that an abducted child is a hell of a lot more important than a Congressional race."

"Do you think the candidate feels that way?"

"I would hope so."

"Because he doesn't act that way." Bell tried the coffee again. "Do you have kids?"

"Two."

"Do you know what I'm saying?"

"I know exactly what you're saying," Molly replied. "But I don't know what's going on in his head. Maybe it's eating him up inside but he won't let it show. He's got this tough guy image to maintain."

Bell looked around the diner. It was mid-afternoon and the place was nearly empty. "It has occurred to me more than once that he's behind this."

"It occurred to me too."

"Do you think he is?" Bell asked.

"No."

"Then what is he doing?"

She drank and then put the cup on the table. "He's trying to get elected."

"And what about his daughter?"

"I think he's convinced himself that these people are not going to harm her. That they're trying to make a statement here. So he's safe sticking to his message."

"I have two sons," Bell said, "and I couldn't convince myself of that."

"Neither could I. But then neither of us is Sam Jackson."

Bell sat quietly for a moment. "It seems that you and I have access to all the same information and that we've pretty much come to the same conclusion about the man."

"I suppose so."

"Then why did you invite me for coffee?"

She nodded slightly, as if conceding a point. "I feel as if I'm violating some sort of professional code here. But there's something you should know."

"What's that?"

"It has to remain confidential," she said. "Otherwise I might never work again."

"All right." Bell was reluctant to make the promise but he felt he had no choice.

"You should know that this theory that the kidnapping is some diabolical plot to drive Sam out of the race isn't quite true."

"How do you know that?" Bell asked. "Better yet—how *can* you know that?"

"He hasn't been forthcoming about that first phone call," Molly said. "Apparently the woman never even mentioned the election. She wants an apology for what Sam said about Laureltown."

"Jesus," Bell said. "Why would he keep that from us?"

"Because it doesn't play nearly as well as a story about somebody trying to get him out of the race," Molly said. "What he said about Laureltown was reprehensible. I'm sure even he knows that. He doesn't want to drag it out into the open again, not when he's in the middle of a campaign. So he plays the other angle instead, which makes him the good guy in the story. The heroic father standing up to the evil-doers."

"So you're suggesting that his phone being off yesterday wasn't an accident."

"Am I?"

"You don't have to," Bell said. "I can connect my own dots. Did you tell the FBI what you just told me?"

"No."

"Why not?"

She shrugged. "Maybe I don't like that guy Dugan."

"You're preaching to the choir here," Bell said.

"Fact is, I wasn't going to tell you either."

"Why did you?"

"Maybe I don't like Sam Jackson either."

"But you're working for him," Bell pointed out. "He's your guy."

"I'm working for the Ford brothers," she said flatly. "Sam Jackson is not my guy."

Bell drove to Pennsylvania that afternoon, to the town of East Stroudsburg. He knew that the FBI had already sent agents to the mall to check the phone for prints and to interview employees and anybody else who might have seen the woman. There was virtually no chance of raising a usable print from a public telephone handled daily by countless people and Bell knew that the woman they were after was too smart to leave hers anyway. She hadn't left any prints in Greenfield or Elmira or Hershey. So far, she hadn't left any sign at all.

Things were slowly coming into focus for Bell after the conversation with Molly Esponda. He had watched Sam Jackson's network interview the night before and he was left wondering just what he was seeing. Now he understood, or at least he was beginning to. He wondered why it had taken him so long, and in fact it bothered him that it had. He feared it was a sign of age; that his powers of deduction were slowing down. Not an encouraging thing for a cop to consider. Whatever the delay in his synapses, he now realized that Sam Jackson was determined not only to refrain from helping the investigation, but to outright hinder it if possible. There would be only one reason for that—he wanted to use the exposure to benefit his campaign. Molly had verified the fact. What her motives might be was another question altogether. There was something about her today that suggested she was being pulled in two directions at once. Bell could have asked her what was behind her decision to talk to him, but he was pretty sure she wouldn't tell him, just as he was certain that she was glad she did.

Bell wasn't traveling to Pennsylvania in search of fingerprints or DNA or security camera footage that didn't exist. He wasn't altogether sure why he was going. But it occurred to him that the stop in East Stroudsburg, and the phone call to Rachel Jackson, had been the first time the woman had gone off script. The calls from Greenfield and Elmira and Hershey had been planned, mapped out. It was no coincidence that the telephones were tucked away in places where the woman's anonymity was all but guaranteed. But the mall in East Stroudsburg was different. The foyer where the pay phone was located was under video surveillance on the lookout for shoplifters. The camera was concealed in a lighting fixture; the woman wouldn't have seen it. She had gotten lucky. If the FBI hadn't had to wait for the warrant for Rachel Jackson's server, they would have had the location yesterday, which meant they would have had the woman on the tape. She had serendipity in her favor. Bell doubted she would have known that the security tapes were erased nightly. She had been careless and gotten away with it.

But why had she become careless? Up until that point, she'd been relentlessly careful, calling from safe pay phones in random towns—playing Keep Away. The call yesterday had been an impulse, Bell thought, a spur-of-the moment-decision. It was easy enough to guess what might have prompted it—the fact that Sam Jackson had his cellphone turned off when the woman tried to reach him earlier. Bell could imagine her frustration. It would have been natural to assume that there were two people in the world closest to the little girl. If one wouldn't talk to her, she'd call the other. And that's what she did.

Bell's mind kept going back to what Molly had told him, about the kidnappers wanting an apology for Sam Jackson's Laureltown rant. What was the connection there? And who was to say there was one? People all across the country—the world even—were outraged by what Jackson had said. They didn't necessarily need to be directly connected to Laureltown to want him to make amends.

It was a two-hour drive to East Stroudsburg. When Bell arrived at the mall, he parked in the lot near the entrance to the Target store and sat there for a time. He could see the pay phones inside the entrance-way. He imagined the woman there twenty-four hours earlier. The call had been quick, less than two minutes. Was she in the store before she called? Did she go inside afterward? Bell doubted that. She would have called and left. She might have been parked where Bell was parked right now. Not that he—or anybody else involved in the investigation—had any idea as to what she was driving.

She'd been heading east after leaving Hershey though. Back to the hub, Bell surmised, wherever that was. If it was Bell, traveling those country roads, with a sudden impulse to make a phone call to the girl's mother, he doubted he would stop at a shopping mall to do it. He'd find a phone in a rural store or gas station, someplace out of town, away from the public eye. But what if she had stopped at the mall for another reason and had a sudden urge to call when she noticed the phones? That could have been the case, especially if the call had been spur-of-the-moment, as Bell suspected it had. If so though, what would it matter? It didn't tell Bell anything new.

He went into the Target and asked for the manager. He was a young guy, beanpole thin, with a large Adam's apple and stylish narrow glasses. He told Bell that he'd already spoken to the FBI, and that they had interviewed all of the employees who'd been working the previous afternoon. Nobody remembered seeing the woman who made the call. How could anyone remember seeing a woman they had no description for?

Bell walked around the store, and then out into the mall. The place was older, and showed its years. Water stains on the ceiling, worn tiling on the floors. There were dollar stores and an Ace Hardware. A food court. A main entrance faced the road out front, with another bank of pay phones. If she stopped only to make the call, why hadn't she made it from there?

Bell went back to the Target store and found the manager again. The man was less polite than the first time.

"I assume you have receipts for all of yesterday's purchases?" Bell asked.

"Well, it's computerized," the man said. "We don't save paper receipts."

"But you have them?"

"Yeah."

Bell checked the notes he'd taken earlier that day, when talking to Heyward. The woman had called Rachel Jackson at two minutes past three. "I want to see the transactions from yesterday afternoon," he said. "Say, two o'clock to four."

"All of them?" the manager asked.

"Why would I just want to see some of them? And print them out, if you don't mind."

"It will take some time."

"Take it," Bell told him. "I'm going to grab some lunch."

Bell ate a hamburger and fries in the food court and then sat there for a half hour, watching the people. At a table a few feet away three men, all in their seventies he would guess, were discussing a golf trip they were planning to Scotland. They were as excited as school children. Good old boys, they'd probably lived here their entire lives. They were small-town guys, Bell thought and, to a certain extent, this was becoming a small-town case. It may have started in New York City but it had definitely moved to the boonies.

When Bell had gotten word earlier that the latest call had come from Hershey, he'd spent an hour at his computer, searching for information on the three towns the woman had called from, looking for a common denominator. All three had chamber of commerce websites, which offered considerable information. All had Lions Clubs, all had Rotaries. Horticultural societies, church bazaars, farmers markets, youth groups, baseball and soccer leagues. If there was a reason the woman had chosen those towns, it wasn't evident to Bell. Maybe she had a personal connection to each—relatives or friends. Bell looked for a common manufacturing link for the three and came up empty. A shared cultural interest—a theater group or writers' retreat—again nothing. He'd even looked at the three towns on Google Earth, hoping to find some distinguishing characteristic that might tell him something. Nothing there, nothing anywhere. In the end he concluded that maybe the woman had chosen the towns at random because that's precisely what they were—random picks—and Bell was looking for something that didn't exist.

When he went back to the store, the manager had the receipts printed out. Bell sat in the Target lunchroom and went over them, again with the familiar feeling of not knowing what he was looking for but hoping to recognize it when he saw it.

When he did see it, he told the manager he needed to talk to the cashier in question. She was a black woman, short and wide, with a bubbly manner.

"I sort of remember her," she said uncertainly.

"What do you remember?"

The woman looked up at the ceiling, as if there might be a clue printed on the tiles there. "Oh, she paid cash. Cuz, like, I remember I said nobody pays cash anymore. She's the last one. Making a joke, you know."

"What did she look like?"

"I kinda remember but not really. She had a hat on, I think. Like a baseball cap."

"What team?"

The woman shook her head. "I don't know the teams."

"Was she tall, short?"

"Maybe kind of average."

"What was her hair like?"

"I couldn't really tell," the cashier said. "Account of the hat and all."

"Anything else you can remember? Any tattoos or piercings? What she was wearing besides the hat?"

The woman showed an expression of fierce concentration before finally shaking her head again. "I'm sorry. So many people go through, you know?"

Bell nodded his understanding. "One more thing. When she left, did you see her use the pay phone on her way out?"

"I can't say."

"That's okay," Bell said. "I can."

FORTY-SEVEN

Back in the city Bell drove to the Jackson house and found Rachel Jackson there alone. No Heyward with his laptop, no radio interviews in the den, no Dugan with his snotty comments. She let him in. She was looking more worn with each passing day, her hair hanging loosely, her eyes swollen. Bell doubted she was sleeping much. When she offered to make coffee, he accepted, more to give her something tangible to do than any need he had for caffeine.

"What size clothing does your daughter wear?" he asked as she put the cup in front of him.

"Size?" she repeated. "She's a nine."

Bell pulled the photocopy of the receipt from his pocket. "We know that the call yesterday came from a Target store in Pennsylvania, at two minutes past three. Well, at exactly three o'clock a woman in that store bought clothes for a little girl. Size nine. She paid in cash."

Bell handed the slip over. Rachel grabbed it like it was a winning lottery ticket.

"Oh my God," she said.

Bell poured cream into his coffee. "I can't sit here and tell you that the clothes were for Vanessa."

"But they were."

"I would say there's a good chance."

229

Rachel sat down, still looking at the paper. Bell glanced around.

"So—the whole lot of them packed up and headed for Wyoming?"

"It's the most important thing, isn't it? I mean, this other matter, the fact that my daughter has been kidnapped, it's just a minor annoyance. We can deal with it at some point down the line. First we need to send Sam to fucking Washington."

"So he crooks his finger and the FBI tags along?"

"That's how it went," she said.

Bell looked at his watch. Four-fifteen. "And no calls today? She's called every day."

"Not that I've heard," Rachel said. She indicated her own phone on the counter. "She hasn't called me. Somebody down at the FBI is tapped into my phone server, just in case. They wanted to leave an agent with me but I said no. They can monitor it from there."

Bell drank the coffee, looking at the phone.

"This means she's looking after her," Rachel said, meaning the receipt. "Don't you think so?"

"Kinda suggests that."

"Maybe they're not bad people," Rachel said, going with it now. "I mean, I've been assuming they were evil but maybe they're not. If they're looking after her. Maybe they—I don't know. I wish I knew what they wanted. She said three things and hung up. Why would she do that?"

Bell was caught now. He'd given his word to the campaign manager, Molly, that he wouldn't reveal what she'd told him. He couldn't go back on that, as much as he wanted to.

"Whatever it is," he said, "I think we can assume it's about your husband. Not you."

Rachel nodded. Apparently she'd come to that conclusion on her own. "Still, I wish she would have told me."

Bell was still looking at the phone, trying to figure a way.

"Maybe you could ask her," he said.

FORTY-EIGHT

Jo watched Sam Jackson's performance on the Rivera show from the living room, the sound turned down so the little girl in the back room wouldn't hear. She wondered if the girl was aware of what her father was. It seemed unlikely; little girls looked up to their fathers, didn't they? Jo never had, but then her father had walked out of her life when she was six and moved to L.A. with his new wife. The fact was that she'd seen him rarely before he left, and almost never afterward.

After the show, she and Henry sat on the porch out front, Jo drinking tea and Henry into his wine. The weather station was calling for rain and the wind was up from the west, the night sky black.

"How are we going to convince him we have her?" Henry asked. "If those phone numbers didn't do it—"

"He knows we have her," Jo replied.

"Then what is he up to?"

Jo remained silent, drinking her tea.

"What are we going to do, Jo?" Henry persisted. "None of this has gone like it was supposed to. We can't keep her forever. I mean, what are we doing here?"

"Helping him get elected," Jo said resignedly.

"Well, that wasn't the idea, was it?" Henry said.

"No. That wasn't the idea."

Henry sighed and had more wine. He could drink bottles of it, it seemed, and not show any effects other than getting sleepy. He was like that with his pot too, although Jo had noticed he'd refrained from getting high since the little girl had arrived, at least in close proximity to the house. A hell of a time for him to become a role model.

"Do you call again tomorrow?"

"No," Jo said. "We have the market in Monticello. Too close to home. And I don't know that we're accomplishing anything anyway. We need a new plan, Henry. The problem here is the guy doesn't care about his daughter. Who the hell would ever have imagined that?"

"But the mother cares," Henry said.

"The mother doesn't know what's going on."

"What do you mean?"

"He never told her our demands."

Henry paused in the act of taking a drink. "Why wouldn't he?"

"I'm guessing because he knows she'll meet them," Jo said. "But I doubt she or anybody else is going to be able to talk him into apologizing to anybody for anything. Especially not when he's running for office."

"So where does that leave us?"

Jo got to her feet and looked out over the field of cabbages and acorn squash in front of the barn. "It leaves us in a bind, Henry. And I have no fucking clue how to get out of it."

FORTY-NINE

The rain came during the night and continued all morning. Jo took a truckload of produce into the market stalls at Monticello, and set up under the awnings there. The storm continued, the wind slashing at the canvas overhead and tipping baskets over. By eleven o'clock, having not made a sale in almost an hour, she decided to pack up and head for home.

When she got back to the farm, the rain hadn't abated and the wind was still up. The creek had expanded, overflowing the pond and encroaching on the pasture field. The goats and the pony had taken shelter under the overhang of the shed and were standing in a row, watching the drizzle beyond. Jo parked the truck and climbed down and then heard Henry shouting at her from the house, where he was leaning out of the screen door. He was waving, beckoning her.

When she went into the front room, the TV was on and Rachel Jackson was standing before a large bank of cameras, alongside a dark-haired man of about forty-five, the man wearing a suit and loosened tie, his hair unkempt. Somebody else, a woman, was talking over the footage.

"...looks as if we're just about ready to go here," she was saying. "All that we know at this point is that the Jackson family has called this press conference. You're looking at Rachel Jackson on the right and the man beside her, we are told, is Detective Derek Bell of the NYPD. It is unclear if Sam Jackson will be taking part in the press conference. As we have stated, this has been hastily arranged. Oh, here we go—"

Rachel Jackson stepped to the microphone and began to read from a sheet of paper. "I have a statement. I was recently contacted by a woman who claimed to have knowledge of the whereabouts of my daughter. We spoke only briefly. I am here today to request that this woman call me back at the same number. I very much would like to talk to you again. Please call me." She hesitated. "Please."

She stepped back and the questions began.

"Where is your husband today?"

"My husband is in Wyoming. He's campaigning."

"Why isn't he here?"

"Because he's campaigning," Rachel said again. "We're in constant touch. The FBI is traveling with him."

"What makes you think the woman who called has your daughter?"

"She said things that made me believe that she does."

"What kind of things?"

"Personal details," Rachel said.

"Do you think your daughter is alive?"

"Of course I do," Rachel snapped. "How can you ask me that?"

"Does your husband believe it?" the same reporter persisted. "Why isn't he here?"

At that point the detective named Bell stepped forward. "We didn't call this press conference to discuss the whereabouts of Sam Jackson. We're only interested in finding this little girl. Mrs. Jackson has assured you that she and her husband are in constant communication on this."

"But Sam Jackson has repeatedly said that he has no proof that these people have the little girl. Has his opinion changed?"

"That's a question for Sam Jackson," Bell said. "We're here today to reach out to this woman. We need to keep the conversation going. We need to bring this little girl home."

There were more questions after that, most of which centered around the fact that Sam Jackson was in Wyoming while his wife was calling a news conference in New York City to talk about their missing daughter. After several minutes of this, the detective brought the proceedings to a halt. Before he did, he mentioned a phone number where he himself could be reached. The number ran on a scroll across the bottom of the screen.

Jo turned the TV off and looked at Henry, who shook his head.

"Sonofabitch went back to Wyoming."

"Yeah," Jo said.

"But she wants to talk."

Jo looked at him. "Like I said before, talking to her doesn't help us. She's got nothing to trade."

FIFTY

The storm passed and by mid-afternoon Jo was standing in the creek at the bottom of the pasture field where it flowed through a culvert under the road. She was in her rubber Wellingtons, clearing a clogged mass of sticks and brush away from the mouth of the culvert in an effort to drain the flooded field behind her. Henry had helped for a while but he tired quickly, as he did these days, and announced he was going up to the house for a nap. It took Jo a couple of hours to clear the logjam and by then she had two wet feet where the creek had flooded over her boots.

She started walking to the house. The sun was shining now and the goats had made their way out into the field, stepping cautiously to avoid the puddles, like infantry moving through a minefield. Jo glanced at her watch; it was nearly milking time. She assumed Henry was up by now; his naps rarely lasted more than an hour. Jo could milk the nannies if she had to but she preferred to let him do it. He had a knack for it.

She was looking forward to a shower and some dry socks. The last time she'd had a soaker she'd been with Grace and they had been catching frogs in the pond. Jo recalled the two of them, sloshing to the house in their wet boots, sitting on the porch and toweling their feet off before pulling on dry woolen socks. How could such a small insignificant moment be so indelible in her mind? She would give anything to live that day over again. Every second, every breath.

Thinking of Grace made her think of the little girl locked in the room of the house and in that instant, she knew she couldn't hold her much longer. She'd wanted to make the girl's father suffer and it turned out that he was the only one who had not. The whole scheme was slowly turning to shit.

She heard someone call her name and she looked up to see a woman standing by the corner of the barn. Her breath caught. One minute she'd been thinking about Grace and the next she was looking at Grace's mother.

"Susan," Jo said, glancing quickly toward the house. "What are you doing here?"

"Nice greeting," Susan said.

Jo's pulse was racing. She realized that the girl could see Susan if she happened to look out the window. "Geez, I'm sorry. It's just that you startled me."

Susan leaned in for a hug. "You're a mess, girl."

"Oh, I know," Jo said, looking at her muddy jeans while urging herself to think. "And I'm late for a meeting in town to boot. I was just heading in for a quick shower. Why didn't you tell me you were coming?"

"You didn't return my call. I felt like a drive. What's your meeting about?"

Jo remembered a pamphlet someone had stuffed in her mailbox a few days earlier. "They want to expand the quarry over near Tiberville. They say it could threaten our groundwater. We have a drilled well here."

"Well, my fault for dropping in unannounced," Susan said, clearly disappointed.

Jo began moving them both toward the lane, where Susan's car was parked. The crash came from somewhere in the back of the house. There was a high-pitched yell that followed. Susan stopped, turned toward the sound.

"What was that?"

"Henry," Jo said. "He's racking his wine off. Probably dropped a carboy on his toe. I don't know what I'm going to do with him."

"That was him yelling?"

"Had to be him. Unless he kicked the cat. We have a new tortoise-shell that's always underfoot."

They walked to Susan's car. "Well, this sucks," Jo said. "Why don't we meet for lunch next week someday. Someplace halfway."

Susan had known her too long not to suspect something but she'd also known her too long to question her. If Jo wanted to confide in her, she would. "Sure, we'll do that."

Jo relented a little, embarrassed by her own deceit. "Hey, how are you anyway? You okay?"

"I know I'm never going to be okay again." Susan hugged Jo, held her tightly for a long moment. "I hope you're okay. Whatever's going on here."

Before Jo could respond she got into the car and drove off. Jo watched as she turned onto the road above and started the long drive home.

"Fuck," she said and headed for the house to find out what the noise had been about.

Henry was in the bathroom with the girl, who was bleeding freely from a scrape on her knee. She was crying and trying not to. Henry, kneeling and wiping the cut with a damp face cloth, looked up at Jo, as if accusing her of something.

"She was in here using the bathroom and she saw Susan and you out by the barn. She climbed up on the vanity to try to open the window." Henry looked at the girl now. "She was going to try to holler at Susan, I guess. She fell and hit her knee there." He indicated the sharp edge of the countertop.

"You shouldn't have done that," Jo told her.

The little girl stared at her defiantly. Henry stood and went into the medicine cabinet for a bandage. Jo looked at the vanity; there was blood and some skin from the girl's knee on the sharp edge of the counter. She waited until Henry put antiseptic cream and the bandage on the girl's knee. The scrape looked worse than it was.

"Okay," she said then. "Out, both of you. I'll clean up in here."

When Henry took the girl back to her room, Jo went into the kitchen for a baggie. Back in the bathroom, she cleaned a nail file with alcohol and then used it to scrape the blood and skin from the counter into the baggie. She sealed it and went to call Daniel.

FIFTY-ONE

They were driving back to Cheyenne from the Powder River Basin, where most of the fracking was happening. They'd been on the road since early morning, in a rented Chevy Tahoe. Molly was in the passenger seat and Sam was alone in the back. He'd requested that she ride in the back with him, to go over things, but she'd refused. She was keeping her distance.

Sam had met with some officials from Great Western Oil & Gas, and he'd assured them that he would oppose any legislation that would curtail the fracking. Afterwards he told the reporters on hand that shutting it down would cost the state over a hundred thousand jobs, a number he'd apparently pulled out of the clear blue sky. Molly could have reminded him that the population of the state was only a half million but she didn't. None of the media types had challenged him on it so why should she?

Their driver was a young volunteer named Clyde Gillespie. He'd shown up that morning wearing a No Surrender T-shirt of his own design and he'd spent the day fawning over Sam at every turn, telling him he was a genuine American hero, and that it was high time that the country realized it. Molly had been resisting an urge all day to slap some sense into the youngster. She doubted that it was possible anyway.

Frank Barton had gone after Sam at a rally in Casper the night before, calling him out for mentioning him in connection with the abduction of his daughter. In response, Sam had done a long interview that morning on the local Fox affiliate, where he'd thrown back at Barton, claiming he was anti-gun, pro–health care, anti-drilling, and pro-choice. He'd talked about everything other than the kidnapping and when the host lobbed the obligatory query on it, Sam had bailed.

"I would love to get into that at this time," he said. "I have new information, just hours old, about the political forces behind the abduction, but the FBI has forbidden me to share this data. Now I know what America is thinking. Since when does Sam Jackson back away from talking about any issue? Usually the answer to that is *never*. But in this case—given that my daughter's life is at stake—I will defer to the expertise of the Federal Bureau of Investigation. I mean, they got the Unabomber, didn't they? And they'll get these cowards too."

Dated reference aside, the stuff about new information was all bullshit, Molly suspected. It certainly didn't come from Agent Dugan, who was following them even now, in a black sedan, with Heyward and another agent in the car with him. There was no new information and no instructions from Dugan for Sam to remain silent. They'd been waiting all day for another phone call from the woman, but it never came. Sam's phone was on; Heyward, with his laptop monitoring the server, made sure of it.

They'd done one event after another, starting at eight in the morning—doing quick drop-ins at malls and factories and gun stores and a half-dozen legions. Wherever they'd stopped, they'd been preceded by an advance crew of volunteers, handing out No Surrender signs and T-shirts and buttons.

Gillespie hadn't shut up since they'd left the Powder River country. He was pimply-faced, with a scraggly and untrimmed effort at a beard. He was a Tea Party enthusiast and he knew a lot about Sam Jackson, or at least the Sam Jackson that presented himself to the public.

"These anti-frackers," he was saying now. "They're like these idiots with their global warming. I got an uncle who lives up north of Cody, place called Ralston. Well, last winter he recorded twenty-two days in a row where the temperature was below zero. Twenty-two days in a row! You could look it up. Now you tell me how there's such a thing called global warming. But if Al Gore says it, it must be true."

In the back seat, Sam was scrolling through his phone, half listening. "Al Gore doesn't know his ass from his elbow."

"Right," Gillespie said. "Couldn't even carry his own state in 2000."

Molly exhaled heavily and looked out the window. They were approaching a service center.

"You know what else?" Gillespie began.

"We need gas," Molly told him.

In fact, they didn't. The gauge read half full, plenty to get back to Cheyenne but Molly needed a break. Gillespie didn't object. They pulled up to the pumps and Molly left the vehicle like it was a burning house. The FBI sedan drove alongside and Heyward and Dugan emerged from the back seat. Dugan walked to the Tahoe and rapped on the side window. Sam powered it down.

"Your wife called a press conference," Dugan said.

"She did what?"

Heyward had the footage on his laptop. They stood in the parking lot and watched, Molly and Sam and the FBI guys all gathered around the hood of the sedan. Gillespie hanging in the background, wondering what they were watching but too wary of the agents to come close.

"Did you know she was going to do this?" Dugan asked when it was over.

"No," Sam said after a moment, loath to admit there was anything he didn't know.

"This doesn't make us look good," Dugan told him.

"She didn't mention the FBI," Sam pointed out.

"Precisely," Dugan said. "It's our case and we don't even get a nod. Instead she's standing there with Detective Dumdum, sending a message to the kidnappers. This is his doing, you realize that. He's feeling left out so he convinces her to go rogue...and get himself a little TV time in the process. You don't come off looking too good either. The wife pleading with the kidnappers on television while you're out here, running around the state."

Molly watched Sam. His lips were tight. She thought for a moment he might unleash on the agent, but he gathered himself.

"She can do what she wants. She always has."

"If she hears from them, we have to go back," Dugan said. "You know that."

"We're going to finish this little tour," Sam said. "We have things lined up. No Surrender is catching on. Ask young Gillespie there."

"We're not asking young Gillespie anything," Dugan said. "If she hears from them, we're going back to New York. Are you going to call her, or am I?"

"I'll call her," Sam said. "When we get back to the hotel. You realize she can't do anything without me. She can't negotiate without me."

"Why not?"

"Because she doesn't have what they want."

Dugan glanced at Heyward, then back to Sam. "You talking about the money?"

Molly watched closely as Sam gave Dugan the same look he'd been giving Gillespie all day. Like he was an idiot to be tolerated when he couldn't be ignored.

"Yeah, the money."

FIFTY-TWO

The cab driver who delivered the package was a recent immigrant from Pakistan. They detained him at the station, putting him in an interrogation room until Bell arrived. The bulky manila envelope had Bell's name scrawled on it in block letters, along with the precinct. Nothing else. Bell looked in at the cab driver and then left him waiting while he pulled on latex gloves and opened the package. Inside was a baggie containing a small smear of blood and skin. Written on the baggie with a magic marker were the initials VJ.

"Who is VJ?" Lynn asked when Bell took the envelope and baggie to show her.

"Vanessa Jackson," Bell said.

Lynn thought about that. "We need to swab the parents."

Bell called Rachel Jackson and asked her to come to the station but he didn't tell her why. She grew anxious, fearing the worst, so he told her simply that they might have a lead. He didn't want to tell her over the phone what it was.

The cab driver's name was Azhar. Bell gave him a cup of coffee and sat across from him. The man spoke English fairly well. Better than a lot of New Yorkers, Bell decided. He was maybe thirty-five, wearing brown pants and a checkered short-sleeved shirt. He was perspiring in the heat of the room.

"A man approached me outside Grand Central Station," he told Bell. "He waved me down. I told him to get into my cab but he did not want to do this. He hands me the envelope and asks of me to deliver it to this station. And he gives me this." Azhar pulled a hundred-dollar bill from his shirt pocket.

"Was he wearing gloves?" Bell asked.

"Yes, he was wearing gloves. In spite of this warm weather we are having."

Bell nodded. Lynn was checking the envelope and baggie for prints. Bell guessed they would find Azhar's only on the envelope and none at all on the baggie. The same would be probably be true of any DNA, but they would have to try.

"What did he look like?" he asked the cab driver.

"A white man," Azhar said. "Maybe the same height as you. Clean shaven. A somewhat heavy man."

"Round face?"

"A round face. Yes."

"Did he look like Curly from the Three Stooges?"

"Stooges?"

"Never mind. What else did he say?"

"He told me I must do as he asks. If I do not wish to do so, I should tell him."

"And you agreed."

"Yes. It seemed a simple thing."

"An easy hundred bucks."

Azhar nodded. "Yes. An easy hundred bucks."

"That's all he said?"

"Yes."

"Where did he go?" Bell asked. "Did he walk into the station?"

"No. He stood there as I drove away. I looked in the mirror and still he was standing there. Maybe he stands there now."

"I doubt it," Bell said.

He left and went downstairs for a copy of the sketch they had of the guy who'd stuffed McIlroy in the trunk of the limo, the guy they assumed had grabbed the kid. The sketch McIlroy had helped render afterward. Bell took it back to the interrogation room and showed it to Azhar, who squinted as he looked at it, tilting his head one way and then the other.

"Maybe," he said.

Bell was thinking it was more than maybe, although the sketches were always an iffy proposition. And this one had emerged from the beer-soaked brain of a limo driver who had just passed several hours in the trunk of a car.

"Now I can go?" Azhar asked.

"Not yet," Bell said. He didn't tell the cabbie that he was in for a long night, by the time they checked out his immigration papers and his employment record and the personal details he'd given. Bell hoped for his sake that everything was in order. He suspected that it was; otherwise the man would have tucked the hundred in his pocket and tossed the package into the nearest trash can.

When he went downstairs again Rachel Jackson was there, waiting for him, dressed in black jeans and a hoodie with some designer's initials on it. Her hair was pulled back in a ponytail and she was wearing glasses. He hadn't seen her in glasses before. Maybe she wore contacts.

"What's going on?" Her voice was thin with worry.

"We got a delivery," Bell said and he took her upstairs to the lab where Lynn had the baggie. She'd already transferred the contents to a glass slide and documented the DNA. When Bell explained the situation, Rachel sat down heavily. Her eyes welled up.

"This is not as ominous as it seems," he said. "First off, we need a sample of your DNA to see if this is even your daughter. And secondly, I wouldn't call this a threat. Keep in mind that at no point has this woman threatened to harm Vanessa. If that was the case—they'd be sending a finger or an ear. I'm sorry, but that's the truth. What this is— if it turns out to be genuine—is a response to your husband constantly saying that he doesn't believe these people have her."

"But that's my daughter's blood," Rachel said. "What—they cut her?"

Lynn stepped forward. "I wouldn't say she was cut. Under the microscope there's no sharp edges. A little bit of skin and a little bit of blood. Looks to me like somebody scraped their elbow."

"Let's do the swab and see what we have," Bell said.

"Is your husband coming?" Lynn asked.

"He's out of town," Rachel said quickly. "Why do you need both?"

Lynn paused. "We can swab him when he gets back."

She swabbed Rachel's mouth and told her she would have the results by the next day. Bell walked Rachel downstairs. He called a cab and they stood outside waiting for it.

"Why are they doing this now?" Rachel asked. "I asked her to call me."

"I suspect this is for your husband's benefit. If the DNA matches, he's finally going to have to admit that these people have your daughter."

Rachel nodded. "He called. He saw the press conference."

"And?"

"He's not happy with me." She looked over. "He says the FBI isn't happy with you."

"We're an unpopular pair," Bell said. "I guess we've got a lot of nerve, trying to find your daughter."

Rachel actually smiled, but it faded. "What happens next?"

"I think she's going to call you again." Bell nodded his head toward the station behind them. "They've gone to a lot of trouble to convince you that they have her. So they'll call. When they do, I suggest you find out what they want."

"And then what?"

"And then give it to them."

FIFTY-THREE

Jo was up early, as she was every day, but still Henry was ahead of her. He rarely slept past six. Of course, Henry was in bed by nine o'clock every night, his slumber fortified by his wine and his dope.

She put the coffee on and while she waited for it she looked out the back window, where she could see him, at work milking the nannies in the open shed. The sun was up but the roof kept both Henry and the goats in shade. The chickens were out of the brooder, picking gravel from the lane, and the red rooster was standing atop some cordwood stacked alongside the barn. He had finishing his morning crowing and was now overlooking his domain.

When the coffee was ready, Jo poured a cup and carried it down the hallway and knocked on the door to the back room. "Are you up?"

There was no reply and Jo wasn't sure if the girl was sleeping, or just not responding because it was Jo doing the asking. As she turned away, she heard a low response of some sort. She unlocked the door and went in. The girl was watching Henry out the window, as Jo had just been doing.

"Do you want some cereal or toast or something?"

The girl shrugged and kept looking out the window.

"How's your knee?" Jo asked.

"Fine."

"We can change the bandage later if you want."

The girl said nothing. Still watching outside.

"Okay," Jo said, giving up. "Let me know if you want to eat something."

She turned and opened the door.

"What's the boy goat's name?" the girl suddenly asked.

Jo turned back. The little girl was actually looking at her, something she hadn't done before, at least not for any longer than a second or two.

"It's not very original but we call him Billy."

"Billy goat," the girl said softly, almost to herself, looking outside again.

Watching her, all that Jo could think about was Grace, and she didn't want to think about Grace, not while she was there in the room with this girl. She didn't want to think that they might be the same, that they might have common interests, that they might have the same fears or joys. That they might look forward to the same things. Jo couldn't stand for that to be true.

"Do you want to go out and see the goats after breakfast?" she heard herself say.

The girl looked over quickly. "What are you going to do with me?"

"Nobody's going to hurt you. Do you think the man with the long hair would hurt you?"

"No," she said. "He's nice. He cooks my eggs the way Suzanne does." She hesitated. "He smells kinda funny."

He smells like a guy who has smoked pot every day for the last forty years, Jo thought. It oozes out of his pores.

"Aren't you afraid I'll run away?"

"I can run faster than you," Jo told her. She waited a moment. "If you want, we can go and see the goats. And I have to gather the eggs from the hens. Have you ever gathered eggs?"

"No. I live in New York City."

"We can gather eggs too. But you have to eat something first."

The girl gave it some thought and then nodded. "Can I have toast and jam please?"

"Yes, you can."

FIFTY-FOUR

Molly was in the lounge of the airport, having a drink, when Bill Ford called. Sam Jackson was there as well, along with the FBI guys, sitting at a table across the room. Molly had seen them as she entered but she avoided them, making her way to the bar instead. Dugan had noticed and she saw him say something to the others and then laugh. They were suddenly the cool kids in high school and she was the outcast. Fuck you all, she thought.

"I've been hearing good things," Bill said when she answered. "He just got endorsed by the miner's union."

"I should hope so," Molly said. "He did everything but slow dance with them. What else you been hearing?"

"His numbers have moved significantly in the past forty-eight hours. Good strategy, going there. Where are you now?"

"At the airport."

"Why?"

"Flying to New York."

"You need to stay there, Molly. Another week of this No Surrender stuff and he could put Barton away. It's working, even if it's nothing but smoke."

Molly had a drink. "You just described Sam Jackson."

"So why are you going back to New York?"

251

"The police received a tissue sample, or something, from the kidnappers," Molly said. "The DNA checks out."

Bill Ford fell silent for a moment. Molly could imagine him digesting the information, figuring first of all what it meant and second, what to do with it.

"So he can no longer say that he wants proof," Bill said.

"Not when they have it."

Another pause. "So what's he saying now?"

"To me?" Molly asked. "Not much. Right this minute he's sitting on the other side of the lounge with the FBI guys. They're all pissed off because Sam's wife and the New York cop called a presser without telling them. Looks like they've formed this good old boys' coalition—them against us."

"Who cares?" Bill said. "We need to know what he's going to do when he gets back to New York."

"Well, he could always give in to them," Molly said. "Of course, that would pretty much jettison the whole No Surrender pose, wouldn't it?"

"I would think so."

"He could always play it the other way. Give them what they want and tell the voters that he would give anything in order to get his daughter back safely. You know—the way any rational human being would play it."

"I doubt he's going to do that," Bill said.

"I doubt it too."

Molly heard somebody in the background say something, and then Bill Ford telling them he'd be right with them. Presumably he had a lot of puppets dangling on a lot of strings across the country. Sam was just one of them, although he wouldn't like to hear it.

"You need to keep me in the loop, Molly," he said when he came back on the line.

"I was going to call you from New York, once I had the lay of the land."

"Maybe the FBI will find them now," Bill said. "With the new evidence, and the phone calls. Surely they have something on these people. That would be a solution we could live with."

"I'll mention it to them," Molly said, looking across the room. "When they've finished their chicken wings."

"We need that seat," Bill told her. "It's not a joke."

"Who's joking?"

FIFTY-FIVE

Bell delivered the news to Rachel Jackson regarding the DNA results around mid-morning. Save the cabbie's fingerprints and the sample itself, there was nothing else of evidential value found on the envelope or the baggie inside. Bell was somewhat surprised at that. Usually the lab would find traces of something—microscopic hairs or skin cells—but the envelope was clean and so was the baggie. Whoever had delivered it had known what he was doing.

Rachel told him that Sam Jackson was on his way home from Wyoming. The FBI was anxious to have a look at the new evidence. They could look all they wanted, Bell thought. It wasn't going to give up any more than it already had.

"Do we need to get word to the woman that we have the results?" Rachel asked.

"I imagine they know that."

"I wish we could be sure. I feel like, I don't know, I feel like we're really close to something happening here. All night I kept thinking I'd have her back soon, maybe even today."

"We could call another press conference," Bell said.

She considered it. "I'd better wait for Sam."

Bell left her and drove to Williamsburg. Since the guy who'd stolen the limo was in all likelihood the same guy who had delivered the envelope, Bell wanted to have another look at the parking garage where the exchange with the little girl had taken place. The chain was back across the entrance when he got there. He stepped over it and walked to the spot where they'd found the limo, with McIlroy snoozing in the trunk. There was nothing there to see, of course, nothing new anyway. Again Bell felt the futility of looking for something that quite possibly didn't exist.

He left his car parked by the entrance to the lot and walked up to street level. Why this neighborhood? Probably because it had an abandoned parking garage, hidden from the street. But there were all kinds of places like that in the city. Was there another reason? Bell started walking. He went north for six blocks and then turned and worked his way back and forth across the neighborhood, moving toward the parking garage. Nothing registered as notable. There were the usual bars and pizza joints and hair salons and tattoo parlors. A muffler repair place. Two body shops and an old brick garage converted to a gym. When he got back to the lot he started south and performed the same maneuver, crossing back and forth.

The farmers market was at full capacity when he spotted it from a block or so away. The street was cordoned off and there were people coming and going from every direction. Those leaving carried paper bags filled with vegetables, bunches of flowers, various pieces of antique furniture and memorabilia. One man held a slat back chair over his head like an umbrella as he made his way through the crowd. Watching, Bell's mind went back to the Google searches from a couple of days earlier, of the towns the woman had called from. He decided to take a closer look at the market.

The manager had a dolphin tattoo on her arm. Bell talked to her in the shade of her office, a converted RV. She told him that almost of all of the vendors were regulars, although occasionally someone from out of town showed up, looking for a spot.

"And you're open seven days a week?" Bell asked.

She frowned. "No. Tuesdays and Saturdays."

The girl had been abducted on a Tuesday. For the first time since he'd started on the case, Bell felt a little electric pulse tap-tapping in his brain. He took his notebook from his pocket and double-checked the date.

"Tuesday the seventh," he said then, "was there anybody here that wasn't a regular?"

The dolphin woman went into the RV and came back with a large black book, a ledger of sorts. She sat and went back through it to the date in question. She tapped the page with her finger.

"There was a guy here that day, selling Quaker furniture that he built himself," she said. "Rocking chairs and harvest tables, stuff like that. He didn't move much. I remember him whining that he never made enough money to cover his stall fee. He hasn't been back. He left me a card though."

She gave Bell the card. The furniture guy was from Connecticut. The info on the card matched that in the ledger. Bell put the card in his pocket as the woman kept looking at the page.

"The only other one that I can see is Pine Ridge Farms," she said, again indicating an entry. "She was here that Tuesday and—" she flipped back through the book. "And the Tuesday before. I never saw her before or since. She had nice stuff, I remember."

"What kind of stuff?"

"Farm vegetables. Tomatoes and corn. Squash, apples."

"You have her name?"

"No," the woman said. "Just her farm—Pine Ridge. I don't ask for a name, unless they pay with a card. She paid cash. I think she said her card was stolen or something. But I have her license plate number."

Bell wrote the number in his notebook. "Did she give you this number or did you take it from the vehicle?"

"She wrote it on the form."

"You wouldn't double-check it as a rule?"

"No. Long as they pay, why would I care?"

Bell nodded and looked about the market. The place was full to overflowing. "Can you show me where she was?"

He found out that the woman had been flanked by a walking beer barrel named André and a hippie artist who called herself Lily. They both remembered the woman.

"She is coming from New Jersey, this woman," André told Bell.

Bell looked at the note he'd just made. "She had New York plates."

"This was her brother's truck," André said. He seemed happy to be the man in the know. "But she is coming from New Jersey."

"What kind of truck was it?" Bell asked.

"The big van," André said. "Like they use to deliver furniture."

"You remember the make?"

"Is Chevy, or maybe GMC," André said.

Bell had a thought. "How did the back door operate? Did it swing on a hinge or did it roll up?"

"It rolls up," André said. "I remember this because this woman has to pull down hard to close."

Bell nodded. The limo driver McIlroy recalled hearing something on rollers. What had he said? Like the rollers they use to moves boxes in a warehouse.

"She claimed she was from Jersey?" Bell asked.

"Newton," André said. "A farm she owns there."

"That's right," the woman named Lily said. She'd been standing by her paintings and now she walked over. "I remember because my aunt lives in Newton. We talked about her."

"This woman knew your aunt?"

Lily had to think about that. "Maybe not."

"What was her name?" Bell asked.

"My aunt?"

"The woman we're talking about."

"Oh," Lily said. "I don't think she said. André, do you remember her name?"

"No. She did not give a name."

"She was camera shy too," Lily said. "I'm always taking pictures. I'm an artist, you see. And whenever I pointed the camera anywhere near her, she'd look the other way. A lot of people are like that though."

"Do you have pictures of her?" Bell asked.

The artist named Lily shook her head, trying to remember. "I'd have to check my hard drive. I might have a couple of her in the background but I don't think so. Like I said, she was camera shy."

"There are always people taking pictures on market day," the dolphin lady said. "People and their phones these days, right? I could ask around."

Bell got a more detailed description of the truck from André and Lily then he took down their contact info and gave them both his card. He told them that they might have to come to the station to do a police sketch of the woman.

"Call me if you find a picture of her," he told Lily. "Anything at all."

He walked to his car and opened his laptop. The market he'd just left was five blocks from where the girl had been transferred from the limo into the other vehicle, whatever that vehicle had been. He recalled that Greenfield had a farmers market, and it seemed to him that both Elmira and Hershey did as well. But that meant nothing. These days, it would be difficult to find a town in the whole damn country that didn't have a market. Still, it was the closest thing he'd found to a common bond.

He'd saved the searches from a couple days earlier and now he went back to them, one by one. It turned out that market day in Greenfield was Wednesday. The woman had called from a laundry in Greenfield on a Wednesday. Elmira's market was open Thursdays, the day the woman had called from the gas station there.

Hershey was the hat trick.

FIFTY-SIX

When he got back to the station Bell ran the plate number and found out it didn't exist. He would have been surprised to discover otherwise. The camera-shy woman with no name who paid in cash and might have been from New Jersey or New York was not about to write down her actual plate number. Even with that, though, there was nothing to suggest that she had anything to do with Vanessa Jackson's abduction. All Bell knew at this point was that she was hiding from something, or somebody. There were thousands of people in the country doing the same thing every day. People running from debt, from abusive relationships, from the past. Bell had no evidence that this woman had been anywhere even close to the three towns where the phone calls had originated. There was such a thing as coincidence in the world. It was a tricky proposition, trying to see clues where none existed, the equivalent of pounding square pegs into round holes.

He sat slumped at his desk, looking at the results of the license plate check on his computer screen. He knew what he had to do next. He had to drive to the farmers markets in Greenfield and Elmira and Hershey, to ask if anybody had seen a woman Bell couldn't even describe.

While he was sitting there the captain walked in and headed for him.

"You working on Vanessa Jackson?"

"Yeah."

"You can stop," Gardner said.

Bell sat up. "They found her?"

"Hell, no," Gardner said. "Sam Jackson wants you off the case. And the FBI's backing him up."

"Why?"

"The FBI says you're a distraction," Gardner said. "They claim the kidnappers don't know who they're dealing with or who they should contact. You're muddying the water. Their words, not mine."

"The FBI hasn't *found* the water yet."

Gardner hesitated. "There's also been a suggestion that you're too close to the wife. And that you're a glory hound."

"That it? Nobody's saying I grabbed the kid myself?"

"Not to me, they're not," Gardner said. "But you're out. It's theirs now."

Bell indicated the screen with the bogus plate number. "I might be onto to something here."

"Give it to the feds," Gardner said.

He walked into his office. A couple of minutes later, Bell followed him.

"I'm taking a week's holidays."

Gardner looked up. "Starting when?"

"Now."

FIFTY-SEVEN

The little girl Vanessa was frightened of the hens at first and Jo had to show her how to shoo them away in order to get the eggs. They'd taken a walk out into the pasture field earlier. Vanessa had tried to pet the goats but the goats were having none of it, particularly the billy, who didn't like people in general and definitely didn't like to be touched by them. The pony—Grace's pony—was of a more affable nature and Vanessa had patted her neck and run her hand over the stiff bristles of her mane.

They walked to the pond to look at the fat bullfrogs where they rested in the mud, and the turtles lined up on the fallen log where the creek flowed into the pond. The grass there was knee-deep and the cattails growing in the pond were five feet tall. At one point, Jo realized that Vanessa was on the opposite side of the pond from her. As Jo started walking toward her, the little girl gave her a look of indignation.

"I'm not going to run."

"Good," Jo told her.

"I know you can catch me." The girl reached out to run her fingers across the fuzzy top of a cattail. "This is sort of like a field trip."

"You go on field trips for school?" Jo asked.

"We went to the zoo in Washington last year. It was pretty awesome."

"What was your favorite animal?"

The girl didn't hesitate. "The pandas. They were amazing."

"I've never seen a live panda," Jo admitted.

"You should go." Vanessa looked around at the farm and sighed. "My mom would like it here."

Jo watched her a moment as she stood by the pond in her jeans and muddy runners. "Do you and your mom do lots of things together?"

"Not really. She's busy all the time."

"What does she do?"

"She always has meetings, with charities and stuff. We'll probably do more things together when I get older."

Jo didn't know what to say to that. "She misses you," she told the girl after a few false starts.

Now they were collecting eggs. Jo showed the girl the various places where the hens sneaked off to lay, beneath the old seed drill in the barn, or in a musty corner of the haymow. When they had all they could find, the two of them sat on a bench outside the brood house. The rooster strutted over to them, gave them a quick look and kept on going.

"That's Buster," the girl said. "He's like an alarm clock."

"You've been listening to Henry." Jo let the name slip before she could stop it.

The girl caught it, of course. She looked up at Jo and smiled. She didn't say anything.

That night Jo sat on the porch, drinking tea and listening to the farm. Henry came out, bottle in hand, and sat down. It was nearly ten o'clock, well past his bedtime. He poured wine into a jam jar and had a drink. Jo waited for him to ask but he didn't say anything.

"Did she have her bath?" Jo asked.

"Yes."

"She asleep?"

"She is."

Jo took a drink of tea, grown cold. "I'll call the mother tomorrow from Cooperstown. If they agree to the demands, we'll let the girl go the next day."

"And if they don't?"

"We'll let her go anyway. We can't win, Henry. All we can do is make sure she doesn't lose." Jo rubbed her eyes with her fingertips. "I had it in my mind that she would be a spoiled brat. I actually thought she might be as reprehensible as her father. What is wrong with me that I would think that, Henry?"

"There's nothing wrong with you. And if there was, it was only temporary."

Jo shook her head. "You know, when we were gathering the eggs— do you know who I was thinking about?"

"You were thinking about Grace."

"I wasn't though," Jo said. "I should have been thinking about Grace. But I was thinking about Susan. What she would say if she knew what we were doing."

Henry watched her as he drank from the glass.

"And what she would say," Jo continued, "is that Vanessa needs to be home with her mother. And she would cuss me out royally while she said it."

"And what would you tell her?" Henry asked.

"I'd tell her she was right."

FIFTY-EIGHT

The call came from a pay phone in Cooperstown in upstate New York. Molly had been in the Jackson house since eight that morning, trying to keep the momentum going in Wyoming. There were only so many TV and radio shows in the state, and she was dredging the river now, trying to get repeats. Sam was once again in his makeshift studio. He'd just finished a live hook-up with some TV show from Casper, a low-budget current events program hosted by a man who'd gotten rich selling mining equipment to the coal industry and now was on television just because he wanted to be. Sam had spent the past five minutes informing him that—at the current rate of immigration—in ten years Muslims would outnumber Christians in the country. Sam claimed that Frank Barton opposed the necessary changes to immigration policy that would prevent that from happening. Neither claim was true but the host—who knew a little about marketing—was buying everything that Sam sent his way.

The call came in on Rachel's phone. The FBI was on site, the usual crew. When the phone rang, Heyward opened the link to the server while Dugan yelled for Sam to come out of the den. Molly followed.

"Is your husband there?" Jo asked when Rachel answered. Her voice, coming from Heyward's computer, was calm.

"Yes, he's here," Rachel said. She had been upstairs when the call came in, and hurried down as the phone was ringing. Molly watched Sam as he moved to sit at the island off the family room. He poured a cup of coffee.

"You got the package?" Jo asked.

"Yes," Rachel said.

"So your husband now believes we have your daughter?"

Sam, spooning sugar into the coffee, smiled as if someone was telling an old joke, one he'd heard so many times it wasn't funny anymore.

"Yes, he does," Rachel said. "Absolutely."

"Okay," Jo continued. "You tell him this is what he's going to do. He's going to pay one million dollars to an offshore account. You'll get the info when the money's ready. And then he's going to drive to Laureltown and he's going to tell the parents of the children who were killed how wrong he was. He's going to tell them it was *not* their fault that their babies were murdered. He's going to ask them to forgive him. Then he's going to go on TV and tell the country the same thing. I would very much like him to be sincere when he does it but I've come to the conclusion that he might not be capable of sincerity. But maybe he can fool the people who listen to him. He obviously *is* capable of that. Okay, you have that?"

"Yes," Rachel said quickly. "Can I talk to Vanessa? Is she with you?"

"Get your husband to do what I say and you can talk to her in person," Jo said. "I'll call you in twenty-four hours."

The line went dead. Dugan looked at Heyward.

"Cooperstown, New York," Heyward said.

"We should have asked her for a memento or two from the Hall of Fame," Sam said.

Molly stared at him in disbelief and then looked at Rachel, who was still holding the phone to her ear, as if trying to extend the contact by sheer will. She seemed not to have heard Sam's remark. When she finally lowered the phone, she turned to him.

"Okay," she said, her voice rising. "How do we set this up?"

"Set what up?" he asked.

"We only have twenty-four hours," Rachel said. "We can go to

Laureltown this afternoon. Somebody has to contact the parents, get them together. You can do the TV thing tonight, right? The network will give you air time."

Sam smiled again, then glanced at Dugan, who was not looking at either of them. He was staring at the floor, like a man who'd stumbled into an embarrassing situation and wished he was someplace else.

"What the fuck are you smiling about?" Rachel demanded of Sam.

"Am I smiling?" he asked.

She turned to Dugan. "Your guys have to coordinate this. Somebody has to talk to the parents in Laureltown." Her mind was in overdrive now. "What if they won't agree to meet? But some of them will. We can only talk to the ones who will. They have to understand that, right? The kidnappers, I mean."

Dugan nodded and glanced at Sam, who took a slow drink of coffee before wiping his mouth with the back of his hand.

"Nobody's going to Laureltown," he said. "You need to slow down, Rachel. We're one step closer to finding these people. And when we do, we'll get Vanessa back, and they'll go to jail."

Rachel approached him. "No. We give them what they want and we can have her back tomorrow. Detective Bell even said that. Give them what they want."

"That scenario would require me to go on television and eat shit," Sam said. "I'm in the middle of a political campaign that has positioned me as the one man in this country who doesn't eat shit. Do you know what the term No Surrender means?"

"Do not tell me that, Sam," Rachel said desperately. "We have to do this. We have to do this and then you can get back to campaigning. I'll help. I'll even go to Wyoming with you if you want. I'll do anything you want me to do. But we have to do this. Please, Sam."

Molly watched Rachel Jackson as she crumbled, there in her own house, in front of strangers, her hands shaking, her voice cracking. Molly turned away and walked out of the room, going back to the den, where she had a radio interview scheduled for two o'clock. From there she heard Sam Jackson answer his wife.

"No," he said.

FIFTY-NINE

Bell, driving his twelve-year-old Ford Taurus, traveled nearly nine hundred miles over a day and a half and by the time he arrived back in New York he knew that the impulse tapping at his brain at the Williamsburg market wasn't the static electricity in the air.

Over the course of thirty-six hours, he learned that there had been a woman selling produce out of a green cargo van at the Greenfield market the day that Sam Jackson had received the first call, and a woman doing the same at the markets in Elmira and Hershey on the days of the follow-up calls. All three markets were within a five-minute walk to the pay phones used by the caller, phones that were tucked away in inconspicuous places. Bell further learned that the woman had vended at each of the markets just once previously. Scouting missions, no doubt.

Bell now had his pattern, and he was partway to understanding the logic behind the woman's actions. She was too smart to use a cell-phone or a computer; he'd figured that out early on. She knew that a pay phone was traceable but wouldn't care, as long as she wasn't caught in the act, and by keeping the calls limited to a couple of minutes, that wasn't a real concern. Placing the calls hundreds of miles apart made it impossible to anticipate where she would call from next.

However, in order to travel relatively undetected from town to town, she required a cover. The truck full of vegetables provided that. None of the markets Bell had visited required a plate number from their vendors, and the number the woman had written down at Williamsburg had proved to be a fake. In spite of that, Bell doubted the woman had been driving across three states with false license plates. It would have invited a cop to pull her over and it would have been particularly risky on that day in Williamsburg, the day that she had used the truck to transport the abducted girl out of the city. Because Bell was now convinced that that was how it had gone down. Why else would she have been at the market, five blocks away from the abandoned parking lot where the limo was found?

He got home at three in the morning and before he went to bed he sat down and made notes of all he had learned on his circuitous trip through Massachusetts and New York and Pennsylvania. He rose at nine and drank coffee while he tried to make sense of what he had written.

He had considerably more information than two days ago, but all that data merely raised more questions. For one—was the woman actually a farmer who decided on a whim to get into the kidnapping business? That seemed a stretch to Bell. It was more likely that she was somebody with an agenda who bought or leased a truck and then filled it with vegetables as part of the act. She couldn't very well pose as an organic farmer without some produce to display. Then again, maybe she was a farmer first and a kidnapper second. Selling at small-town markets could have inspired the plan to travel about undetected. Who knew which came first? It was the chicken and the egg, an apt reference for someone posing as a farmer.

Bell had attempted to get a description of the woman and in that he had been given a lot of information, all of it useless. According to the people who claimed to have seen her, the woman driving the truck was either in her late twenties or mid-forties or early sixties. She was blonde or brunette or redheaded. She was dark, possibly African-American. She might have been Asian, or had a Swedish accent and she weighed somewhere between one hundred and three hundred pounds.

Sitting at his kitchen table with his coffee, Bell knew what he needed to do next. Now that he had a description of vehicle, he needed to go through all the available street videos from the day of the abduction to try to find it. And hopefully pick up a valid plate number. And he would have to do it while supposedly being on vacation, and without the blessing of Sam Jackson and the Federal Bureau of Investigation. Or his own boss at the NYPD.

While he was considering the delicate nature of the task, his phone rang. He looked at the display and then answered. Rachel Jackson was on the line.

"Why are you calling me from Whitman's Diner?" Bell asked.

"I can't use my cell," she said. "Unless I want the FBI listening."

"And you don't want the FBI listening?"

"Can you meet me?"

They met in the park a half-hour later. She was waiting for him, by the bandshell she'd mentioned. It was cool and damp and she was huddled in a blue windbreaker, a cap pulled low over her eyes. Bell joined her on the bench and listened while she told him about the phone call she'd received earlier, the call from the woman he'd been following, albeit a few days behind. Apparently she had called this time from Cooperstown. It was a pretty good bet that Cooperstown had a farmers market, and that today was market day. Not that it mattered, Bell knew, because the woman wasn't in Cooperstown anymore.

When Rachel told him what the woman had asked for, Bell sat quietly for a long time, relieved that it was finally out in the open. He didn't have to feign ignorance anymore.

"An apology," he said then. "That's what this is about?"

"Seems that way," Rachel said. "More than the money. I always wondered about the money. A million dollars. Sam's worth fifty times that, probably more. Why are they asking for peanuts?"

"You and I have different definitions of peanuts," Bell said, "but I see what you mean." He looked across the park. The place was full of people, in spite of the weather. There was a dozen or so guys playing touch football, teenagers it seemed, and a few had their shirts off. The foolishness of youth. After a moment he turned to Rachel. "Did the woman say she's from Laureltown? Is she connected somehow to the shooting?"

"I thought about that," Rachel said. "What if she's one of the mothers? What if she took my kid because she lost her own? Maybe she has no intention of letting her go."

"If that was the situation, she wouldn't be contacting you at all," Bell reminded her. "You said she promised she would let her go. Don't you believe that?"

Rachel took a few seconds then nodded. "I do."

"Why did you call me?"

"Because Sam won't do it," Rachel said. "He won't apologize to those parents. He won't even consider it. And he sure as hell is not going to go on TV to say he's wrong." She laughed, quickly and bitterly. "He's the man who doesn't surrender. Don't you know that?"

"This is his daughter," Bell said.

She started to reply then stopped, forcing herself to be quiet. Bell had seen her do that once before. She was edgy, her knee bouncing, eyes darting about the park. He decided to tell her about where he'd been the past two days. She sat huddled in the windbreaker, listening, her teeth chewing on her bottom lip.

"I've been to the Williamsburg market," she said when he finished. "Vanessa and I went there to buy flowers a couple of times. So this is the woman? You're sure?"

"Put it this way," Bell said. "If I was absolutely certain, I'd ask the state police to put out an APB on that truck right now, assuming it's traveling from Cooperstown back to—well, we don't know to where. But all I have is a vague description of a green truck, maybe a GMC, and no plate number. And keep in mind I've been removed from the case."

"It's too coincidental though," Rachel said. "Are you going to tell the FBI this?"

"I'll tell them if they want to listen. But that doesn't solve the problem with your husband. He needs to change his thinking."

Rachel shook her head. "You have to understand. He doesn't operate as a person. He operates as a persona. I don't think he knows how to separate the two. And now, with this campaign—"

"He feels like he can't back down," Bell said.

"I hate to say this but I really believe he'd prefer that this would end in a confrontation. The FBI against the kidnappers." She looked at Bell. "Because that would be a big news story. And it would be a victory for Sam."

Bell got to his feet. "I hope you're wrong about that." He hesitated, thinking of what he was about to say. Thinking that maybe he should leave it alone. But he couldn't: he needed to know so he could better understand the situation. "By the way, we still need Sam's DNA for the lab work. You remember Lynn asked you for it?"

Her face went blank and she looked away from him. He kept waiting for something but it never came. It seemed as if she would rather sit there forever than respond. In the end it was Bell who broke the silence.

"Does he know?"

"I didn't think so." As she spoke, she was watching the kids playing football. "Now I'm not sure."

"Who's the father?"

"Doesn't matter," she said. "A guy I knew. A guy I saw…briefly." Only now did she look at him. "I have a shitty marriage, Mr. Bell."

He smiled. "Yeah, I picked up on that."

She didn't smile back. "I have a shitty marriage and I'm not a good person. I told you before that I haven't been a good mother. But I am going to change that. If I get a second chance, I'm going to change. Do you believe me?"

"I believe you."

She nodded. "I need a second chance. I need to have my baby back. I don't fucking care about my marriage. This is the straw that breaks it. I'm a weak person to have put up with him for so long. I know that."

Bell stood there a moment longer before he nodded. "Okay. But you are not a weak person, Rachel."

"What are you going to do now?" she asked.

"Try and find your daughter."

SIXTY

Sam had no problem convincing the network to give him a spot on Rivera's show again, especially after he promised to identify the people responsible for his daughter's disappearance.

Agent Dugan went with him to the taping and this time Molly tagged along. As for the appearance, Sam was obviously working off an agenda. He didn't shave beforehand and he wore dark pants and a blue chambray shirt, the sleeves rolled up. He looked like a reporter working a story or a cop who'd been on a stakeout for days. Or—more to the point—a grieving, sleepless parent. He always kept his hair neatly combed and now, minutes before going to tape, Molly saw him run his fingers through it, mussing it just slightly.

Rivera, once again the stick figure in the act, led off by asking Sam if there were any new developments. Sam squinted at him, feigning fatigue, and when he began to speak his voice was hoarse and strained. Molly had no idea how he managed that.

"We are now in contact with the terrorists who took my daughter from me. As I have suggested all along, they are a bunch of spineless cowards. But now we know what their goals are, these cowards. They are the individuals determined to take away our Second Amendment rights. They've decided that they need a spokesman for their aims and that I should be that man."

"Hold on," Rivera said. "What are they asking for?"

"What are they asking for?" Sam repeated. "Well, first of all they want twenty million dollars. That's predictable enough. But they also want me to go on TV and tell my fellow Americans that they have to give up their guns." Sam looked directly into the camera now. "How do you like that? They want me, Sam Jackson, to go on television and tell each and every one of you to turn in your firearms. They want Sam Jackson to tell you that the Second Amendment is a piece of garbage. Now, I know we have a drug problem in this country but whatever these guys are taking is beyond the pale."

"Who are these people?" Rivera asked.

Sam shrugged. "You need to ask somebody on the other side of the aisle that question, Ronald. Because these people are definitely in the employ of somebody who wants to take me out, politically speaking. Like I said before, the timing of this is the key. What these idiots, these cowards, don't realize is that they've chosen the *last* man in this country who would knuckle under to them. Keep in mind my campaign slogan—No Surrender. That they would choose me for this clumsy piece of extortion just shows you how imbecilic these people are."

"Are you still talking to them?"

"Oh, we're talking," Sam said. "We're talking all right."

"Some pretty inflammatory things you're saying," Rivera said. "Aren't you afraid of angering the individuals who are holding your daughter?"

"Did you just ask me if I'm *afraid*?" Sam demanded. "I'm afraid of nothing. But these people are afraid. Cowards are afraid by nature. And they're growing more afraid every day. Which is why I think you're going to see them hand my daughter over. Deliver themselves to the mercy of the law. As we used to say when this country still had some backbone—the jig is up."

"You have to admit that you have no proof that this is political," Rivera said.

"I do have proof."

"And...that proof is?"

Sam paused a moment. "I spoke to one of these individuals less than an hour or so ago. A woman. That's another thing—these cowards choose to hide behind a woman's skirts. They won't come at me man-to-man. Anyway, I was talking to this…addled woman…and I asked her just what she hoped to accomplish. And she told me that her main goal was to deny me a seat in our Congress. In those very words."

Molly was in the green room, with Dugan and a half-dozen people, staffers and others. As Sam issued the last falsehood, she looked over at Dugan. He stared straight at the screen, refusing to meet her eyes. She had the impression that he was okay with all that Sam was saying. Molly got to her feet and went outside to call Bill Ford. She needed to tell him what was going on.

Although she was pretty sure Bill Ford would be okay with it too.

SIXTY-ONE

Bell walked into the captain's office and sat down. Gardner was reading something in the newspaper. It could have been police-related or it could have been an opinion piece about the Jets being one and seven on the season. Bell waited until Gardner set the paper aside and looked over at him.

"Detective Bell. Spending your vacation here at work, I see."

Bell told him about his road trip to Greenfield and Elmira and Hershey. He told him about the woman. He told him his theory about the market at Williamsburg.

"We need to go over the street videos again from that day. I have a rough description of the truck."

"Where are we going to get the manpower for that?" the captain asked. "You know how much work that is."

"Well, I'm here," Bell said.

"Yeah, and I also know that the union's going to squawk if they hear you're working your vacation."

"Then I'll end my vacation."

"That's fine," the captain said. "Then I'll remind you that you're off the case. Why not just drop this in the FBI's lap? They have more money than we do. They have more of everything."

"I don't think so."

"You not getting along with the feds?"

"We have philosophical differences."

"Get past them. We need to cooperate. You need to cooperate."

"Right."

"Now go fishing or something," Gardner said. "You're on holidays, for fucksakes."

When Bell left the precinct, he realized he hadn't eaten since getting up that morning. He went to McGee's for a steak sandwich and a beer. It was mid-afternoon and the place was largely empty. Two middle-aged men, both sporting huge bellies, shot pool on a coin table in the back. Bell thought about the limo driver McIlroy and his buddy, the fictional Bill Driscoll, shooting pool across town. That's how it all had started. A chance meeting that was anything but that.

He drank his beer and went back through his notes while he waited for the sandwich. His phone rang as he was eating. It was Agent Dugan.

"Rumor has it you need some help."

"Rumor has it my captain has a big mouth," Bell replied.

"We need to see what you have," Dugan said. "You've ID'd a truck?"

"I have a lead on a truck," Bell said. "I don't have an ID on a truck."

"I need to see whatever you have," Dugan said. "We're at Jackson's house. Get your ass over here."

"I'm having a beer."

"Drink it and get over here."

"I'm pretty thirsty," Bell said. "I might have two beers."

"Don't make me send a couple agents after you."

"I guess I can relax," Bell told him. "I've seen how good you are at finding people."

He hung up and ordered another beer and went back to his notes. He read what he had written the day he'd visited the Williamsburg market. Afterward he'd called the guy in Connecticut who made the furniture and ruled him out as a suspect. Further down the page he'd written the word "pictures" with a question mark. Now he picked up his phone and called the market manager, the woman with the dolphin on her arm. When she answered he reminded her who he was.

"You said you were going to check to see if anybody had any cell-phone pics from the market that day."

"Right." She paused. "You know, I couldn't find anything. Sorry."

The pause suggested to Bell that she hadn't followed up. "Well, keep asking. Maybe do another round of the regulars?"

"I will," the woman said. "Absolutely."

"Sure you will," Bell said when he hung up. He found the number of the artist named Lily and called it. She answered on the first ring.

"Lily Walker."

Bell told her why he was calling.

"Oh, I found some pics but nothing that can help, I'm afraid," she said.

"None of the woman?"

"I have a couple but you can't see her face. One is where she's lifting a hamper of something from the back of the truck. Her head is turned. And I think there's one more but I cut her head off completely. You can see her torso. Does that help?"

Probably not, Bell thought. "I'll come by and have a look. It'll be in a couple of hours. I have another stop first."

SIXTY-TWO

The scene at the Jackson house was the same. Heyward with his laptop, Dugan his attitude. Sam Jackson was in the den-turned-studio with Molly, the campaign manager. Rachel Jackson was not in sight but a few minutes after Bell arrived she came downstairs. Maybe she heard his voice.

As Bell began to give Dugan his story Sam Jackson came out from the den to listen, remaining on his feet and regarding Bell like he was selling something door-to-door. Bell sat at the dining room table while he talked. Rachel brought him a cup of coffee without asking and then sat down across from him.

"And that's about it," Bell said when he finished. He refrained from telling Dugan about Lily and the photos. There was probably nothing there anyway, and he didn't want Dugan sending someone to talk to the woman in place of Bell. She was his contact.

"Tell me again what you have on the truck," Dugan said.

"I know it's green and at least two witnesses said it was a GMC," Bell said. "Big van, probably a seven-ton."

"No plate number?" Dugan asked. He'd already asked before.

"If I had a plate number, I would have run it by now."

"You say you got back in the city last night?" Dugan said. "If we had this information five hours ago we would have had choppers in the air after the woman called from Cooperstown. In all likelihood we'd have this truck in our possession right now. The driver too."

"There was a call from Cooperstown?" Bell asked. He could feel Rachel's eyes on him.

Dugan stalled a moment, caught. "Yeah, there was."

"Too bad I didn't know that," Bell said. "I've been out of the loop. But you knew that, didn't you, Agent Dugan?"

Dugan gave Bell a look before turning to Sam Jackson and shrugging. Now it was damage control. "Could be something. Could be nothing more than coincidence. What did he come up with—a green truck and a woman nobody can identify."

Sam nodded, as if agreeing on what to order for lunch. "But next time she calls, I want somebody in a chopper looking for that truck."

Bell stood up. "I guess my work here is done." He saw now that the campaign manager was in the room, leaning against the doorway to the den and watching him with a wry expression. Rachel stood as well. It seemed as if there was something she wanted to say before he left.

"Leave your notes," Dugan told him.

"Then they wouldn't be my notes anymore," Bell said. "I told you what I know."

Dugan stepped forward and tapped Bell on the chest with his forefinger. "We can't stop you from digging around but you'd better goddamn well keep us informed, pal."

Bell grabbed the agent's finger and twisted it backward before pushing it away. Rachel stepped forward and interrupted them, offering a folded piece of paper to Bell.

"Keep us all in touch. Here's my cell number."

Bell hesitated. He had her cell number, and so did the FBI and everybody else in the room. He glanced at the number and saw it was different than the one he had. He put the paper in his pocket.

"You find this woman, you'd better hand her over to us," Sam told him. "I'm not sure I like the way you operate."

"Well, we don't have to impress each other," Bell said. "I don't care what you think of me. And, since I'm not a resident of Wyoming, you don't care what I think of you."

He noticed that Molly was smiling as he left the room.

SIXTY-THREE

Lily Walker's house smelled of patchouli oil. It was located on a narrow gravel road north of the city, a few miles from West Point. There were chickens in the fenced-in back yard. Bell had knocked on the front door and the woman yelled for him to come around back, where he opened the wooden gate and waded through the hens to walk up onto the porch. She met him there and let him in.

"Front door's got a broken hinge," she said. "You can open it but it's a pain in the ass to close."

They sat at a narrow harvest table while she showed him the pictures on her laptop, but not before she went through a gallery of her paintings first. She was drinking gin in a highball glass when Bell had arrived—he could smell the gin—and she'd offered him a beer, or glass of wine, and he had declined both. He was looking at the visit as a quick side trip, one that wouldn't produce anything but one that he had to make. After a couple dozen pictures of flowers on easels he spoke up.

"The woman in the green truck."

"We're getting to that," she said. "I just thought you'd enjoy seeing some of my work."

Bell made a show of looking at his watch. The woman, not to be outdone, made a production of searching for the pictures, even though she'd been expecting Bell's visit. She finally brought the first one up. Bell was looking at a shot of André the sausage-maker, standing proudly in front of his display of meats, hanging from their racks. In the background Bell could see a woman, slim, dressed in khaki pants and a tan work shirt, standing up in the back of a truck. Her head was cut off in the photo.

"Okay," he said.

Lily clicked the mouse and found the second picture. The same woman, her back turned partly to the camera, was lifting a hamper basket of acorn squash from the truck. Her face was obscured; Bell could make out a couple of strands of light brown hair beneath a navy baseball cap. He was about to ask Lily if she could print the two photos for him, even though there was very little to see of the woman in question.

Before he could speak, Lily scrolled the picture upward slightly and, in that instant, Bell lost all interest in the woman because there, clearly at the bottom of the photo, was the truck's license plate. It was not the number the woman had given the dolphin lady.

Bell wrote it down, thanked Lily Walker and headed back to the station.

SIXTY-FOUR

Molly left the Jackson house that afternoon and headed back to her hotel. Sam Jackson and agent Dugan remained at the residence. Dugan seemed to think that the kidnappers would call after they saw Sam on the Rivera show that evening. Molly wasn't quite so sure. If she was a kidnapper, she doubted that any of the lies Sam told would encourage her to make contact; in fact, the opposite would be true. But then she wasn't a kidnapper, she reminded herself. She was just an employee of Bill Ford, undertaking an increasingly unpleasant task. The only satisfactory part of the relationship was that she was being well-compensated. Which sounded like something a prostitute would say. She tried not to think about it.

Back in her suite she spent the better part of two hours on the phone to different aides and volunteers back in Wyoming. The numbers were up, the coverage was ever-expanding. They were handing out No Surrender signs and T-shirts and pins faster than they could make them. The word of the day seemed to be momentum. Molly knew it to be an elusive entity. Momentum. It was hard to find and harder to sustain. You couldn't buy it or rent it. It had its own whims, like a rainbow or a hurricane. It could be unstoppable or unstartable and nobody possessed the formula for either.

Molly poured bourbon in a glass and sat down on the couch. She'd changed into yoga pants and a T-shirt when she got back to the suite and now she sat there, the glass resting on the arm of the sofa, staring across the room.

She tried to imagine herself as someone who only knew the Sam Jackson of sound bites and truncated media interviews. Would she be tempted to vote for him? On one level, it was a compelling story—a man whose daughter has been abducted, standing firm in the face of whatever evil was behind it. Who wouldn't consider a man like that? The maverick, the independent. Gary Cooper in *High Noon*, taking on the bad guys all on his own? Of course, in this instance, Molly wasn't persuaded because she knew who he was, what he was. But the people of Wyoming didn't and that was all that mattered.

As she was thinking about it, the man who would be Gary Cooper called. He was downstairs, he said, and he wanted to talk about the campaign. He used the word momentum.

"I'll come up to your suite."

"The hell you will," she said.

She changed her clothes and went down to meet him in the bar. He was sitting at a corner table, scotch in hand. He'd shaved since the taping of the show and changed into a dark blue suit. Molly sat and ordered a glass of red wine.

"We need to go back," he said after she gave him an update on the situation in Wyoming. "Build on this. This will carry us right up to the election."

"But can you go back?"

"I can do whatever I want," he told her. "You haven't figured that part out? Smart woman like you?"

Molly would rather not have her intelligence heralded by a man like Sam Jackson. As compliments went, it was insulting.

"What's the FBI going to say?"

"They go where I go," Sam said. "They're working for me, not the other way around. We tie up whatever we need to here, and then head back tomorrow. As long as this thing with my daughter is unresolved we can cherry-pick whatever media outlets we want. Left, right, center—it doesn't matter. They all want me now."

This thing with my daughter, Molly repeated to herself. She started to respond and her phone rang. She took it from her purse and answered. It was Bill Ford. He'd just watched the Rivera interview.

"Matter of fact he's sitting across from me," Molly said when he asked about Sam. "We're talking about heading back to Wyoming tomorrow."

"Who is it?" Sam asked but Molly ignored him.

"The interview?" she said. "Oh, for the most part it was all bullshit but what did you expect? Bullshit baffles brains. Where would we be without it?"

"Who are you talking to?" Sam demanded, his voice growing loud.

"It's Bill Ford," she told him.

"Let me talk to him."

"He wants to talk to you, Bill," Molly said into the phone. "Okay, not a problem. Catch up to you later."

She ended the call and looked at Sam. "He was tight with time. He says to keep up the good work."

"I asked to talk to him," Sam said sullenly.

Molly shrugged her indifference as she had a drink of wine. "Tell me something—what happens to this campaign if they release your daughter tomorrow? What happens to No Surrender then?"

"I'll tell you what happens," Sam snapped. He was still pouting at being ignored by Bill Ford. He drained his glass in a gulp. "No Surrender shifts from being a concept to being a reality. I go from being the guy who preaches no surrender to the guy who *didn't* surrender."

"And I suppose," Molly said, "that we'd have a great photo op. You and your daughter, the tearful reunion. All that."

"For sure."

"I think the voters would like to see some pics of the two of you together," Molly said. "Because, if I can recall, I haven't seen a one so far."

SIXTY-FIVE

The farm sat in a little valley through which a narrow creek meandered, emerging from some spindly pine trees growing along the southern reaches of the Catskills. There was an old frame farmhouse on a rise, and a barn that looked to be of the same vintage, alongside a newer outbuilding of painted steel that appeared to be a warehouse, and a large shed in the back with an overhanging roof. There were goats in a pasture field beyond the shed. A brown and white pony grazing. Chickens roamed the property at will. An orchard of a couple of acres, the trees heavy with apples, grew to the north of the house.

The green GMC truck was backed up to the warehouse. With the binoculars Bell could see the plate number clearly.

He had parked on the two-lane blacktop a quarter mile away, leaving his car beneath a rise in the road, out of sight of the farm. He'd been there since before dawn, thinking that the woman might be heading for a market somewhere, to sell a little produce, and maybe make a call from a pay phone in the process. The truck hadn't moved though. Bell had waited, hunkered down in some cottonwoods alongside the road, watching. Just past daybreak an older man with long hair tied back in a ponytail had come out of the house and walked to the shed to milk the goats. He'd gone back inside and a little while later a woman had appeared. She was built somewhat like the woman

295

in Lily Walker's headless photos; Bell would not have been surprised if she was the same person. What did surprise him was the fact that the woman had a little girl with her. Both were carrying baskets of some sort and they went into the henhouse.

Bell lowered the binoculars. The girl was roughly the same age as Vanessa Jackson and from that distance she looked like the girl he'd seen in the photos. But why would Vanessa Jackson be free to wander around the farm? It was pretty damn quick for Stockholm Syndrome. Too quick, in fact, even for someone that young and impressionable. It couldn't have been the Jackson girl, which meant that the woman obviously had a daughter of her own. That was an interesting twist. Was she keeping the kidnapped girl at the house and if so—how could she explain that to her own daughter? Maybe the Jackson girl wasn't even at the farm. Bell hadn't considered that.

Twenty minutes or so after the woman and the girl went back into the house with their baskets, the woman came out again. She climbed on an old gray tractor and hitched it to a trailer, loaded with empty bushel baskets, and drove the rig into the orchard. A few minutes later the old man came out of the house and walked out to join her. They spent the rest of the morning picking apples from wide wooden ladders.

Bell had brought along a thermos of coffee and a ham sandwich. He watched the two all morning long, occasionally taking a break to walk back to the car to sit down. Once he fell asleep for a few minutes and when he woke up, he'd forgotten where he was. Remembering, he hurried back to the rise. The woman and the man were still in the orchard. Bell watched and wondered what to do. He was reluctant to approach the house unannounced. He didn't need anyone panicking at this stage of the game.

The two went inside a few minutes after noon, and a half hour later the woman emerged. She walked to the warehouse, where she'd parked the tractor and wagon and proceeded to load a half-dozen bushels of apples into the back of the cargo truck. She got into the truck and drove off, heading north. Bell jogged back to his car and followed.

She drove into the town of Monticello and parked at the rear of a grocery store called Mountain Foods. Bell drove past her as she got out of the truck and kept going, turning into a lot across the street. He watched as the woman rang a bell on the loading dock and then thirty seconds later a man appeared. He had a red beard and long hair, done in a braid. The two of them unloaded the bushel baskets and carried them inside.

When the woman came out a little while later Bell was leaning against the front fender of the truck, waiting for her. Stepping down from the dock, looking at some paperwork in her hand, she didn't see him until she was a few feet away. She was tanned and fit, in her thirties, brown hair and eyes. Her name was Jo, according to the DMV. Not Joanne or Joanna. He watched as she gave him the once-over, her eyes wary. Bell was wearing jeans and an old Yankees T-shirt, Jeter's number. He didn't look like a cop, or maybe he did. It didn't matter now.

"Headed to the market?"

"There's no market here today," the woman named Jo said. She opened the truck door.

"But there's always a market somewhere," Bell said. "There's one in Greenfield. One in Elmira." He paused. "Hershey, Pennsylvania has a market."

She stopped, staring at the truck's interior. "I don't know what you're talking about."

"Yeah, you do."

She closed the door. Before turning to him, she took a moment to scan the area around them. Seeing if he was alone.

"Who are you?"

"NYPD," Bell told her. "I've been watching your house since dawn. I didn't want to approach you there because I didn't know the situation. I didn't want anybody panicking." He paused. "I still don't."

He waited for her to say something. She was looking at the ground now, at the cracked concrete of the loading area.

"He's never going to apologize," Bell said. "You must know that."

She looked at him, then past him again.

"Did you see him on TV last night?" Bell asked.

Jo waited a long time and finally nodded.

"That's what you're dealing with."

"Am I under arrest?"

"Not at this moment," Bell said. "I was hoping that you and I could find a way to resolve this situation without involving a whole lot of law enforcement."

"How would we do that?"

"The little girl's mother would agree to anything to get her daughter back. I have a feeling that you and her could figure something out. I'm sure you know exactly how she feels. You're a mother yourself, right?"

Jo gave him a puzzled look. "No, I'm not."

"I just assumed," Bell said. "I saw you with the little girl this morning."

Jo hesitated. "That was Vanessa."

"That was Vanessa?" Bell repeated. "So—she's free to come and go?"

"Not really. It's complicated. It's—it doesn't matter. Tell me how this would work."

"I need to talk to Rachel Jackson."

"What about the asshole?"

"We leave the asshole out of it." Bell was beginning to like the woman, in spite of everything. "I assume you've figured out by now that he's more interested in getting himself elected than getting his daughter back."

"Yeah, and all I'm doing is helping him along."

"Which wasn't your intent, I'm sure," Bell said. "Tell me something—what's your connection to Laureltown?"

Jo exhaled heavily. Bell got the impression that she'd been holding everything in for quite a time now and it was all coming out in a rush. He thought she might start crying.

"My goddaughter," Jo said.

With that, Bell thought he might start crying.

"All right, let me talk to the mother. You realize she doesn't have to tell anybody anything, not if the two of you can come to an agreement. She's not required to press charges. The police don't need to know your name."

"You know my name."

"I've been removed from the case. I'm just here as a concerned citizen."

"What about *him*?" Jo asked. "She'll tell him."

"He might be the last person she would tell," Bell said. "Okay, I need to go talk to her. I need you to trust me on this but I also need to trust you. Give me your word you won't grab the girl and try to run."

"I got no place to run to," she told him.

She turned and opened the truck door again. Bell started to walk away but stopped. He came back as she was climbing into the cab, pulling shut the door. The driver's window was down.

"Two things I have to ask," he said. "First, why did you use your real plates that day in Williamsburg? That's how I found you."

She shrugged. "Phony plates, I was afraid I'd get pulled over. With the kid in the back, I couldn't take that chance."

"I thought so," Bell said. "Number two—who's the man who helped you grab the kid? I know it's not the old guy at the farm."

"No."

"Who was it? And don't tell me it was Bill Driscoll."

"I won't," she said and started the truck and drove away.

SIXTY-SIX

Bell drove back to the city. When he got there, he parked and dug the number from the pocket of his jeans. He sent her a text.

Can you talk?

The reply came back in less than a minute.

Call me in twenty.

He waited the twenty minutes and dialed the number. She answered on the first ring.

"Where are you?" he asked.

"Walking," she said.

"Everybody at the house?"

"Yeah. What's going on?"

"I found her."

"Oh my god."

Bell gave her a moment. He could hear her breath quickening.

"Oh my god," she said again, this time exhaling in relief. "Is she okay? Where is she?"

"She's fine," Bell said. "I saw her. It was from a distance but she's fine. Now listen—would you be willing to get her back with no questions asked, no charges laid, nothing?"

"Of course I would. Tell me what to do."

"All right," Bell said. "We need to do this right. We don't want the FBI in on it and frankly, we don't want your husband either. This is not going to be a raid that's set up to make your husband look like a hero. I think the woman will hand Vanessa over. This woman is not evil, Rachel."

"I'll do whatever you say."

"I was thinking we could do it tonight," Bell said. "You need to understand that you're going to get a grilling like you won't believe when you bring her home. They're going to want details and I mean details. You can't give anything up."

She didn't say anything for a moment. "Sam's going back to Wyoming in the morning. Dugan will be going with him. But you say I can get her tonight? Where is she?"

"She's upstate." Bell was quiet for a moment, thinking. "You know what—let's wait until tomorrow. Give us some distance between the principals."

"Are you sure she's okay? I mean, where she is, she's okay for another night?"

"She's safe, Rachel. Safer than she'd be with a dozen agents kicking in the door. Let's wait. I'll set things up and text you in the morning."

"Hold on," Rachel said quickly. "This woman—now she doesn't want anything?"

"I wouldn't say that. It's just that she knows she's not going to get anything."

The line went dead and Rachel put the phone in her pocket. She'd been walking through the park when Bell called and stopped while she talked to him. Now she stood there, on the corner, while her heart raced and her thoughts swirled. It took her several minutes to gather herself, to come to the realization that in twenty-four hours Vanessa would be back home. She wanted to believe it but in believing in it too much she was afraid she might jinx it. She would try not to think about it then. She might as well decide not to breathe.

She went back over the conversation with Bell. He had actually seen Vanessa. And apparently he'd come to an agreement with the woman who had her. But what else had he said—that the woman knew she wasn't going to get anything?

Trying not to think about Vanessa coming home, trying not to jinx it, Rachel thought about the woman instead, about what she had done and what she'd wanted. And what she wasn't going to get.

After a while she walked over to Fifth Avenue and hailed a cab. She told the driver where to take her and they headed downtown.

SIXTY-SEVEN

Sam came home shortly after ten o'clock. Rachel was sitting on the living room couch, drinking a glass of chardonnay, waiting for him. Her jacket was thrown carelessly over the back of the couch. She didn't know where he'd been and she didn't care. It seemed as if the interviews were escalating, never-ending. Rachel had stopped answering the landline days ago. The message box was full so anyone trying to get in touch with Sam that way was out of luck.

She could tell he'd been drinking as soon as he walked in. He could hold his liquor better than anybody she'd ever known, but still she knew. His eyes grew hooded and he carried himself differently, recklessly. He was probably surprised to see her there but he didn't let on. If she was at home at this hour, she was usually in her room, watching TV or reading. He moved past her and splashed some scotch in a glass.

"What are you doing up?" he asked without turning.

"Having a glass of wine," she said. "In my own home. Which is empty for a change."

He walked over and sat down in a leather chair. He took out his iPhone and scrolled through his messages. Rachel watched him for a while, her heart rate climbing.

"Why are you trying to aggravate the people who have Vanessa?"

she finally asked.

"What?" he asked absently.

"You heard me."

He typed a text before putting the phone aside. "Is that what you think? And here I thought they were trying to aggravate me. Kidnapping my daughter is not an effective way to get in my good books."

"You're telling lies and calling them names." Rachel reminded herself to remain calm. To breathe. "What can that accomplish?"

"What lies?"

"Jesus," she said. "You don't even listen to yourself, do you? The shit you say on TV. The shit you say every day to get elected."

Sam gave her a quizzical look. "What are you doing? You don't care about the campaign."

"I do when Vanessa's involved," Rachel replied. "Why are you pretending they took her as a political act? There's nothing political about this. Nobody told you that this has anything to do with you running for office. You lied."

Sam, drinking from the glass, shrugged. He wasn't going to have this conversation with anybody. And especially not her.

"That's the thing about you," she said. "You don't care. You're supposed to be this man who is passionate about his country—and you couldn't fucking care less about it."

He was nodding now, taking it in, feigning disinterest but she knew him better than that. He was getting close.

"Do you have any idea how you came across on that show last night?" she asked then. "You sounded like a complete idiot. Babbling away about conspiracies and spineless cowards and how you're running the investigation. It was cringeworthy, Sam. It was fucking laughable. Is that how you're going to get elected? By acting like a clown?"

That was it. He got to his feet and walked to the bar. He poured more scotch, even though he'd barely made a dent in the first measure.

"What's next, Sam? Put a red ball on your nose?"

"You self-righteous little cooze," he said softly as he turned toward her. "Who do you think you're talking to? What do you know about what I'm doing? You smug little Bennington bitch, with your charities and your three-hour lunches and your fucking five-acre clothes closet. What do you know about any of this?"

"I know it's all an act."

"Of course it's an act," he snapped. He walked toward her. "That's how you get elected. Do you have any idea who I'm courting out there? I'm courting a whole state of mouth-breathing morons. To do that, I have to stoop to their level. Is that too fucking complicated for you? Are you just as stupid as they are? What is with you tonight?"

"Nothing," Rachel said. "Maybe I'm a little out of sorts because my daughter's been abducted. It doesn't seem to bother you much. Not as long as you can use it to help you in the polls. Just like you used those kids in Laureltown."

"Fuck Laureltown," Sam said. "That was some maniac who went over the edge."

"But you said the parents were to blame."

"The parents couldn't have stopped it," Sam said. "Nobody could stop it."

"Then why did you say that?"

"Have you always been this stupid and I just never noticed? I said it to stir up shit. I said it for ratings. That's the way this country works these days. And if I *hadn't* said it, then Bill Ford wouldn't have tapped me for this campaign and I wouldn't be on my way to Washington. So I'd say it worked out pretty well."

"And the twenty-two dead kids?" Rachel asked.

"Fuck 'em. Nothing but collateral damage. The world's over-populated as it is."

Rachel set her wine glass on the coffee table. She got to her feet and took her jacket from the couch. "Okay, that's enough."

He stared at her. "What's going on with you?"

"That's enough," she said again and went upstairs.

SIXTY-EIGHT

Jo waited until after they'd gathered the eggs to tell her. They carried the baskets into the house and washed the eggs with warm water before drying them and putting them in the cartons. Ordinarily what would happen next was the tough part, the part where Jo put the little girl in the room again and locked the door. Locked the door and went about her day, trying not to think of the child there, all alone and still scared, in spite of how things had changed.

Today was different.

Jo stacked the eggs by the back door, ready for the cooler in the warehouse. She kept one dozen, though, and brought it over and handed it to the girl, who was sitting at the table, folding the drying towel.

"These are for your mom."

"What do you mean?" the girl asked.

"You're going home today."

"No way."

"Yes."

"Oh my gosh."

The tears started and Jo turned away so the kid wouldn't see her cry.

SIXTY-NINE

It had been the cop's idea that they meet someplace neutral after Jo had suggested that they simply come to the farm.

"If she doesn't know where your farm is, she can never tell anybody where your farm is," Bell had said of Rachel Jackson. "No matter how hard they push."

Jo chose the schoolyard in Mooretown, twenty-four miles away. What had begun in a schoolyard in Laureltown could end in one, under circumstances that couldn't be more different. After setting up the meet, she and Bell had a long conversation about Daniel's involvement, although Bell still didn't know the name. The detective reminded Jo that Daniel had stolen a limousine and kidnapped both the driver and the little girl. He would have to answer for that.

"Keep in mind, you don't know his name and you never will," Jo told Bell, ending the discussion.

In fact, Jo had talked to Daniel the night before. When he heard what was about to happen, he agreed that it was for the best. Jo suspected that he was actually relieved.

She and Vanessa were at the school a half-hour early. It was a sunny day, and cool. They sat on the swings and waited. The little girl put the carton of eggs in the shade of a shagbark hickory tree. Before leaving the farm, she had given Henry a hug and told him to take care of Buster and Grace's pony. At that moment she could have asked Henry for the farm and he'd have given it to her.

The sedan pulled into the lot and Rachel Jackson was out of the car before it stopped, sprinting across the yard to lift her daughter into her arms, both mother and daughter crying and then laughing.

Jo hung back, watching. By the car, the cop Bell was doing the same thing. Jo didn't know if the girl's mother would speak to her or not. She had ample reason to despise her. Bell hadn't told her Jo's name, for the same reason that they hadn't met at the farm.

After a minute or so, Rachel looked over to Jo and then started toward her. Behind her, Vanessa headed across the yard to retrieve the eggs.

"Thank you," Rachel said as she neared.

"I should not be thanked for anything," Jo said. "What I put you through. I'm so sorry. It was a stupid thing. A stupid idea."

Rachel shook her head to refute this. She reached into her jeans pocket and produced a flash drive. She handed it to Jo, who looked at it, puzzled.

"What is this?"

"The best I can do," Rachel said.

Vanessa was beside her mother now. "Look, Mom...eggs and I helped gather them."

Rachel smiled, her eyes wet. "Let's take them home."

SEVENTY

Two hours after getting the news that Tim Rutherford wanted him on *The Press Box* that Sunday, Sam was on the charter back east, leaving Molly to cancel all his weekend events in Wyoming. She had counseled putting Rutherford off a week but Sam wouldn't hear of it.

"And give him a chance to back out?" Sam had asked. "No way. You heard what he said two weeks ago. Let's see who's full of hot air now."

The show was live from the NBC studio in Washington. Sam knew that Rutherford lived on a farm outside McLean, allegedly a property owned at one time by his great-great-grandfather. Who knew if it was true? But it served Rutherford's pose that he wasn't a New York guy, just a folksy reporter from the country. Garrison Keillor with a political bent.

Sam arrived wearing khakis and a brown shirt, the sleeves rolled up. He knew that Rutherford would be shirt and tie and he wanted to make the contrast clear. A woman met him in the lobby and took him to makeup. He was in the chair when Rutherford stepped into the room. He hadn't dressed for the show yet and was wearing jeans and a chambray shirt. Cowboy boots. Sam recalled that he and his wife raised horses of some kind. Like most talking heads, Rutherford was smaller in person than he appeared on TV. Even with the boots, he couldn't have been any taller than five-eight or so.

"I just heard the news that your daughter's home," Rutherford said after offering his hand.

"She is," Sam said.

"That's wonderful. You and your wife must be overjoyed. I can't imagine."

"No, you can't," Sam said.

"I didn't hear any details."

"You're not going to get any from me. It's private."

The fact of the matter was that Sam himself didn't know what had transpired. The news had broken while he was on the charter the night before. He'd made a quick pit stop in New York and found Vanessa at home. Rachel was acting superior and distant; she wasn't saying anything other than Vanessa was safe and the subject was closed. The media had been informed only that the little girl was home and that there would be no further statement. The case was closed. It wasn't, not to Sam, but he had to get on the shuttle to Washington. He would get some answers when he got back that afternoon.

"I can tell you one thing," he said to Rutherford. "I got her back on my terms."

"That's good."

Sam turned in the chair for a better look at Rutherford, while the makeup woman tried to stay with him, applying the base.

"So what's going on here? Why am I suddenly worthy of *The Press Box*? Don't tell me your numbers are dipping."

Rutherford laughed. "If they were, I'm not sure *you* would be regarded as a tonic for that."

"You might be surprised. In the end, it's all about the numbers, isn't it?"

"I hope not," Rutherford said. "I'll see you out there."

The studio backdrop was spare, with some early American artwork and a few bookshelves. The man had won several Emmys but none were in evidence. False modesty. Two oak chairs, with deep brown leather padding. It was a three-camera set-up, all very familiar to Sam. There was a sound booth to the left of where Sam sat, with the director and a few others inside. Sam settled in and waited as Rutherford did a rather abbreviated intro. In fact, everything about the host seemed a bit rushed, uncharacteristically so, as if he had a job to get out of the way.

"Let's go back to 2000," he began, turning to face Sam. "At that time, you—"

"Before we start," Sam interjected. "I just want to say what a pleasure it is to be here, Tim. After all this time."

"Well, we're happy to have you," Rutherford replied. "Now if we can go back—"

Sam smiled. "I must say, though, you look much bigger on TV."

Rutherford took a moment before returning the smile. "What looks large from a distance, close up ain't never that big."

"What's that?" Sam asked.

"Bob Dylan."

"Right," Sam said, enjoying himself now. "From the left-wing Big Book of Quotes?"

Rutherford allowed his smile to pass. "In 2000 Hillary Clinton announces her candidacy for a Senate seat in New York. You called her an opportunistic she-devil. Is that correct?"

Sam shrugged, leaning back in the chair. "Probably. Sounds like me."

"Opportunistic," Rutherford said. "Why did you think that?"

"First of all, opportunistic is pretty much a synonym for Clinton, isn't it?"

Rutherford looked at him evenly, saying nothing.

"Okay," Sam said. "I know what this is about. Although I was expecting something a little more original from you, Tim. This is the parachute issue, right? Hillary landed here from Arkansas and now I've jumped feet first into Wyoming, and you're trying to establish a parallel between the two. Let me tell you the difference, Tim. Hillary moved to a large-population blue state from where she could best mount her failed assault on the White House. She and Bubba decided the road to Washington went through the Empire State. She didn't care about New York, she only cared about D.C."

"And you care about Wyoming?" Rutherford asked.

"That's right."

"Why?"

"Why do I care about Wyoming?" Sam asked.

Rutherford nodded. "What makes Sam Jackson's parachute any different than anybody else's?"

"It's simple," Sam said. "I'm not *in* the loop. I'm not a guy who's spent his life currying favor and kissing rings and making the *right* connections, all in order to someday get himself elected. I didn't find this candidacy, it found me. I understand the people in Wyoming, but more importantly—they understand me. We're in this together."

"You feel a bond with them?"

"Of course I do. They understand hard work. They know what this country used to be. They know what No Surrender means."

"Do you think the people in Wyoming hold you in high regard?"

"Yes, I do."

"And do you hold them in high regard?"

"Yes, I do."

Rutherford nodded to the sound booth. "I want to play you a recording."

Sam glanced in the direction of the booth. Before he could speak, he heard his own voice.

"*—any idea who I'm courting out there? I'm courting a whole state of mouth-breathing morons. To do that, I have to stoop to their level. Is that too fucking complicated for you? Are you just as stupid as they are?*"

Sam turned on Rutherford, who was sitting forward now, his eyes focused. "That is your voice, Sam Jackson? That is you, talking about the people of Wyoming?"

"That is *not* me," Sam said. His breathing became ragged.

"It is though," Rutherford told him calmly. "It is you." He looked toward the booth once more. "We have more. Let's listen."

As the tape began, Sam got to his feet, jerking the microphone from his collar. "This is bullshit! It's a fucking set-up. I will sue you and this fucking show and this fucking network."

When he was gone, Rutherford turned to the camera. "And we'll be back."

SEVENTY-ONE

Molly sat back on the hotel bed, remote in hand, and punched in Bill Ford's number. It rang a half-dozen times and went to voice mail. She hung up and called again. The third time he answered, his voice thick with sleep, his tone belligerent.

"It's five-thirty in the morning here, Molly."

"Turn on your TV," she said.

"Why?"

"Do it."

"Christ," he said. "What channel?"

Molly smiled. "Oh, I'd say just about any channel. *The Press Box* got it first but everybody in the country has it now. Keep flipping—you're going to hear his voice."

Molly leaned back against the pillows and waited. She was feeling better than she had in weeks. Then she heard Sam Jackson's voice, coming though the phone. Bill Ford had found it.

"*—a whole state of mouth-breathing morons. To do that, I have to stoop to their level. Is that too fucking complicated for you? Are you just as stupid as they are?*"

Molly waited. She could imagine Bill skipping through the channels, trying to gauge how bad it was. Once he was fully awake, he'd know how bad it was. He wouldn't need a remote for that.

"What happened here?"

"His wife recorded him," Molly said. "I don't know all the details but the little girl is home. The wife recorded him, drunk and going off on his electorate. The girl was released and the tape ended up in Tim Rutherford's hands. You connect the dots. All of a sudden Sam Jackson is deader than Davy Crockett."

"Shit," Bill said. "What can we do?"

"*You* can look for a new candidate," Molly told him. "But at this point that would be throwing good money after bad. As for me, I'm going home."

"You're quitting?"

"It's over. But I have an idea for one last photo op."

"What?"

"Sam Jackson—waving a white flag."

"You think that's funny?"

"I think it's hilarious," Molly said as she hung up the phone.